When Wicked Runs:
West

Written by Marissa Miller

Based loosely on:
Alice's Adventures in Wonderland
Through the Looking Glass
Peter Pan
The Wonderful Wizard of Oz

Acknowledgments

Thank you to the original creators of these characters and worlds:
J. M Barrie for *Peter Pan*
Lewis Carroll for *Alice's Adventures in Wonderland* and *Through the Looking Glass*
L. Frank Baum for *The Wonderful Wizard of Oz*

This book is a work of fiction, using the characters and locations from the above books.
The plot is completely original.

Thank you to Shannon for starting this story with me for fun, and allowing me to make it my own. Thank you for helping me recreate Dorothy, the Mad Hatter, and the March Hare. Your nonsense and shenanigans are greatly appreciated!

New Edition Note from the Author

Welcome to the new and improved version of the *When Wicked Series*! I hope you will enjoy this fun, mashed up, twisted retelling of some of our favorite classic children's books.

Initially, I had published another original version of this series' first and second books. There was a different interior format, content, and they featured alternate cover art. After the books had been out in the wild for a bit, I started to realize a few things.

Primarily, the books were being classified by the cover and interior format as middle grade rather than the intended young adult. This prompted the decision to redesign my covers. As I leaned into the idea of a cover revamp, I realized that I also had this special opportunity to reevaluate the storyline and apply changes to the books in a rewrite after seeing it out in the world.

Obviously, its not typically an option to rewrite or revise once a book is published, so although it is unorthodox, I am extremely grateful to be able to go back and give the storyline the extra attention to best serve and perform for the readers.

The original books will no longer be available for sale, and will be replaced by this revamped version of the series. The main, umbrella plot line concept is still the same, but I am proud to say that it is more in depth, and altered for the better. The original version of

West was roughly 38,580 words, and this new and improved version roughly now is... 66,942 words!

This whole process has been a beautiful growing experience for me, full of many ups and downs. I feel that I, as a writer and author, am stronger for it, and that my When Wicked books also reflect that same growth and strength.

Thank you to everyone who has read both versions, for following along my bumpy journey. And, thank you to those who are joining for the first time, for choosing to give my series a try.

I hope you all enjoy the adventures awaiting you West of the signpost as we take a tumble into Wonderland with Alice, Peter, and Dorothy.

-Marissa Miller
When Wicked Series, 2022

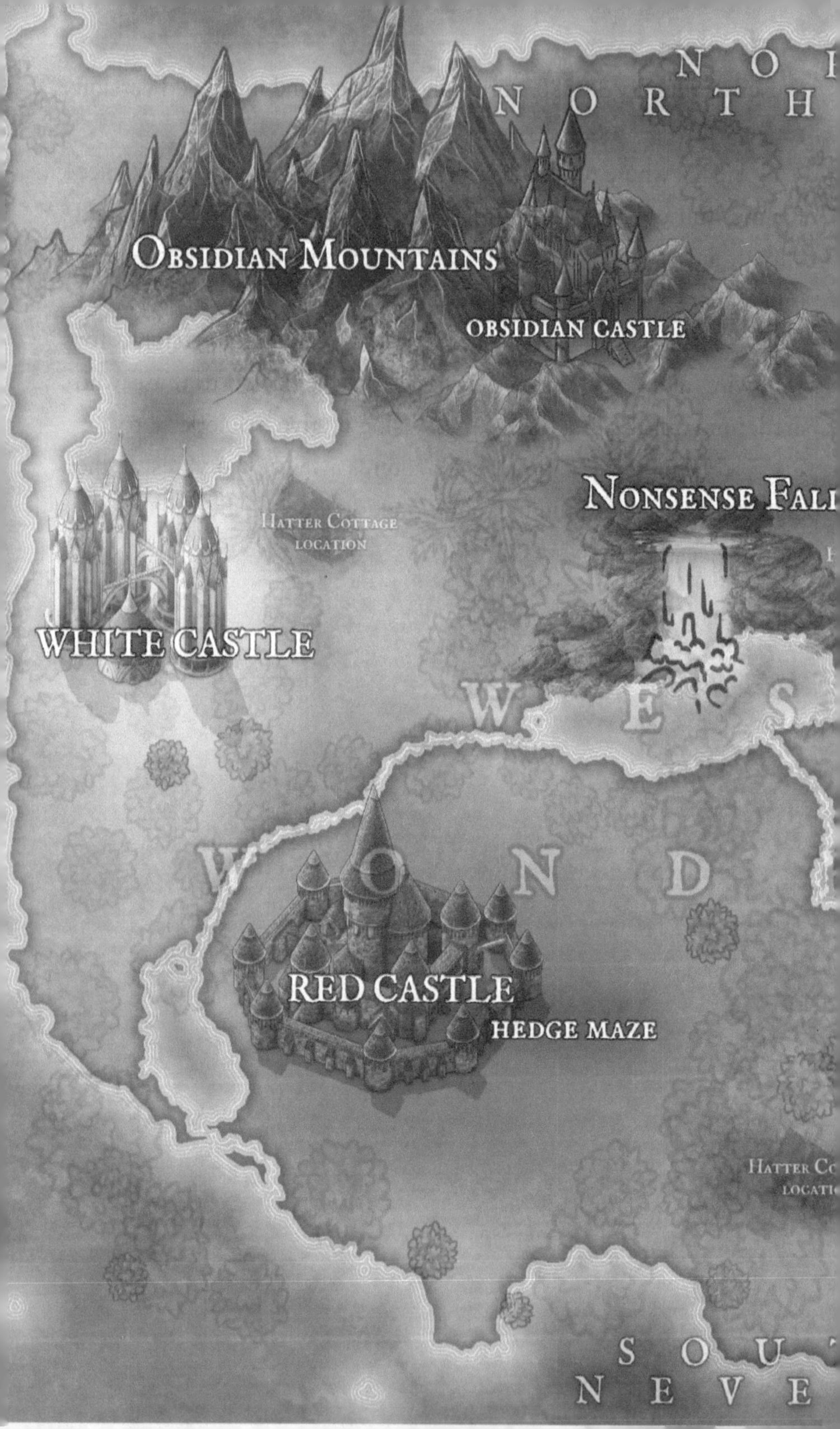

OBSIDIAN MOUNTAINS
OBSIDIAN CASTLE
NONSENSE FALL
HATTER COTTAGE
LOCATION
WHITE CASTLE
W E S
W O N D
RED CASTLE
HEDGE MAZE
N O
N O R T H
HATTER CO
LOCATI
S O U
NEVE

H TO
RN GATES
COTTAGE
ON
AGE
FUNGI FOREST
IS
RLAND
Hatter Cottage
location
TWEEDLE COTTAGE
ALICE'S CABIN
SIGN POST
TO
LAND

When Wicked Series,
Book One
When Wicked Runs *West*

The ticking of the clock pounded against my skull as I stared out the kitchen window into the garden. I had been waiting close to an hour to tell everyone about the curious burrow I had discovered outside the woods earlier that day, but no one was the least bit interested. Instead, everyone was focused on preening over my sister and her new engagement.

I drummed my fingers on the window sill, wondering why there was such a fuss going on about a proposal that had already been discussed at length for months, and the wedding wouldn't be until the following year.

"Do you suppose Alice will be too old to be a flower girl? She's not in the nursery anymore and will be soon beginning her proper education," Mother was asking, and I couldn't help but roll my eyes.

"What nonsense. It's not as if anyone has even *asked* me if I'd like the position in the first place," I grumbled into the palm I was leaning on. I understood the concept that there was a fondness that could develop between a boy and girl, and that they would likely at some point choose to spend all their time together, but what didn't make sense to me was how everyone lost their head over it. It did happen everyday, didn't it? So what made it so special anyway?

Adult topics didn't seem the least bit interesting to me. Certainly, the unusual burrow I had found was more interesting than discussing flowers. Talking flowers might be another matter, but all the different ways of arranging white roses? How dreadfully dull.

"Alice, dear. Please go try on that new red dress we got for Eleanor's party," Mother instructed me, without so much as looking in my direction.

"You got her a *red* dress?" My sister, Eleanor, asked. Her brow crinkled slightly, creating the signature crease that told of brewing dissatisfaction. "But, that isn't one of the colors."

"I like red," I grumbled to myself as I slunk from my position at the window. I paused as a small movement caught my eye out in the garden and I spotted two long white rabbit ears poking out from behind a shrub. "Oh! A rabbit is in the garden!"

"She insisted on the red one. I don't think anyone will really notice," Mother continued to Eleanor, ignoring my comments about the rabbit.

I continued to look out the window, completely enthralled, when the rabbit's head appeared in view and it made eye contact with me. We blinked at each other a few times, and then my mouth dropped when the rabbit stepped out into full view. It was standing erect on its hind legs like a person, and was wearing a proper waistcoat, complete with a dangling pocket watch. It grasped at the watch and opened it to check the time.

"Oh! In the garden, there is a—" I started, pointing frantically at the window, but no one was paying me any mind.

"Alice, the dress," Mother repeated, her tone leaving no room for discussion. I puckered my face into a scowl and reluctantly pulled away from the window. I felt my cheeks flush with irritation as I wandered up the stairs to my bedroom, where I tugged open my wardrobe and retrieved the red dress Mother had bought for me yesterday.

It was a sort of russet red, a simple style, and had a little bit of sparkles dappling the chest. I had picked it out, and since it was the only dress I had shown any real enthusiasm for, Mother had agreed I could wear it to Eleanor's party this weekend.

My mind still on the peculiar rabbit lurking about in our garden, I raced back down the stairs with the dress in hand, and plopped it down in front of Mother and Eleanor, and took a mere two steps towards the window before I was called back.

"It seems rather simple for the event," Eleanor commented, the crease over her brow deepening ever so slightly.

"It's much smarter once it's on. Alice, I asked you to try it on for us, not throw it about to become wrinkled. Please, go try it on," Mother chided, extending her arm to hand me the dress, once more without making any real eye contact.

"Yes, Mother," I sighed, and took the dress to the washroom to change. I tugged the dress on, and fastened it, pausing to look at my reflection in the mirror. The dress fit well, but had a little pocket of room to grow, mostly in the chest, where Mother insisted I would have to start accounting for any day now. There was a slight red splotch on my cheek beneath my round sky blue eyes, where I'd had my hand pressed to my face for the better part of an hour. I rubbed slightly at the other cheek, hoping to even out the complexion a little.

My long blonde hair was a bit disheveled from pulling the dress over my head, so I quickly ran my fingers through it to smooth it over. There was a lengthy black ribbon on the counter where I had left it this morning. I grabbed it and tied it around my head, nodding in approval at my reflection as I finished pulling the two loops atop snug. It was my favorite hair ribbon, and so long as I kept my hair out of my face, I was more or less allowed to use it as I pleased. A small freedom these days, it would seem.

"That should suffice!" I spoke to my reflection, imagining that she was her own person in a world of her own on the other side of the glass. "Best hurry and finish the parade up so I can go see that curious rabbit."

Mother and Eleanor both gave me quick once over glances in my new attire before Eleanor gave her reluctant approval and they launched back into their conversation. Seeing the opportunity to slip away, I quietly announced I was going out into the garden to find the white rabbit I'd mentioned seeing earlier.

When no one bothered to respond to me, I smiled and with the stealth of a cat, slipped out the back door and raced into the garden to look for the rabbit. I jumped when I heard a foreign voice muttering behind me.

"Late, late. Oh, this is making me terribly late," I gasped as the voice was irrefutably coming from the pacing white rabbit at the edge of the garden.

"Goodness!" As soon as the exclamation left my lips the rabbit went rigid and blinked three times at me before turning tail and racing away. "Oh dear. Wait! Please wait! I don't mean you any harm!"

I sped after the rabbit, and scrambled over the small cobbled wall that separated our garden from a small hill that led to a little creek. Beyond that creek was a wide expanse of meadow that stretched until the edge of a large wooded area. That also just so happened to be the exact area I had been exploring previously and discovered the curious burrow my family had no interest in hearing about.

The rabbit cleared the creek with a long leap from his powerful back feet, and I followed suit shortly after. "Please, I just want to be friends!"

I raced through the meadow with reckless abandon. I ignored the sharp blades of grass scratching my legs, as I pressed forward after the white rabbit. No matter how much harder I pushed myself to run— run away from my family home, out the garden, down the creek banks, and through a flower-speckled meadow where my elder sister had once read me stories— the rabbit remained the same distance ahead of me. Unreachable.

Finally, it stopped outside the very burrow I'd previously investigated, resting on the edge of the woods. It turned and squinted its large black eyes at me, still standing tall on its hind legs, and most definitely fully adorned in a proper waistcoat and trousers. In its tiny front paws, it again clasped a pocket watch.

This creature's appearance had been the single most exciting thing that had ever happened to me, and surely no one would believe me if I ever told them without some sort of proof. But, aside from that, I could see a real talking rabbit and have a chance to ask why it was all dressed up and, in any case, what it was running late for. If I could only just catch his attention, I was certain we could be friends. Or perhaps he was lost and needed help finding a way back to some marvelous world where such things as animals and flowers *could* indeed speak as humans did. Oh, how exciting a world like that would be. Far more intriguing than the one I currently found myself in.

"Wait!" My breath puffed with effort as I grew closer to the burrow. "Please, wait for me." I suppose I should have probably been afraid to be getting so close to a talking animal. As far as I knew, talking animals only existed in stories, so finding that to now be untrue, I had no real idea how one would behave in the real world. And yet, my insatiable curiosity compelled me to find out.

The dapper rabbit waited until I was a mere ten paces away before shoving the watch into its pocket and diving into the burrow. I skidded to a halt and inspected the entrance a bit closer this time, wondering if I might be too big to continue my endeavor of befriending the rabbit. The hole was larger than I had expected, and I could fit through easily if I wanted, but I hesitated.

I looked over my shoulder at my home in the distance. The sun would set in about another hour, and with everyone fussing over my sister and her new engagement, I doubted anyone would miss me if I were to see this investigation through. They rarely ever noticed when I was late to dinner anyway.

While this rabbit could very well turn out to be a foe, it was also equally possible that it could be a friend. If I were to return with something as miraculous as a magical talking animal as a companion, surely they'd have to pay attention to me then! Even if it turned out to only be my imagination, it would certainly be more of an adventure than staying cooped up inside. An adventure and a friend. Oh, how I longed for both, even if I had to dream up the whole thing, it would be real to me either way, I decided.

My heartbeat quickened at the idea, and I turned back towards the burrow. Dropping to my hands and knees, I slowly crawled into what turned out to really be more of a small dirt cave, ducking and weaving around small stones and dangling tendrils of roots. The damp, musty scent of earth curled around my senses.

"Late, terribly late indeed. I need to hurry this along…" The echoing voice of the mysterious rabbit sounded from further into the burrow.

I felt a small prick of anxiety telling me that it wasn't such a good idea to keep crawling further into a dark hole, and further from any source of light. I was just contemplating turning around after all, when my eyes caught sight of a small shimmering silver light ahead. It seemed to shift in size as it flickered, and I swore I could hear clinking teacups and someone laughing.

"What in the world?" I crawled closer to the dazzling light, and as I did, I realized that the source looked like glittering silver glass twinkling in the air like starlight. "Mr. Rabbit?"

When no one responded, I instead heard someone shuffling a deck of cards, crows cawing, and distant dull cannon fire. It sounded as though it was coming from the star glass in front of me, and without thinking I reached forward to grasp one of the shards.

The next moment, I found myself falling into a dark hole. I opened my mouth to scream but no sound came out as the darkness encircling me began to illuminate, and I realized I wasn't so much tumbling *down* as I was more precisely falling *up*. My hair shifted from flying wildly above my head to flowing softly about my shoulders, and my skirt stopped fluttering around my legs to instead puff out like a balloon filled with ambient air.

I marveled at the walls slipping past me as they flickered from black into various hues of sparkling silver. It looked soft to touch too, like the way dirt becomes soft after being put through a sifter several times. Walls of stardust, and I was a shooting star cascading through it.

As if reading my mind, the walls narrowed and I reached out both arms to drag my fingers through the fine particles, gasping in delight as they cleared a trail through the dust, flickering away into darkness once more.

Only briefly did the thought cross my mind that it would be

terribly difficult to climb back out of this hole before my feet landed softly on the ground, and the beautiful walls of starlight faded away. I inspected the dirt splattered fabric of my brand new dress, knowing I would get quite a scolding when I returned to the house. Then, I blinked slowly, my mind having a moment of trouble discerning where I was.

I was no longer in a fantastical rabbit hole outside the woods. I was nowhere near the babbling creek, and certainly not anywhere close to my house. In fact, I wasn't terribly sure I was even in England anymore. But how could that possibly be? Surely, I couldn't have actually tumbled into the magical world I had been idealizing only moments before. Such things simply didn't happen.

"Perhaps I hit my head, or fell asleep during one of those dreadfully boring party discussions. Yes, and this had all just been a marvelous dream," I began to rationalize aloud to myself, wringing my fingers together to quiet my mounting nerves.

Instead of the bottom of a rabbit hole, I found myself on a dirt path. It was flanked by a field of golden wheat strands swaying against a soft breeze. Just ahead of me was a crossroad, marked with a singular signpost with four different signs that each read off an alternate direction.

North was expressed in a mechanical font that lacked any nuances of creativity or splendor while *West* was written in a type of handwriting that immediately reminded me of what a clown's handwriting might look like. Though old looking and splintered, *East* had an elegant wispy swirl to its letters, which was in direct contrast with *South* which looked to have been written by a child's crayon. However, it was not the signs that made me scrunch up my face with a certain element of confusion, fear, and curiosity. It was the vaguely transparent cat, grinning broadly at me from the post.

Two

Alice

"**S**taring is rude, you know," The cat was very fluffy, with white fur and orange running from the top of his head down into his tail. He had two large perfectly round green eyes that took in anything and everything. However, all of that was relatively normal for a cat. What made *this* cat different was that I could see the signpost through his body, and he had an exaggerated grin that stretched far longer than any natural cat would. Unlike the talking rabbit, this talking cat was not wearing clothing either.

"Rude?" I bleated to the new talking animal. I felt my body still, so as not to startle the cat away like I had with the rabbit, but energy surged through me with excitement.

"Ah, but I'm not rude. Simply mad," The cat replied with a delighted laugh that sent chills down my spine. Oddly, I was not afraid though. In fact, if feelings were visible the chills would have sparkled like ice.

"You do not appear mad to me. Actually, you appear quite pleased, Mr...." I trailed off, not knowing what to call this strange creature. Perhaps it was bad manners to address talking cats by name here… Wherever *here* was, anyway.

"Cheshire," The cat answered my question, a piece of the

surrounding wheat stock between his teeth. "The Cheshire Cat."

"What is it that a Cheshire Cat does, precisely?" The question babbled from my lips. I was growing more and more curious, and just like flames, the curiously melted away the chills. I had wanted to catch the talking rabbit, but a talking cat was just as captivating.

"As he pleases," The cat answered simply, and sprang onto the Northern sign, sprawling dramatically on it.

"Well, my name is Alice—" I started, but the cat interrupted me.

"I haven't much interest in names. That is Caterpillar's fancy. I, myself, prefer *di-rection*." He emphasized the diction of the word direction as if it would only make sense for a cat to be interested in such a thing. "Which way are you going?"

Trying not to feel dejected that it didn't seem like this cat much wanted to be my friend after all, I looked at the signposts. "I hadn't really thought about that yet."

"Shouldn't you?"

"I suppose I should, and I really ought to be finding a way home."

"Where is home?" The cat's tail flicked as he spoke.

"I'm afraid I don't exactly know."

"Marvelous! Then you wander freely. So, pick which direction you will wander to find home first."

"I just pick?" I scrunched my face with contemplation as I once more inspected the different signs. Perhaps the cat had a point. If I didn't know which way to go, the only logical thing to do would be to pick a direction to start and go from there. But, I really ought to think it over thoroughly. There was the chance that I was dreaming and would be waking soon anyway— so why not have an adventure? There was also the chance that I really had found myself stuck in some sort of strange foreign world, and I'd better pick a direction I could be comfortable in while I looked for a way home.

"Pick up sticks?" The cat echoed me, though not quite accurately, his eyebrows raising inquisitively.

"Well, I am only twelve… Though I suppose age does not matter much to you any more than names do. But, in this case, it pertains to which direction I ought to go," I started to explain the direction I had landed on to the cat.

"Go on," He prompted, flopping into a different dramatic pose, his paw pressed thoughtfully to his face.

"Well, you see—"

"Do I? How wonderful!"

"Uh, yes." I ignored the cat's interruption. "Well, I figure the writing of the signs must have something to do with the places they lead to. Since I am just a little girl I feel I should follow the sign that says South so that I might find other children," I explained logically, noting that the different signs also pointed to different sets of forests as well. At least with other children around, I wouldn't be so lonely, and maybe their parents would be able to help me get home.

The Cheshire Cat gave a hearty laugh. "That's no way to choose a direction!" He chuckled.

"What do you mean? I think it was perfectly logical!" I defended myself in dismay.

The cat shook his head. "Where I come from, logic gets you nowhere."

"So I should not go South? Well then, how about East?" It looked like it would be a respectable place.

"Perhaps. Do you prefer to stand on your head?" He rolled over to balance on his head.

"Well, no, I can't stand on my head," I answered honestly,

though mounting confusion was pooling inside my mind.

"Go West."

"West? Alright, I suppose I shall go West then," I agreed, feeling relieved at having chosen a direction— or having a direction chosen for me in any case. If the writing alluded to clowns, it might very well be an enjoyable place to play in on my way home.

But the cat shook his head. "Don't go that way. No one ever goes that way."

"But you just said…"

"How do you feel about tea?"

"Tea? I thought you only cared about directions?"

"*Tea* is most certainly a direction." The Cheshire Cat rolled his eyes. "If you aren't fond of tea, I would go East."

"But, I am very fond of tea." I could feel my curiosity turning into irritation. This conversation was beginning to seem as pointless as the ones back home did.

The cat, on the other hand, looked thrilled. "Fond of tea? Oh, well then, you must go West!"

"Alright. I am not sure what game you're playing, but I am done with this nonsense. I am going West," I said firmly, and trotted off in the direction that the West sign pointed to.

"If you find any catnip, bring me some, will you?" The cat purred in a dreamy voice that echoed with distance.

I kept on my path and did not look back, ignoring any sense of foreboding that was gathering around me. What ever would I find going West? I really had just wanted to stop spinning in circles with that cat. I wondered if the rabbit had gone this way, and if it too would be so terribly nonsensical to converse with. Then, I chided myself for not thinking to ask the cat if he had seen the rabbit. If I found him, I could ask how to get back to my garden. But, odds were, even if I did go back to ask the cat, he probably would just confuse me all over again. So, best to stay moving in one solid direction for now until I could find someone else to ask for better directions.

Thankfully, the day was warm and the sun was still shining overhead. The air smelled vaguely of berries and flowers, and I could almost taste the sweet scent on my tongue. Soon the dirt path began to turn in a peaty forest floor, and trees began dotting the ground along the sides of the path, turning into the forest I had seen from the signpost. There was something strange and subtly magnificent about it though, and I finally noted that their trunks were not brown, but the further I walked, the more they began to transition into trunks of other pigments like russet, magenta, and mauve. I marveled at the sight as I walked until I saw a large wooden sign that said *Wonderland* posted on a plum and brown speckled tree trunk.

"Curious," I mumbled to myself. I hadn't the faintest idea of where I was headed, and I suppose that should have alarmed me. Instead, I swallowed down my fear when I thought of how else I could be spending my time right about now, alternatively; Being ignored and paraded about in dresses only to be ignored again.

So, I made it a little game to think about what kind of dimension I had fallen into. Perhaps it was an underground system of caves that only *looked* like the outdoors, but was really running beneath my family's estate, unbeknownst to them, of course. Or, perhaps I had fallen in a hole so deep that I came out on the other side of the world, flying through the sky like a star after all.

When that game had run its course, I began to try and deduce what kind of place Wonderland would be. The sun was beginning to slink away behind the treetops, leaving more shadows than light in the twilight hour. It would be time for supper back home, and surely my family would be noticing my absence. They would come to find me once they remembered I had mentioned the burrow to them earlier, I consoled myself as the hairs on my arms began to rise.

The more I wandered, the more lost I began to feel. Every time I chose one path to travel down, as soon as I turned around again, the dirt path had been swept up by some invisible broom. The trees seemed to bend in closer to me, their foliage growing darker and darker with every step I took. I kept putting one foot in front of the other. Maybe this place fed on fear or something.

"I do suppose I should probably find something to eat, but best to be careful so I don't accidentally poison myself," I said aloud to no one in particular. It was fully dark now, and I knew I should stop for the night, but I was also having trouble discerning what I could potentially eat. My stomach rumbled with hunger as I squinted in vain at a bunch of berries I had managed to find. Perhaps I had made a mistake by listening to that cat at all, and then just impulsively going this way anyway.

I'd come across a large tree that rested right in the middle of my path. It was plastered with signs that read things like, *this way*, *that way*, *BACKWARDS*, *around* and the occasional *up* sign that was actually pointing down. I studied every sign, as my eyes adjusted to the gloom, and the moonlight began filtering through the trees, wondering whether I should go this way or that way. I saw movement in the corner of my eye, only to see nothing but trees around me. A sense of icy cold wrapped itself around my body and then was gone as quick as it had appeared. I could have sworn I had seen a vague flash of purple and white blur by, but shrugged it off as a trick of the light, and went back to squinting at the signs.

Then something caught my ear. Music and laughter. I turned towards the sound, noting it was coming from the deeper shadows off of the path. Perhaps I had wandered close to the Southern border by mistake! I ran towards the sound.

I slowed to quiet my steps as I approached an illuminated clearing, where a quaint little pink and yellow cottage resided. In front of it were the two most curiously round twins I had ever seen. They looked vaguely egg-shaped but rounder still. They were using each other's stomachs to bounce off of one another and they were laughing hysterically. I thought briefly of the laughter I had heard coming from the shards of starlight—as I had decided to think of them as— but it wasn't the same. I waited in the shadows of a tree and watched to see any indication of whether these round fellows would be friendly or not. A soft breeze carried the faint aroma of biscuits, and my mouth began to water.

"It's rude to spy," I heard a voice behind me, and I jumped, bumping my head on a low hanging branch. I spun around to see the same transparent cat I had met at the crossroad.

"I'm not spying!" I whispered, knowing good and well that I was. "Anyways, are you *not* spying on me?"

"I prefer the term 'observing,'" The Cheshire Cat said in a long-suffering meow.

I squinted at him. Why had he shown up again? "I don't mean to be rude but—" I started, but the cat's eyes widened with interest.

"Really! What do you mean then? Have you found my catnip?" He asked me with a lazy grin. Something told me this cat was not all there, not including his obvious physical transparency. I wondered if I could see his brain through his skull.

"No, I have not found you any catnip!" I could feel my temper rising, but I did not want to anger a potentially psychopathic cat. I'd bet they had sharper claws than regular cats.

The Cheshire Cat pouted woefully for a moment then pounced from his perch to dive into thin air, vanishing entirely. I peered around the tree and could not see any sign of him.

"Have you met the Tweedles?" I heard his voice, followed by seeing his fluffy orange and white tail curl around my nose like a mustache. I looked up to see the cat was sitting on my hair, bapping lazily at the loops of my bow. I reached up and removed him, setting him on the ground in front of me. He smiled.

"No, I have not met the Tweedles," I half huffed with annoyance. "They seem occupied."

"The Tweedles aren't good company anyway. They tell stories that make no sense at all. And they give gifts that turn everything upside out and inside down," The cat was explaining when a thought suddenly occurred to me, and made his presence less discouraging.

"Wait! You were at the crossroad when I arrived."

"Yes." He blinked one at me, then fixed me with an unyielding stare.

"Can you show me the way back?" I asked, feeling hopeful despite myself. I really did not trust this cat further than I could throw him. Then again, if I threw him, he would probably disappear and wind up on my head again. I was unsure of how that bit would fit into my trust metaphor. I shook my head to clear it.

The cat yawed and flopped on his side. "No," he said. "But I'm sure the Tweedles could."

I frowned. "But I thought you said the Tweedles were not good company," I argued.

"The Tweedles? Oh! They tell the most wonderful stories. There are always lessons to be learned in each one."

I groaned. Once again this cat would be of no use to me. Even if he didn't mean me any harm, and was friendly enough, he really wasn't very helpful at all. I would have to approach the bouncing twins in front of me to find out anything else.

"Do you know Bill?" The Cheshire Cat asked suddenly, sitting up. Perhaps he would be helpful after all.

I shook my head. I had not met anyone named Bill. I hadn't met anyone besides the Cheshire Cat at all, in fact. Though I had had the sensation that I was being watched once it got dark. Maybe it had just been the cat following me.

The cat purred, "Then if you'll excuse me, I have a lizard with a ladder to find." And then he was gone.

Lizard with a ladder? Curiouser and curiouser. I took a deep breath, gathered my courage, and stepped out of the shadows only to bump— or rather bounce— off of one of the round bellies of the twins. They had stopped their game and were waiting for me. They must have overhead the cat. I brushed myself off and straightened up, extending my hand. Confidence was an attractive quality when making new friends, or so I had been told by my sister.

"How do you do? My name is Alice," I began. The twins narrowed their eyes and glanced at each other. I felt my courage evaporate. Then their mouths spread into huge grins and they both grabbed my hand at the same time and shook it vigorously. I could feel my teeth vibrating.

"How do you do and shake hands!" They both sang out, releasing my hand and bouncing about. I couldn't help but wonder if they were any saner than the cat.

"Yes, I was wondering if you might be able to help me. You see I have lost my way and…" I trailed off when I realized the Tweedles were not absorbing anything I was saying. They linked arms with me and led me to the front of their house.

"Would you like to hear a story?" One babbled.

"Or watch a play?" The other one asked.

I shook my head politely, "no… uh, thank you. I really need to find my way…You see, I'm quite lost."

The Tweedles gave each other a knowing squint with those plastered smiles on their round faces. Something about their facial expressions unnerved me.

"Perhaps I ought to just leave you two to your privacy and go back the way I came," I said, taking a step back. But one of the Tweedles patted my hand while the second one ran in an excited circle and then disappeared into the cottage. His exit was followed by a series of loud clangs and bangs.

The remaining Tweedle led me to a nearby log and sat me down. "Tweedle-Dum will be right back. He's grabbing you a gift that should help with your travels," the first Tweedle said sweetly.

A gift? What was it the Cheshire Cat had said about the Tweedle's gifts? Oh never mind with that cat! It was his confusing nonsense that got me lost in Wonderland to begin with. We waited in silence. I glanced around my surroundings, hoping to remember this place as a landmark.

There were tall dark trees that resembled a mixture of pine and oak trees and little flurries of random flowers scattered here and there. I noted the cottage had a short chimney pumping gray smoke above the treetops in rhythmic swirls, fading away into the dark sky. There were mushrooms scattered across the ground too. They had red tops with white polka dots that looked like the common drawings of cartoon mushrooms back home. I wondered why the Tweedles had not removed the mushrooms from their yard when the rest of it looked straight out of a picture. I was about to ask, simply to make polite small talk, when Tweedle-Dum returned from within the cottage holding a small trinket in his gloved hands. Had his hands been gloved before?

"Here we are! A compass ma'am, for your adventures in Wonderland," Tweedle-Dum announced, presenting me with a small silver compass attached to a chain. "May I?" He asked, gesturing to my neck.

I bowed my head in compliance and he slipped the necklace on. I tugged my blonde hair free from underneath the chain and grabbed the tiny compass in my hands, bringing it close to my face to inspect it. My skin felt tingly.

The first thing I noticed was that the compass was not pointing North like a normal compass would. Instead, it's an elaborately swirly and crooked arrow pointed west. I figured this must just have been due to my having already ventured so far into Wonderland. Still, if I followed the compass South I could find my way to Neverland. Then at least I would be around more sane company. Or if I went East, I'd likely find the signpost again, and I could wait to be found there.

"Thank you! This should help me find my way," I gushed, grinning at the Tweedles.

"Oh, and we couldn't help but hear your belly rumbling while you were in the bushes," The second Tweedle chirped at me.

"So we have a basket of goodies to tide you over on your journey. They are of varying sizes, of course." Tweedle-Dum nodded along. "Tweedle-Dee makes excellent treats."

Tweedle-dee shoved a basket abruptly into my arms. I couldn't help but think that the mentioning of size was an odd detail to praise a treat with, and noted that I hadn't seen Tweedle-dee leave to retrieve the basket, nor did his brother have it when he first came out. But, my belly was rumbling, and I looked at the food appreciatively.

"Thank you, really. You've been very kind and helpful. If you'll please excuse me, I'm afraid it's gotten terribly late and I best be on my way." I turned and waved over my shoulder as I was swallowed up once more by the trees.

The Tweedles waved in unison then returned to their bouncing game. I looked at the compass around my neck as I walked a ways to what I perceived to be towards the east. Tiredness pulled at my eyes and I rubbed at them, trying to stifle a yawn. I kept listening every once in a while to hear if anyone was calling my name, looking for me. Surely, by now, they should have gone searching for me and looked at the burrow.

But after a few hours of hearing strange honks and coos in the darkness, a wave of crankiness had settled over me as I trudged to stop.

"I have absolutely no idea where I am!" I groused to myself, plopping down where I stood. I hadn't come across anyone else other than the Tweedles or that Cat. Perhaps I should have asked the twins for more specific directions back to the post since I was fairly certain the compass they gave me must be broken.

I pawed through the contents of the basket and picked a pink frosted treat to eat. I glowered at it in my hand, feeling a mixture of gratefulness at having anything to eat at all, but also vaguely annoyed that it seemed like no one was looking for me.

"You'd think my absence would mess up Eleanor's precious party, and that should be motive enough to find me. Or if they had been actually *listening to me* for once, then they'd know where to look for me!" Resentment burned in my chest. It had been my recklessness that had gotten me lost, but part of me felt like no one had even noticed I'd left or cared enough to find me.

I looked at the compass glumly and squinted when I saw the needle twitch down to a southwest position. It most definitely had to be broken. I groaned and bit into the biscuit. The next thing I knew, my head was whizzing through the trees, and I felt a terrible jolt tear through my body.

"Ah!" I yelped, dropping the biscuit as I now sat with my head above the treetops. "How in the world…?" I trailed off and realized now what the Tweedles must have meant about the biscuits being *different sizes*. Talking cats, rabbits with waistcoats, and now a giant girl lost in the woods. This was a different world entirely. Of that I was certain now.

I took one last feeble look around me from my new vantage point to see if I could spot anyone in a search party looking for me. But the night was still. My eyes landed on the signpost standing tall in the distant moonlight. No one was coming for me.

Tears began sliding down my cheeks as I reached through the branches for the now tiny basket full of biscuits. If pink meant big, perhaps blue would turn me back to my rightful size. I crushed most of the basket with my clumsy oversized fingertips but managed to find a blue biscuit and popped it into my mouth.

Sure enough my body began to shrink, and as I receded back through the tree branches I fell a chasm of hollowness spread through my chest. I was my true size again, sitting where I had started, but I felt so terribly *small*. I looked at the compass dangling from my neck and ripped it off in frustration, flinging it with all my might into the bushed. To my surprise, when I dropped my head to my knees a moment later, I felt a small tingling down my spine, and the silver compass was once more fastened about my neck.

"What *is* this place?" I curled into myself, succumbing to my tears, until my heavy eyelids finally overtook me.

"Hey!" My eyes popped open and I quickly scrambled backwards at the sound of foreign voice.

"What?" I squawked, blinking rapidly to adjust to the bright light of morning. When the bleariness had cleared, I was staring into two soft green eyes very close to my own. I peddled backwards again.

"Oh, good! You're alive." Facing me was a grinning boy. His hair was a rich reddish brown, his eyes glimmering with mischief. He had a sprinkle of freckles over his nose that gave him a sort of charm. Still, I did not appreciate the fright he caused me and I was not in the right mood for any more mind games.

"Who are you?" I wobbled to my feet, warily sizing up the sanity of my latest acquaintance.

"Straight to the point, I like that!" The boy laughed. He was wearing torn and muddy trousers, and threadbare stained shirt, which had at some point been crudely patched in various places. He stuck out a thumb and gestured cheerfully to himself. "The name is Peter. You're the first person to have shown up here in ages! Want to be friends?"

"Friends?" I blustered in surprise. "You want to be friends with me?"

"Well, sure. Why wouldn't I?" Peter shrugged, and I felt a small smile beginning to curl at my lips. A light feeling started blooming in the chasm of loneliness that had opened the night before. "Well, aren't you going to tell me your name, Love?"

"Are you from England?" I asked hopefully, hearing that he was the first person I'd met who sounded like he was from where I was from.

"Nope. I'm from South," Peter answered, cocking his head to the side curiously.

"Oh," I puffed in defeat, then realized he was still waiting on my name. What a terrible friend I was already turning out to be! I stuck my hand out. "Oh! I mean, how do you do? My name is Alice Liddell. Lovely to meet you."

Peter stared at my offered hand for a moment and then grabbed it, giving it a single solid shake. "Alright, Alice." When he released my hand he suddenly lifted a foot off the ground and hovered.

"You're flying!" I gasped, though I suppose I should not have been surprised that boys could fly if rabbits had watches and cats could talk. I had been a mile tall not twelve hours earlier.

Peter ignored my astonished outburst and floated in front me, laying lengthwise in mid-air, propping his head up with his hands. "So, what made you choose West?"

"I met an interesting cat when I arrived," I frowned, wanting to know how he was flying. "He gave me some rather poor advice. I had to pick some direction, and he got me all confused, so, I decided to go this way. Why?" I asked, glancing at his face to read his reaction. Perhaps he knew the Cheshire Cat.

Peter smirked. "Advice from a cat? Not in Wonderland. He's always playing tricks here. You'd be better off listening to your own advice, I think."

I thought about the advice my brain had given me since seeing the white rabbit. It told me not to go out into the garden, not to leave the garden, cross the creek, or follow the rabbit into the hole. I apparently was not on speaking terms with my intuition.

"I give myself very good advice," I said with a smile. "I just very seldom follow it."

Peter laughed, and I immediately recognized it as the same laugh I had heard in the burrow. Perhaps he would know how to get me home after all!

"Do you know how to get back to where I came from? It was a burrow on the edge of a forest," I asked, staring intently at my new friend.

But he shook his head. "Sorry, Love. I haven't the faintest idea of what you're talking about. Afraid I haven't frequented any burrows as of late. In fact, I've only recently even started exploring this direction for myself."

"Oh," I sagged. "I'm afraid I wandered a bit too far from home while following this strange rabbit that came to my garden. I heard him talking and just wanted to be friendly, but I think I just scared him away. I was also feeling a bit cross with my family and needed to get away. Anyways, I accidentally fell down this rabbit hole and ended up here and now I am quite lost. I'm trying to find my way back home."

Peter rubbed his chin thoughtfully for a moment before finally dropping his feet to the ground again and looking inquisitively at me. "Why?"

"Why what?"

"Why do you want to go back home?"

"Well, because it's *home*. It is where one is always supposed to return eventually."

"Maybe you needed a new home and that's what brought you here. You said you were cross with your family so what's waiting for you back there if you were to go back?" He asked matter-of-factly.

I opened my mouth to reply but paused in surprise at the feeling that had entered my body. Surely he couldn't have a point could he?

"You can't pick what family or life you're born into, but if you're not happy with it, what is stopping you from picking new ones?"

"Well, I'm afraid I don't think it really works like that."

"Worked for me!" Peter folded his arms and rocked back and forth with a broad slightly crooked smile. This smile was friendly and warm though, and not the least bit unnerving. The warm feeling grew a little more as I looked at the boy's face.

"They didn't even come looking for me," I sighed, dropping my gaze to my feet. "If they'd just listened to me earlier they would have known where to look to find me."

"Hmm. Well, Alice, now I've found you and I'm right here! We can look out for each other and have adventures. What do you say?" Peter lifted off the ground and tilted himself upside down so he could make eye contact with me. "We can explore Wonderland together."

I bit my lip and rubbed my arm, feeling a strange heat spread over my cheeks— and not like when I lost my temper either. How peculiar. Peter, who I had known for a fraction of an hour, wanted to be my friend, speak with me, listen to my answers when he asked me questions… and he wanted to spend time with me. Compared to the cold dark feeling of being all alone, his company made me instantly feel warm and happy all the way down to my toes.

I reached up to adjust my bow, which I had just suddenly realized must be all askew from sleep, and nodded slowly. "Alright, I think I would like that very much, Peter."

Peter's crooked grin grew even bigger and he buzzed about me for a moment with enthusiasm. Perhaps he's been just as lonely as I have. He seemed pretty happy though, so surely he couldn't have been completely isolated. He jerked his hand to gesture to follow him, so we headed further into the strange land together.

"Alight! I only just decided to explore Wonderland recently, so here's what I know so far. I wouldn't drink any tea in here."

"I thought this was the direction for those who are fond of tea?" I asked, nonchalantly running my fingers through my long hair to unsnarl it.

"All the tea comes from the March Hare, who lives next to the Mad Hatter. And he gets their water from a place called Nonsense Falls. I had some tea from them when we first met. It took a bit to kick in, giving me enough time to think there was nothing to it. But, then my head was fuzzy for days. I think I might have even agreed to marry a mouse!" Peter's face was animated and expressed each word he was saying.

I couldn't help but laugh at the notion. "Sorry that the wedding didn't work out," I played along.

He beamed back at me. "I wasn't ready for the commitment. Being twelve is rough! I'll give myself a few years to figure all that out first." He gave me a wink. "Maybe grow a little and see where I'm at when I'm thirteen— if I ever get that old. That, and I have this distinct fascination with cats." He furrowed his brows and gave a whistle. "That didn't go over well."

"I imagine not!" I thought of the signposts and how there had been a sort of nonsense font for West which led to Wonderland, apparently a place where tea made you want to marry mice. Where did the child's handwriting lead to? "What is in the South? You said that's where you're from, right?"

"Neverland!" His whole face lit up with enthusiasm as if the name itself were some sort of splendor. "It's a place, sort of like Wonderland, where you never grow up. You age as you choose.

There are pirates, and treasure, and fairies, and mermaids. There are the Lost Ones too," He explained, clearly seeing my curiosity spark again on my face.

"Real fairies? I had no idea that they really existed!" Something in saying the word *fairy* out loud felt contrived and fake, yet there was something about the way Peter spoke that made me believe. That, and everything else I'd experienced so far made me think nothing in my wildest imagination could be untrue at this point. "And what— or who— are the Lost Ones?"

"Children like you and me. They pick South at the crossroads and live in a parent-free world where they can stay young boys forever."

"Boys? Haven't you any Lost *Girls* in Neverland?" I asked, feeling the odd hope that the answer was no. Something in my heart wanted me to be the only girl around these parts. It would make me special. Something inside me wanted Peter to think I was special. It was a very peculiar sensation indeed.

"We had one once," He declared with a sigh. My hope faltered for a moment then he continued, "But that's a tale for another time."

"Wait, why don't we just go South to where you're from?" I offered, feeling again like South, which had been my first choice, was where I ought to have gone to begin with.

"I've already been all over South. We can explore West together for the first time. It's an entirely different experience, Love."

I thought about this for a moment, then decided to let it be. "So West is Wonderland, South is Neverland…What is East then?"

"To the East, dear Alice, lies the so-called *Wonderful* World of Oz," Peter explained, placing one hand on my shoulder and gesturing with his other.

"If it is so wonderful then why are you not in Oz?" I asked, thinking Oz was a particularly odd name.

Peter smirked, a cold glint sparking in his eyes, but then it was gone, and gave an exaggerated grimace. "There is a tendency to be an abundance of witches to the East. Some Good, others Wicked. Plus that's usually where most of the adults end up, and they aren't much fun in my experience."

"Witches and fairies… Oh my. Alright then, what is North?" I asked, feeling it was a logical question, but Peter dropped to the ground from where he had been floating alongside me and, for the first time since we met, he actually looked serious.

"No one knows about the North. It's sort of the one rule it seems. No one ever goes North. From what I've gathered, Glinda guards the Northern Gates and she's a very powerful witch."

"Are there any witches in Wonderland?" I asked, suddenly feeling very small and afraid.

"Only a few," Peter said briskly, leading the way down a new fork in our path again. His answer did not reassure me at all. "There's the Wicked Witch of the West…She's a bit frightening, but she's got weirdly pale skin and an eyepatch, so she'd be easy enough to spot. Then there's the Queen of Hearts, or the Red Queen, as she is sometimes called. She's the one to avoid. She likes to chop off people's heads, I hear. But, I am getting most of my information from those tea enthusiasts, so hard to say."

"Goodness!" I exclaimed, wrapping my fingers protectively around my throat at the idea.

Peter snapped his fingers. "That reminds me! There's a Good witch too. The White Queen."

"Well, at least there is some hope then," I sniffed in relief, but Peter's smile and shake of his head dashed my hopes.

"No one has seen her in ages though. She might be dead

for all we know. That happens a lot around here, you know. Death. Dismemberment. It's something you kind of become casual about," Peter said matter-of-factly.

"How on Earth do you get used to death and dismemberment?" I demanded.

"That's just it, Love," Peter said with a wink. "You're not on Earth anymore. Sometimes it's what helps you survive. Once this pirate attacked me and some of the Lost Boys and, while fighting, he lost his hand! A crocodile ate it. Now he wears a hook instead. Good ol' Captain Hook. You would think he had changed his name after the incident, but the irony was it was *already* his name!" He mimed the sword fight in the air as he spoke. To my surprise, his shadow stretched to counter his jabs.

"Perhaps I ought to go back the way I came after all," I fretted, feeling more uncertain of my decisions than ever. Peter had just confirmed for sure that I was in an entirely different world than my own.

Peter shook his head. "You chose West, and directional decisions mean something around here. You've gotta explore it. I promise you, it's not all bad. It's pretty wonderful, really. That is why they call it *Wonder*land, I'd bet."

I looked him in the eye and could see my own round blue eyes staring back. He seemed to mean what he said. A question rustled at the edge of my mind. "Peter, if you are from Neverland, a place that sounds so magnificent, what have you been doing in Wonderland?"

Peter shrugged. "I don't know. It just seemed like the place to be to make a new friend today." He paused to inspect a small pouch looped to his trousers, and cleared his throat. "I've got to get back to the South now,"

"Can't I just come with—" I began, my stomach dropping. Seeing my bewildered expression at the idea of him leaving me alone he leaned forward and whispered, "You know, you're kind of pretty."

"What?" I gasped in embarrassment. No one had ever said such a thing to me before, let alone a boy. The heat flushed my cheeks again in a full blush.

"We're friends now so I'll see you around again soon. I'll be sure of it. Find out some new interesting stuff to tell me about when I get back. We are going to have a blast together, you and I. I can already tell!" He gave me one last wink and then shot into the sky and disappeared in the growing dark of the impending night.

I could only stare after him sullenly and hope he meant what he'd said about coming back. His compliment had taken me by surprise but made me smile all the same. I liked that he called me pretty. His simple flirtation, fueled by pity or sincerity, was enough to at least take the edge off of my rising panic. I felt a little more sure of myself, and I wanted to have something to share with him if he did come back.

Still, I knew what was *not* pretty, and that was my head on the Red Queen's chopping block. I lifted my chin and took in the whirling rainbow of foliage around me, then set off with a confident stride to navigate this maze of a world. Perhaps the faster I explored it, the faster I could leave it.

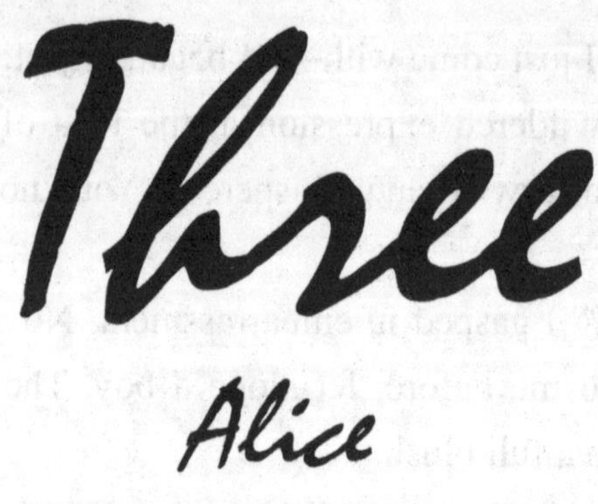

Wonderland seemed to be a relatively docile stretch of wild woodland, from what I had seen. I ducked and weaved around thickets and branches, and chose paths to follow at random. I tried to make it a game with myself to guess what I might find around each new bend.

The day was stretching on, and I grew weary from being on my feet for so long. I was hungry too. I'd saved both a few blue and pink biscuits, figuring I could take a bite of both at the same time and hopefully avoid the growing and shrinking experience. Unfortunately, though my thought process did turn out to be true, I was still filled with the rapid sensation of muscles being stretched too far and too fast.

I spotted a patch of flowers and decided it was as good a place as any to rest my head for a while. The petals were all such beautifully vibrant colors, and the variety of flowers was astonishing— such the opposite from the plain white roses that were fussed over at home. I crouched down in the flowers, letting their swaying stalks obscure me and my red dress from view, then I closed my eyes.

"She's as ugly as a weed!" A small voice called out. One of my eyes popped open. Had I simply been dreaming? I closed it again.

"Look at her scraggly petals! Repulsive," The voice jeered again. It was by far the first and most hostile tone I'd come across since arriving in this land.

Both my eyes opened this time as I was quite certain I was not dreaming. Something reached out and touched my hair. I slapped it away and sat up, looking around in an unhelpful flurry, causing everything to blur together in a mixture of greens, browns, blues, violets and reds.

"She tore my leaf!" Another voice wailed.

Leaf? I looked down to see a daisy glaring up at me. I leapt back in surprise.

"I beg your pardon…" I started to apologize but was interrupted by another insult.

"She's got the face of a toad. A toad sprawled amongst our lovely petals. How vile." A violet picked up a thorn and reached forward and stuck me with it.

"Ouch!" I yelped, jumping to my feet and pulling the thorn out. A small trickle of blood ran down my arm. I felt a tug on my hair, then a hard yank.

"You call this yellow? Pitiful. You are an ugly, ugly girl," A sunflower scoffed, throwing my blonde hair back over my face.

I blew it off of my nose. Then, following the first two flowers' lead, the rest of the violets and sunflowers began attacking me. They pulled at my dress and yanked my hair and poked me with thistles and thorns. The other flowers shied away from the altercation, making the collection of swaying stems separate and flatten like a great wind had knocked them down.

A soft ticking seemed to ring in my ears, and I felt my temper flare. "Enough!" I shouted and plucked one of the advancing flowers straight out of the ground, ignoring its screams and flung it down on the ground, hard. "You horrible, nasty things!"

I watched with a sense of sick pleasure as all of its petals fell off. It was like an odd side-effect of losing my temper. The aggressing flowers released me. At the same moment I was silently cursing the boy I'd met for not warning me that I could be killed, not by vicious monsters, but by a thousand thorn scratches, I heard that familiar laughter behind me. *Peter.* I spun around to find him sitting on a branch watching my battle with the flowers.

"You!" I yelled up at him, balling my hands into fists. "You should have warned me about this place!"

Peter stopped laughing and floated down to stand in front of me. "Warned you? How was I supposed to know you were going to tick off a bunch of wild flowers?"

On impulse I punched him in the arm. I felt the powerful satisfaction of seeing the surprise in his eyes and his other hand holding the arm I had hit. That meant it hurt.

"It's not funny! I have been wandering around aimlessly for hours, no one I've met seems to even be sane here, and then I get ambushed by dandelions!" I spoke crossly. "And, after convincing me to go on adventures *with you*, you left me to fend for myself. You should have taken me with you. Or, at least told me what this place was really like." I reached up and fixed my ribbon that the flowers had knocked askew, and inspected my many new little wounds.

Peter's eyes wandered to my necklace, which was glinting as the dappled sunlight hit it. "Where did you get that?" He pointed at the compass, ignoring my outburst. "Not the Tweedles, I hope."

I furrowed my brows together and lifted my chin defiantly.

Peter took that as an answer and gave a half chuckle, half groan in response. "Oh, Alice, why did you go and accept a gift from the Tweedles?"

I felt my cheeks flushing with irritation. "Because, no one has told me anything about anything here! And, I am quite sick of it. It is not like I received some sort of manual of the blasted place," I growled.

Peter raised an eyebrow and then leaned back against a tree. "You've got quite a fiery personality, don't you? Fair enough. I forget new arrivals don't know much," He said, and before I could get upset about him implying I did not know much, he continued. "Did you at least check to see if it's a direction compass?"

"Isn't that what a compass is?" I had a bad feeling. What if this was some different type of compass? It had reappeared around my neck when I'd tried to throw it away the night before. I suddenly felt self-conscious, wondering if maybe the flowers had been right and I did have the face of a toad now.

"I don't know about Wonderland specifically, but I've seen my share of trinkets that aren't what they seem. Plus there are different types of directions here," Peter explained, and I wondered if maybe the Cheshire Cat had been right and that tea really was a direction after all. "There are regular directions, moral direction, mood direction, lost direction, opinion direction, love compass…. Etcetera. Let me see it."

I lifted the tiny compass up for him to inspect. He rubbed his chin in concentration. I crossed my fingers behind my back, hoping that I hadn't taken a piece of cursed jewelry.

"They gave you a different compass. You can tell because the pull to the North is all wonky. I can't tell specifically which kind though," He said finally. "I am not familiar enough with magical trinkets. I just know the basics. But, whatever it's for, seems like you are a little off kilter, Love."

Splendid, I probably did look like a toad. "What do I do then? Take it off?" I reached for the chain, hoping Peter would know how to keep it from going right back.

He shook his head. "It's already been around your neck so it will take effect either way, and the silver compliments your eyes or something. Plus, it'll be bound to you from contacting your skin, and keep showing up, until it has either completed its purpose, or someone destroys it. But, I believe the destroyer would be killed… I don't really remember all the rules, plus those rules only apply to certain ones. I'd say we could ask the Tweedles, but I doubt they even knew what they gave you themselves. So, we will just have to wait for it to start showing its effects. Until then, why don't I show you Wonderland the proper way?"

I did not feel relieved about the news about the compass, but something in the way Peter grinned at me and extended his hand made me feel safe. I had that odd sensation of fondness creep into my belly once more. I nodded and took his hand. He pulled me closer and a flush of heat shot through my body.

"Hold on tight!" And, with that, he lifted me into the air and we soared over the top of Wonderland.

I clamped my jaw shut to avoid screaming until we had leveled out. I was impressed that he could carry me so easily, since he was about my age. He must be pretty strong. I took a deep breath and let it out, exhaling my fears with it so I could enjoy the view and feeling of flying. This was an experience I could never dream of having back home.

The tree leaves were a richer green than I had ever seen before, and there with flickers of every color imaginable rushing through the streams. Purple mist sprayed from waterfalls and tiny pin dots of creatures bustled here and there. There was a maze made of hedges in front of a castle with rounded crimson tops.

We passed through a cloud. I expected it to be made of water like real clouds, but it was soft, like down feathers, as it brushed my skin. Now I knew why Peter had said it was not all bad. Here, in the daylight, I felt intoxicated by its beauty. I noticed two other castles, one made of white marble and the other looked like it had been carved out of obsidian rock straight from the craggy mountain it was attached to.

"What are those castles?" I pointed below us.

"The white one belongs to that Good witch I told you about, but it's been abandoned since she vanished. And the dark, unfriendly looking one belongs to the Wicked Witch of the West. I hear she keeps an army of flying monkeys there with her," Peter replied cheerfully.

I realized what a small dark piece of Wonderland I had seen. There was so much beauty beyond just waiting to be explored. And there was a fair bit of history laying in these woods, and in each castle. This place felt like stepping into a fairytale.

"Can you teach me to fly on my own?" I piped up again, as I trailed my fingers through another puff of cloud.

Something stole the smile from Peter's face for a fraction of a second. "I could, but I sort of took flight lessons off my list of friendly activities. I can just carry you when we want to fly. It's easier to chat anyway."

"Oh, alright." I wondered what had made him afraid to teach others to fly. Perhaps someone had not been very good at it and had gotten hurt or something.

"Don't worry! I won't drop you," He laughed, then that mischievous look crossed his face again and he added, "at least not on accident."

I blanched. "What do you mean on—" I stopped short, shifting into a scream of terror as he let me drop from his arms, plummeting through clouds towards the treetops.

"Watch this!" He crowed and dove past me, catching me by my arms and legs again. I instinctively flung my arms around his neck and gripped hard. "Got ya!"

"Why?!" I demanded, shaking. "That could have killed me!"

"Only if I didn't catch you. I knew I would. Trust is a big part of flying. Do you trust me?" He smiled at me, and I looked into his eyes.

I opened my mouth to object, but no words came out. To my complete surprise, holding his gaze as I was, I felt nothing but trust. How could that be when we'd only just met? Was this what true friendship was supposed to feel like?

I nodded slowly, loosening my hold about his neck. "I do, actually. I trust you, Peter."

"Want to make it a game? I promise I know my limits and won't let you get hurt," He offered, still staring into my eyes. The green of his was quite lovely to look at.

I blinked and looked away. "Alright, I trust you," I repeated.

"Great! I'm going to toss you straight up and you can pretend to be a bird. Then I'll catch you when you come back down. Are you ready?"

"I suppose so!" I bit my lip, wondering why I had agreed to such a nonsensical thing. Even more perplexing was the infectious enthusiasm and excitement that was filling my chest.

"Ready?"

"Ready!" I agreed, and my body tensed in anticipation.

Peter tossed me upward, and zipped into position beneath me. As I whipped through the air, I felt something break loose within me. It was something foreign but happy. I felt free.

Peter was my friend now, so I would not always be alone. Something told me I would see that cat again too. I pushed my worries about which type of compass dangled around my neck to the back of my mind.

The compass would take effect one way or another so in the meantime why not have an adventure? It didn't look like I would be home in time for tea anyway. The advice they always gave lost children was to stay put until someone found you. It wouldn't be my fault if they couldn't be bothered to look in the right places.

No more stuffy parties, long dull conversations about nothing important, or bothersome rules. I had a *friend* here. I was soaring through the sky with him. Forget a single unusual burrow, that no one wanted to pay any mind to. I had an entire *land* to explore here, and Peter wanted to explore it with me.

At the peak of the toss, I threw my head back and cawed like a bird as loud as I could, before giggling the whole way down back into Peter's waiting arms. He beamed at me.

"I can't believe you actually let me throw you in the air! You've definitely got an adventurous side that I think I can get along with just fine," He laughed and then cupped his mouth to give his own mighty crow. "We're going to have some adventure together, you and I."

"Perhaps we were meant to find each other," I joked, and pointed towards the ground. "Can we go back to the ground now?"

"Already?" Peter looked deflated.

"We need to pick someplace for me to return to—Somewhere to be my new home here." I clung to Peter and reveled in the breeze dancing across my face. I would get back to my own world, eventually. And, *eventually* could wait a while as I indulged my curiosity.

Peter's grin could have rivaled the Cheshire Cat's. "Let's go!"

We landed softly on the ground in a clearing of brightly colored trees, their trunks nearing a reddish violet hue when the light hit them. I scanned our surroundings and spotted a low hanging branch that was sturdy and thick.

"There, that branch looks good." I walked over to get a better look, and as I approached, I thought I saw something flicker in the shadows deeper in the woods. It was like a glint of light bouncing off crystal. The same chill I'd felt before meeting the Tweedles enveloped me. I tugged absentmindedly at my compass.

"Are you going to hang from it or something?" Peter asked, floating over to me, his body upside down to mirror his question.

"Of course not!" I laughed. "This will be a good support beam to make a house."

"A house?"

"Yes. It will have to be small, of course, and it won't be anything fancy. But, I just want to be able to feel safe when I go to bed."

Peter looked at me thoughtfully for a moment, his expression looked vaguely awestruck. "Wow, you really are planning on staying," He mumbled to himself, so quietly I almost didn't catch it.

"I don't really have another choice, seeing as I can't go back to where I came from. Besides, I think I'll have a lot more fun here with you than I ever could at home— I mean in my old world," I corrected myself, deciding I ought to shift to viewing Wonderland as my home for the time being. It would keep the anxiety of being in a foreign place from eating at me that way.

"Of course! I have my own hideout back in Neverland.

Made it myself, so yours should be no problem," Peter mused, and began floating around, picking up various branches and foliage. He disappeared into the shadows and returned with a clump of lichen and vines.

"Goodness." I stooped to inspect the materials when he plopped them at my feet.

"If you can start tying the small branches together, we can layer them up to make a roof,. Then we can stack larger branches over that. If it rains, you should stay pretty sheltered. Plus, the thicker we can make it, the warmer you'll stay," Peter explained, before buzzing off into the woods again. He called over his shoulder to me, "I'll be right back! I am going to go find the big pieces."

"Won't you need help carrying them?" I shouted after him.

"Nope!"

"Well, if you say so," I mumbled to myself and sat on the ground to begin tying and weaving. He was strong enough to not only carry me, but toss me high in the air as well. I pictured him carrying a log in each hand, the toned muscles in his arms flexing ever so slightly to reveal their brawn.

"Whatcha thinking about?" Peter's voice sounded behind me.

"Ah!" I squeaked, certain I had just turned three shades of pink in embarrassment. Why was I thinking of such things? I certainly never would have noticed something like that before. Was this feeling why Eleanor started spending time around boys? "Nothing!"

"Are you feeling okay? Your face is all red." He stuck his face close to mine to inspect it then grinned. "You weren't thinking about *me*, were you?"

"No! No, of course not," I snapped, tugging harder than

necessary at the vine I was gripping. It snapped and hit my hand. "Ouch!"

"It's okay if you find me handsome. I've been told that before. That's why I called you pretty earlier. It just means you've got a good look about you." He floated on his back, flashing me a very cheeky grin.

I glowered at him. "Where are the big pieces you said you were getting?"

"Over there, Love!" Peter chirped and I turned back towards the tree I'd picked, gaping as I saw a bunch of broken logs leaning against the branch like the steeple of a church.

"What? But how did you do that so fast?" Perhaps my image of him hauling logs wasn't so far fetched after all. I pushed up to my feet and circled around the little fort in progress. There was a glittering residue on the bark.

"It's pixie dust," Peter came to me.

"Did it teleport the materials here with magic?" I asked in awe.

Peter laughed like I'd suggested something ridiculous. "No, no. Fairies don't use their dust for magic like that. It's what makes them fly. Me too." He patted the pouch at his hip. "Only witches and wizards use *actual* magic, and I try to stay very clear of all that. You'd be better off avoiding magic too."

"So you made the logs fly here with you. Clever." I nodded, appreciating the ingenuity. I tried to bury the feeling that I really preferred the idea he'd carried it all by hand.

We spent the rest of the day assembling the make-shift house, weaving branches, stuffing moss and leaves in the cracks, and placing large branches and logs. Peter managed to find us some decent food that didn't alter our size and I'd scarfed it down eagerly until I was full. By the time the sun was setting, leaving us in a twilight glow, Peter and I were collapsed on the ground from our efforts.

"That was a lot of work," He groaned, throwing an arm over his face.

"Been a minute since you've broken a sweat, eh?" I teased, rolling onto my side to look at him. The ground was cool and refreshing beneath me, and the air was fragrant with moss and random—non-talking— flowers I had tied together to make a sort of wreath at the entrance.

He smirked. "Peter Pan never has a reason to sweat, Love."

"Don't you sweat when you're afraid?" I laughed, and Peter rolled over too, propping his head up with his hand.

"Nah. I don't have fears, just fun," He answered happily.

"Everyone has some fears, Peter." I rolled my eyes. Perhaps he was just trying to sound tough.

"I left all my fears behind a long time ago." He didn't smile when he spoke, and a somber look clouded his face as he flopped back onto his back and gazed up at the changing sky. "The only thing I really avoid is growing up."

"How long have you been a boy, then?" I recalled him saying before that in places like Wonderland and Neverland you could age as you chose.

"Quite a while now," He answered, but didn't elaborate further.

"Well, I think I will choose to get older while I am here." I sat up and looked down at my new friend.

He pulled a face. "Why would you want to do a thing like that? You want to grow up and become a witch, and run off to Oz?"

I laughed. "No, nothing quite like that. You see, I have a

sister back ho-- er, where I am from originally. She is several years older than me, but I remember when she got to be around my age and the time before she became a full blown adult. I think I should like to go that far, and stop just before I'd be an adult. Even if it simply stopped the very day before I'd turn eighteen."

"It can work like that?" Peter looked puzzled.

"I don't see why not. There were things that were nice about those years for my sister." I paused, bringing up the memories in my mind.

"Like what?" Peter pressed. His face looked so earnest and searching. Hadn't there ever been anyone to share this sort of thing with him?

"Well, I am not sure how it is for boys," I admitted. "But, she was in what she called an 'awkward stage' around this age that I am now. I suppose I can understand it. My arms and legs are bit out of proportion."

"That will probably help you be a good runner, climber, and swimmer though," Peter countered, his green eyes now reflecting that stars overhead.

"I suppose, but she also got…" I paused and blushed. "Well, she got prettier too. Something about her seemed to come into itself and complete. Now she's considered very beautiful."

"Does she look like you?"

"A bit. She has brown hair though. Our faces share a resemblance. I think I will probably turn out a little taller too."

"In that case, you'll probably be beautiful too," Peter said matter-of-factly. "But I don't want to be beautiful so I think I am good as I am." He cracked a smile and batted his lashes at me.

"I don't think you'd have to worry about that," I laughed, and the movement knocked my ribbon so it slipped down around my neck and my hair fell forward to frame my face.

"You said yourself that you don't know how it is for boys. Last time I grew a year, some bad stuff happened."

"I think those are called growing pains," I sighed, and tried to picture the young men that had been around during my sister's teenage years.

"I don't think that was it," Peter mumbled, his eyes reflecting memories of another time and place.

"Well, I don't have any brothers, but I did see some young men grow up," I offered hastily, pulling him back into the moment.

"Okay, so how did it work for them? What was the benefit?" Peter looked skeptical, but since he had so far stayed a boy for so long, I was surprised this topic held his interest to this extent.

"Let's see. They got bigger, and stronger, and usually they got more handsome too."

"Do they get meaner?" Peter asked and the question took me by surprise.

"No, not necessarily," I blustered. "Not in my experience, anyway. Why would you think that?"

"No reason, really." Peter shook his head and shrugged. "Bigger, stronger, and more handsome, eh? Could you stand it?" He winked at me, and I punched him in the arm, causing him to erupt with laughter.

"Cheeky bat," I grumbled with a smile. "I think I'd be just fine. In any case, I don't think I could stand myself if I ever became as dreadfully dull as my sister did when she became an adult. So I simply must never become one if I can help it. But, I'll take the improvements where I can before then."

"You'd start liking thimbles probably too. I guess they're alright though. I never did really get a proper explanation about them," Peter chimed in, half to himself.

I thought of the sewing Mother would do, and figured thimbles did make more of an appearance in adulthood. Curious how he'd learned about thimbles in the first place though. Perhaps that other Lost Girl had one with her or something. Or, maybe thimbles were more common in this land.

"Maybe…" Peter started, bringing me back to the conversation, then paused and his face crinkled in deep contemplation. "I could give it a try. But only a little bit, just to see if you really know your stuff. There are times I'd like to be bigger and stronger, and maybe faster too. I could defeat whoever I wanted in a duel like that."

"You mean you want to grow up?" I blinked at him, fully taken aback.

"Whoa, hold on, Love. I do *not* have any intention of being a grown up. But, I can get my head around the bigger and stronger part. *If* what you said is even true. I could grow until I see fit to stop. Plus, like you said, if I don't ever grow to eighteen, I won't be an adult. Adults are bad news."

"I suppose it would be quite the adventure for you. Certainly something new. But, you don't have to feel pressured because of me." I reached out tentatively to pat his shoulder, then pulled back awkwardly.

"Why would I do that?" Peter sat up and faced me square on. "You're my friend right?"

I nodded emphatically.

"So, we are just trying something new together. I'll just stop if I don't like it. You'll quickly find out I don't do anything I don't want to do."

"If you say so…" I looked away for a moment. "Alright, we can take it day by day and see how it goes. We can even make it a game! I can guess how tall you'll grow."

"Alright!" Peter smiled enthusiastically and floated to his feet, extending a hand to pull me up too. "What can I measure for your growth?" He looked me up and down.

"Uh," I squirmed under his gaze. "I suppose I should grow a bit taller too, but nothing quite like you. Here, I can make a tick mark in the tree to track both our progress. My mother did that for a while in the doorway to the pantry."

"Pantry? I'd measure your pantry? What's that?"

"Never mind." I waved away the question and grabbed a rock. "Okay, stand against the tree and I'll mark your height."

Peter complied cheerfully, squaring off against the tree trunk. As I got close to him, I realized he was alright a good bit taller than me.

"I think you'll easily grow beyond six feet tall. I think I'll only grow a couple of inches." I scored the tree at the top of Peter's head and shooed him away so I could mark my own height. "There. Oh! Your voice will likely get deeper too."

"Will I sound like this?" Peter dropped his tone to a booming, throaty sound. It reminded me of what a goblin might sound like.

"No, I should hope not. You'll sound similar to how you do now, just a little… stronger, I suppose."

"Stronger is nice," Peter mused then squinted at me. "Is your voice going to get deeper?"

"No." I shook my head.. He really didn't have much experience with girls after all. "But, I might become more clever."

"Brawn and brains, eh? Great, we will back the perfect pair! But, I reserve the right to cease growth at any point, and save you from yourself if things go awry." He threw his arm over my shoulders as he spoke and I smiled.

"No adults for either of us! You've got a deal, Peter," I chirped happily, then tried and failed to stifle a yawn. "I'm afraid I am quite tired."

"Well, Love, I suppose I shall leave you for the night. I gotta get back to South anyway. But look," He turned me towards the little fort. "Look what we made. Isn't it great?"

I looked up fondly at Peter and back at the structure. "It sure is."

"Welcome *home*, Alice."

Four
Dorothy

Summer had begun and a lot was happening as it was a very special summer. This was the year that my Aunt Em had decided it was time for me to try to make some friends aside from everyone out at our family farm.

"I have a singularly wonderful friend already," I had insisted when Aunt Em and Uncle Henry broached the topic with me at dinner one night.

"Sorry, Dorothy. As singularly wonderful as Toto is, you need a little more from a friendship than I'm afraid a dog can give," Uncle Henry had replied kindly.

"Look, Dorothy," Aunt Em had chimed in, setting her silverware back down on the table. "We agreed that doing everything at home was best when you first got here. It was intended to give you time to adjust to your new life here."

"Exactly," I had agreed cheekily, only to be deflated a moment later.

"Well, Sugar Cube, you got here when you were eight years old. You are sixteen now. That's a mighty long time to have adjusted," Uncle Henry had pressed. "We think maybe trying to spend a little more time in town might help you make some new friends. Maybe even a summer job… We could lighten your farm chores a little. Your cousins can pick up the slack. What do you think?”

And so, there I was, a month later, standing behind a counter in the town market, waiting for my day at work to be over so I could get back to the farm.

It wasn't that I was so attached to staying in Kansas. On the contrary, I was looking forward to some unknown grand adventure I might have in the future. The problem was that the only way I could have an adventure, outside of Kansas, was for me to stay focused. Plus, I felt safer sticking closer to home where things were sturdy and familiar. I could control my own trajectory straight over a rainbow if I wanted to.

I hadn't much experience being social, and I didn't see the point in starting now. There would be time enough for that later when I was where I was going to be long term. For now, I worked hard, studied a lot, and my adventure would come when I got to be an adult and went away to college. And, I was going to have to pave my own way to that dream.

By being schooled at home, I could finish as much coursework as I wanted, as fast as I could manage. I could spend all day with the farm animals, and my dog, without any sort of dramatic encounters of flexing muscles and batting lashes. Moreover, I could just exist as I wanted to, without really being told what to do. I could dream and plan my future as I wanted it.

“Ahem,” I was snapped back to reality by the sound of a familiar cough.

“Uncle Henry!” I cheered.

“Hey there, Sugar Cube!” Uncle Henry beamed back at me, clutching a picnic basket. “I know your shift is just about to finish up and I had a few things to deal with here. I thought I might bring your singularly wonderful friend to walk you home."

Right on cue, Toto's head lifted the lid of the basket. His big brown eyes twinkled happily against his black fur as he stared up at me.

"Er, don't tell your Aunt Em. I know you're supposed to be interacting with people-folk but, I figured we could ease you in a little bit better," Uncle Henry said quietly as he handed the basket to me.

"And I love you all the more for it," I gushed and leaned forward to plant a kiss on my uncle's cheek.

"Gale!" My new supervisor barked out. "You're free to punch out. Looks like most people are headed to some musical something or rather in the park. You'll probably want to go too."

"Well... I suppose I am expected to go," I mumbled under my breath before adding, "Thank you."

"Are you going to go to the park then?" Uncle Henry piped up as I punched my time card.

"I guess I will stop by and see what it is all about," I agreed amicably.

"Excellent. I'll see you at home." He waved goodbye as he exited the store.

"Well, Toto, I guess this is our adventure for today. Who knows, maybe it'll be exciting after all," I cooed to my dog as we stepped outside.

Toto gave an inquisitive yurp from his basket. I set it down, allowing him to hop free as I straightened out my blue gingham dress and tucked a strand of hair that the wind had plucked from my braids.

Toto led the way towards the park and I followed slowly as I amped myself up to the engagement. I could hear the music starting to filter through the trees and decided to shortcut through a dense patch of growth.

This would be my first mistake that day.

No sooner had I spotted an opening to go through, than I plunked my foot down on someone's pretty pink dress— complete with a muddy footprint.

"Ugh! What do you think you're doing?" Came the indignant squawk of the dress' owner.

With a small internal scream, I pried my way through the remaining brush to face a young blonde girl, with perfectly quaffed curls, and a pinched nose. I immediately recognized her as Miss Felicity Arroyo— who everyone referred to in Midwestern stead simply as Miss since her family was rich and everyone treated them as too superior to forgo formality. She, naturally, wasn't alone either, and was surrounded by a full assembly of her closest cohorts. All the peers thought she was so exotic because she wasn't from Kansas, and was able to take trips to Europe with her family.

"I am sorry. The wind knocked some leaves in my face. I didn't see—" I started to apologize, but Miss Felicity cut me off.

"But why were you in the leaves in the first place? You aren't from school. Are you some kind of hobo?" She scoffed, her pinched nose wrinkling with scornful satisfaction.

"Certainly not. I was just finding a shortcut," I huffed in response. I could feel my cheeks turning pink with embarrassment.

"Mmm. I don't think so," Miss Arroyo chuckled, her eyes squinting with disdain. "Look at those shoes! Anyone in those wretched things must be a hobo."

Her friends snickered at her jibe, only encouraging her to go further.

"And, I think," She took a step closer to me. "You should do us a favor and go back into the bush!" She crowed and shoved me.

"Ack!" I squawked loudly as I toppled back into the clump of foliage, throwing the picnic basket to some unknown location.

Toto leapt into defense mode of his owner and charged forward to land a hearty chomp on Miss Arroyo's pretty pink satin skirt. He gave his most fearsome growl, and clawed at Felicity's porcelain legs.

She screamed bloody murder. "Get this mangy mutt off me!"

"Toto, release," I commanded unenthusiastically, feeling like the little witch had deserved exactly what she had gotten. I once more clamored out of the bushes with growing indignation.

Toto did exactly as he was told and came to sit by my insulted feet. Meanwhile, all of Felicity Arroyo's friends had clustered around their swooning leader as she inspected the tiny claw marks— hopefully permanently— marring her perfect skin.

"You mark my words, Dorothy Gale…"

"Oh, so you do know who I am then. And that I live on a farm outside of town and not in these bushes?" I quipped back as I picked up my dog.

"Of course we know who you are! We always make note of who the *freaks* are," Miss Arroyo rasped angrily, returning to a looming position in front of me. "You are a weird, dirty, hermit that doesn't belong with society and that's why your family keeps you shut up at the farm."

"Oh, right—"

"And, after your family pays for my dress that you ruined," Miss Arroyo gestured to the skirt that the growing wind was blustering around her legs. "I am going to make sure that you and little vermin regret attacking me. My family can destroy yours."

I blanched and hugged Toto close to my chest. "You… you

can't do that," I spluttered weakly. This was my second mistake that day.

"Is that a challenge, Dorothy? Just you wait. I'll get you back for this."

"You are wicked, Felicity Arroyo!" I shouted back at my new nemesis.

A flash of dry lightning cracked overhead, and the growing wind ushered in a sudden cluster of dark rolling clouds. The trees began creaking and people in the park were struggling to hang on to their hats. The blades of summer-green grass rippled like waves, and the bows of greenery bobbed up and down. Seconds later, the whirling air was split with the sound of a wailing siren, warning that a twister was on its way. Feeling my anger and hopelessness boil inside me, I turned and fled back through town. This was my third and final strike of mistakes that day.

More lightning illuminated the black sky as townspeople closed up windows and barred their doors. Everyone was heading for their cellars, and common sense would have told me to stop and ask to hide out in one in town. But, when the storm passed, I didn't want to be anywhere near Felicity Arroyo and her threats of destroying my family. Maybe Aunt Em and Uncle Henry could help. So, I kept running back towards the farm, leaving the scrambling town and sirens behind me.

I bolted down the dirt path, now swirling dust and gravel around my legs, that would eventually lead to my family's farm. Though normally I appreciated the distance, in that moment, I cursed living quite so far out of town. A loud snap made me jerk my head to the right as I saw a tree starting to break at its trunk, the wind blowing it over.

"The twister," I puffed, and gripped Toto tighter as I bolted towards the farm house. "It's coming."

The farm was within sight now and I just needed to make it to the cellar. I willed my stinging legs and bursting lungs onward. My hair had all but unraveled from my neatly plaited braids, dragging strands through my mouth and slapping my eyes. But, I had to keep going. The strong gusts threatened to carry me with them as I finally approached the house, and I saw the swirling dark cyclone on the horizon, torrent chaos looming. There was an unsettling shimmering fog rolling around inside it, and I couldn't fathom what was lurking within that tangle of screaming clouds and darkness. I spotted Aunt Em and Uncle Henry's pickup parked in the driveway—confirming to me that Uncle Henry had made it home safe— and sprinted the last stretch to the cellar door.

I pulled the latch to safety but it wouldn't budge. I banged on the door and called the names of my aunt, uncle, and cousins, but my voice was drowned out by the screaming of the wind. Lightning cracked overhead, a terrifying flash illuminating the approaching destruction.

"They can't hear us Toto," I whispered to my dog. "We will have to hunker down in the house." Abandoning the cellar, I threw open the front door to the house, noting that the wind had already ripped our screen door clean off its hinges.

Toto was protected underneath the bulk of my body as I curled into a ball between the sofa and the coffee table. The twisting wind crashed against the house and shattered all of the windows in a single blast. It howled through my hollow home with a vengeance.

I threw my hands over my head and I wished with all my might that Toto and I could be anywhere but there. Just somewhere, anywhere, safe.

I began sliding involuntarily for a moment and, with a

sickening feeling, I knew our tiny house was airborne. Furniture smashed against the walls, and their fragmented remains reverberated against me. I tried to shield Toto from the worst of it. Then, *thud*. We made an impact with the ground and everything was suddenly entirely still.

Five

Alice

I awoke to sunlight filtering through the pin-hole gaps in my makeshift roof, and rubbed my eyes groggily. Reaching for a small sharp stone, I scratched a new mark in the wood beside the little bed to indicate the start of another new day in Wonderland.

"Two thousand, three hundred and seventy two," I said aloud. That's how many days I had spent in Wonderland. That was how many days no one from home came looking for me, found me, or seemed to care. And, that was the number of days since I'd finally made new friends and met my favorite person in either world. That was nearly six and half years ago.

My fingers twirled absently around the cursed compass that still dangled from my throat. Peter and I had never noticed any overnight dramatic changes to my personality, so we concluded that the magic must be buried deep within the compass and required a catalyst to unleash it. He had revealed he didn't much care for magic so it made sense that we never really looked into it any further as long as it wasn't doing anything.

Every now and again I would have some nightmares about unleashing a great deal of anger, and giving into some of my darkest thoughts, leaving nothing but destruction and death behind me.

Sometimes the nightmares would be of no one here in Wonderland caring that I vanished, just like my own family had done. I knew it had to be anxiety over not knowing what was lurking within the compass, but each time I'd have the dreams, it left me feeling very unsettled. I didn't want anything bad to happen to any of my friends— most of all, Peter. And I definitely didn't want him or anyone else forgetting me so easily.

"Good morning, Love!" As if on cue, Peter's head poked through the doorway. "Decent?"

"It'd be too late now, if I wasn't" I sighed, but smiled and sat up. We had expanded the fort into a very tiny cabin over the last few years. After I had managed to help this Carpenter fellow stop a Walrus from foolishly pulling a few sleeping oysters from their beds in a small pond close to the Southern border, he had obligingly helped renovate my home. It had been an odd day, even for Wonderland.

The Tweedles had gifted me with a bed— this time I made sure there was nothing cursed about it— and The Mad Hatter and March Hare both gifted me with a great number of dishes. The Carpenter had managed to work a crude water system for drinking nonsense-free water, but for bathing I had to go to a stream.

"You know, I still don't know what the big deal was. You've seen *me* shirtless. You see me without a shirt all the time, actually."

"It's different!" I scowled at him and crossed my arms.

"Oh, right. Because you have—" He started to gesture to his chest.

"Peter!" I threw my moss-stuffed pillow at him. It had been six and a half years since we had first met, and we had both stopped aging ourselves a little over a year ago, leaving us both infinitely about seventeen years old. It gave us both the growth we'd talked about, but also gave us a good year of barrier between our infinite childhood and adulthood.

He dodged my pillow attack easily and floated into the room fully. "Fiery as ever today, I see."

I reached blindly for something else to toss at him, then stopped when I saw what I was holding.

"I didn't say I didn't like it, Love," Peter laughed, shaking his head. "But you don't need to go breaking the snow globe I gave you."

In my hand, I held the enchanted bubble Peter had gifted me in my first year here. It had been for our Christmas lesson, when I taught all my friends here about holidays and we'd had a holiday party and played a secret Santa game. Peter had somehow managed to acquire what would equate to a magical snow globe in our world, so we could go inside and play in the snow until the magic ran out. He'd given me my very own winter Wonderland, and it was a very dear and precious memory to me.

Now, it couldn't be entered into again, but instead was a priceless keepsake. I smiled fondly and set it back down on the little shelf by my bed. "How long are you going to milk that one?" I teased, throwing my legs over the edge of my bed and stretching.

"When someone else does something more amazing," He gloated, plopping on the bed next to me.

I shoved him playfully. "I know. It was a very splendid gift. Now, why are you pestering me first thing in the morning?"

"Don't I always?" He bumped me back with a broad shoulder. "Wait, what do you mean *pestering*? You can't wait for me to show up every day! The adventures don't start until I get here!"

He poked me in my ticklish rib, successfully achieving a burst of giggling from me. "How do you know I haven't been adventuring on my own?" I asked dramatically. "Maybe that's why I am so tired when you get here *so early*."

"You have to maximize the day, Love. And you wouldn't dare adventure without me." He leaned back to slouch on his arm.

Life adventuring in Wonderland had been wonderful. I'd seen so many amazing things, and had gotten to meet a lot of curious, but interesting company— such as Dodo, the infamous Bill and his ladder, The Mad Hatter and March Hare. I never did find the white rabbit again, and we decided to assume he had run off into the Queen of Heart's territory, which so far we avoided.

And, it was true. I had shared each of those marvelous moments with Peter. We had such fun together, and it made me look forward to what nonsense we would get up to next. Peter had easily become my favorite person to spend my days with. Then, days turned into months, and months into years. Even though I occasionally would remember my family, I would push it away before it could overwhelm me. They'd never found me, and I couldn't go back. So, I had to make a life here.

I liked to think there was a part of Peter that truly fancied me as I did him— that same fluttery feeling in my stomach as when we had first met had only spread in rampant flapping and occasional palpitations. After all, he was willing to grow up with me—At least a few years, anyway. Apparently, that's a pretty big deal, not to just Peter specifically, but the entire motif of Neverland as a whole. He'd insisted it was fine all the same, so long as we stopped before getting to be actual adults. It just made me happy that he'd made such a big decision based on wanting to spend time with me.

It was a difficult sensation to decipher without anyone to discuss it with. All I knew for certain was that I enjoyed the time we'd spent together. I really did go to sleep thinking of our time together, and awoke eager to see what we'd do next in this crazy place.

I tried to advise myself not to trust him completely. He was mischievous and impulsive, and had led me into danger more than once. Then again, I could be short tempered, overly curious, and equally as impulsive. We were either a very good match for each other, or we'd be the death of one another.

Still, as time went on, and he did indeed grow bigger and stronger, I could not help but notice that he was also most definitely growing into a handsome young man, who also unwaveringly helped me out of danger each time we faced it. Thoughts and memories over the past few years swirled in my mind. Time had moved so quickly.

I jumped to my feet and headed for the door, looking coyly over my shoulder at Peter. "You're wrong! I've been having moonlight adventures with… Bill!"

Peter feigned indigent hurt and anger, smashing his fist into the bed. "You wouldn't dare! Why would you need his ladder when you have me to fly with?"

"His ladder is better than flying," I goaded and made a break for the door.

"You've gone too far now!" Peter crowed and zipped after me.

I ran as fast as I could through the woods, now a relatively familiar terrain. I had learned that there were certain parts of Wonderland that reordered themselves, jumping to various locations in the land. Like the Hatter's cottage. It would pop all around Wonderland.

Peter whizzed through the air behind me, catching up in an instant. He made a dive to tackle me, and I stepped to my right to dodge behind a tree, sending him tumbling through the empty air.

"Bloody hell," He swore at his fumble, though his face was bright and full of mischief.

"Ha!" I cheered, and raced away deeper into the woods, the vibrant foliage blurring around me, until I erupted into an open clearing that seemed more like a small meadow in the middle of the densely wooded land.

I paused to catch my breath from my sprint and pulled my long hair back from my face with my faithful black hair ribbon. While my red dress was now torn, a little too small, and threadbare, my ribbon had actually held up rather well.

"Got you," I heard Peter whisper in my ear, and the next thing I knew was on the ground tumbling through the soft grass. An explosion of tiny creatures fled our human tumbleweed, and when we finally stopped rolling Peter had me lightly pinned.

"Hey!" I protested. "No fair, you fly faster and you're stronger than me."

"True. Now, take it back!" He insisted, his crooked smile stretched to its limits. He narrowed his eyes playfully.

"Never!" I howled, squirming wildly. "You might be faster, bigger, and stronger, but best not forget that I have gotten more clever."

"Take back that midnight climbs on Bill's ladder is better than flying with me," He laughed and began poking at my ribs again.

My eyes began watering from how hard I was laughing. "No," I gasped. "You can't make me."

"I beg to differ, Love. Your brains can't beat my brawn here." He paused his tickle attack to gloat.

I stared up at him hovering above me and my heart did that strange palpitation thing it sometimes did. I rationalized it was still beating so hard from the run and wrestling about. But his green eyes were so bright, the way his messy mop of auburn hair shaded them, the freckles on his permanently sun-kissed nose, and that charming crooked smile… I forgot myself for a moment and the next thing I knew, I had leaned up and planted a kiss on his cheek.

His eyes widened with surprise and his grip on me slackened until he reached one arm to touch the spot where I had just kissed. "You gave me a th—"

"Ah ha!" I cut him off before my mortification could kill me right there on the spot. I wondered if I could actually blush so much that it would boil me alive. Why in the world had I done that? Stupid! I had to play it off. I took Peter's off guardedness and surprise to my advantage and knocked him off of me before jumping to my feet.

"Why did you…?" He was still staring at me, completely dumb struck.

I squirmed inwardly, hoping I hadn't just somehow done something so terribly strange that it ruined our friendship entirely. "I told you I had gotten more clever. You shouldn't underestimate my ability to get away next time," I said quickly.

"So, it was to get away?" Peter asked slowly, rubbing his chin thoughtfully..

"Of course it was." I looked down at my feet subconsciously and began fiddling with my compass.

Then he seemed to give himself some sort of mental shake and started laughing. He grabbed my hand and brought me back onto the ground beside him. "Well played! I guess you really are more clever. It definitely surprised me."

"Clearly," I joined in the laughter. "But, you are right."

"About what?" Peter looked lazily at me.

"Bill's ladder isn't as fun as flying with you, though I do

wish you'd let me fly on my own sometime," I pressed lightly.

But Peter shrugged it off. "How would I be there to catch you if we did it that way?"

"Fine," I sighed. I'd already brought up that if I was flying I wouldn't *need* him to catch me when we'd discussed this before, so I didn't push it further. Instead, I changed the subject. "Now, what did you have in mind to do today when you first showed up?"

"I thought we could go searching for Mome Raths today. Dodo told me he'd seen them around Nonsense Falls," Peter suggested, sitting up.

"Did he now?" I sat up after him and quirked an eyebrow. The Dodo's information was always rather embellished.

"Okay, I know what you're thinking, but Cheshire was there and he said they'd been there too!"

"Oh, now you've really convinced me," I said sarcastically and rolled my eyes.

Peter bumped me with his elbow. "He did! Or, at least, I think he did. Anyways! We can always see when we get there.

"Or we could go explore Neverland since we are already close to the South?" I offered with a cheeky smile. Even after all my time here, Peter still had managed to get out of showing me his precious Neverland. I often wondered why, but tried to remind myself that the one time I had gone there on my own to find shoes for the Hatter in a pirate chest, I'd nearly been drowned by mermaids. So, he probably was just being protective or something.

"But, the Mome Raths! We've been here ages and still haven't caught one," He countered, including overly animated gestures of grandeur.

"Nonsense Falls is on the other side of Wonderland!" I laughed. "Bill's nightly visits make me very tired, you know. He is a very chatty lizard.”

“Very funny, Love.” Peter rolled his eyes and floated into the air. “It’s not too bad as the bird flies. And it’s even faster when I fly. Plus, we would have been closer if you hadn’t run the opposite direction.”

I threw my head back and groaned. “Alright, I have wanted to find one of those elusive Mome Raths. I guess that makes it our explorer’s duty to find one.

“Quite right!” Peter cheered and flew in an excited circle. He tugged me up and into his arms for flight. “To Nonsense Falls!”

I smiled and shook my head. “To Nonsense Falls!” I echoed his cheer, pointing dramatically forward. “Charge!”

~*~

Our quest to find a Mome Rath had not been successful by the time Peter dropped me back off at home and I’d crawled into bed. We had seen evidence that the creatures had been there, and were likely just hiding very well, so we had called it a day, eaten some dinner, and decided we would try again tomorrow.

“Today was a good day!” Peter had called as he left. “Try not to get too tired with Bill tonight. We’ve got an early day.”

“I kissed his cheek,” I whispered to myself as I sank into my bedding. “*Why*, Alice?” I pushed my palms against my eyes and groaned.

“Are you going to answer yourself?” The familiar feline voice purred in my ear.

“Cheshire!” I scolded as the fluffy cat materialized on the shelf next to the globe. “I told you, I don’t like when you randomly materialize in here and eavesdrop.”

"Is it eavesdropping when you're not speaking to anyone else?" He laughed heartily.

I pursed my lips in frustration but didn't reply. He'd only confuse me into agreeing with him. Instead, I asked him a question. "What brings you here tonight?"

"Oh, I felt a dreadful chill and could have sworn it was purple. Or was it green?"

"Chills don't have color." I tilted my head but smiled at the cat. "Besides, it never really gets too cold here. You know that. It must have been in your head."

"In whose head?"

"Yours."

"Oh, no. It doesn't get cold in my head. And it only gets hot in yours."

"What?" I gasped, wondering how in the world Cheshire could possibly have any insight to the heated feeling in my nightmares.

"Starts with a chill and ends with a fire," The cat purred lazily. "Dream wisely."

Then, he faded away, successfully leaving me confused like he almost always did. Was he trying to warn me of something? I also felt a little unsettled, and wished Peter was still close by. I'd feel safer with him here.

"Best to just go to sleep," I advised myself, willing away the ambient eeriness surrounding me as I sat alone in the darkness. I tugged my blanket closer around me for comfort. "Goodnight, Cheshire," I called softly, just in case he was still lurking around.

Despite the underlying sensation of cold fear that ran through my body, I managed to drift off to sleep fairly quickly, and as I did, the coldness grew until I was shivering as my dream began to materialize. I was standing alone in foggy darkness.

A loud ticking noise echoed through the space, startling me. I whirled around trying to discern what was happening. When the tick sounded again, I realized it was coming from my compass. I gripped it tightly and brought it up to my eyes to see it slowly swiveling from northwest to the East.

My teeth chattered, and when I looked back up, I saw a large floating bubble in front of me. Inside of it I saw my family's home. It was snowing there, and the lights were all dark. It looked so depressing. I watched as I saw movement in the window and caught a quick glimpse of my sister—older now— staring miserably through the glass out towards the meadow beyond the garden. Her left hand was holding back the curtain and I realized, with a small intake of surprise, that she wasn't wearing a wedding ring.

"Eleanor?" I called, but like a bit of cloud, my breath disturbed the bubble and it popped. I was once more standing all alone, but this time I was in a small clearing of Wonderland. Another tick sounded, a blurry cloaked figure shuttered into view in front of me. A pale hand reached forward and tapped the face of the compass, then the arrow dropped to southeast.

A terrible heat started building in my chest and I dropped to my knees. I knew this feeling. It was anger, resentment, and bitterness. It was every moment I had ever felt alone and insignificant. I erupted into flames and the fiery force of it scorched everything around me. I heard a cry of pain and turned around to see Peter on the ground, his body badly burned.

"No!" I screamed and raced to his side. I was still crackling with fire as I kneeled beside him. The stench of burning flesh stung my nose and I had to swallow back a gag.

"Get away, *witch*. Your magic is Wicked," He groaned,

trying to push me away, only to be burned again. His eyes were glossy with betrayal and pain "Alice, how could you?"

"Peter, I'm so sorry! I didn't mean to, I swear," I sobbed. "I just got so angry… I couldn't control it."

But Peter's eyes had gone still and lifeless and I screamed, scrabbling away from him. I hugged my knees close and tried to rationalize to myself that this was just a nightmare and I could never hurt Peter in real life. It was just a terrible, terrible dream and I only needed to wake up.

I felt a cold chill go down my spine, quelling the fire with it, and a foreign voice hissed behind me. "It's activated. Where will you run?"

I gasped, but when I whirled around to see who had spoken to me I saw the hooded figure blow away in a puff of smoke. The wisps were purple.

My eyes snapped open when I felt a soft touch on my shoulder, and saw Peter looking down at me with concern. I was awake again. I bolted upright and threw my arms around him.

"Are you alright?" He asked, hesitantly returning the hug to reassure me. "I was on my way here and I heard you scream, but when I got here you were still asleep."

I tried to slow my breathing. "Yeah, I'm alright. I just had a bad dream. You got hurt."

"You got that worked up over me getting hurt?" He asked in surprise.

"Of course I did!" I pulled back and looked imploringly into his eyes. "It was my fault you got hurt."

"Don't worry, Love." Peter smiled at me and patted my hand gently. "Look, I'm right here and I'm just fine. You haven't hurt me a bit."

"Yeah," I sighed in relief. "You're right."

"Do you still want to go look for Mome Raths at the falls?" He asked, his hand still resting over mine.

"Yeah, sure. I want to," I said in a hurry, snatching my hand back self consciously. "Everything is fine. I'm fine. Let me just splash my face, straighten my hair up, and we can go."

"Sounds good," Peter nodded and worked up a smile, though I wasn't entirely sure I had convinced him.

"See, if Bill had been here, I'd never have had the dream at all," I joked, pouring a little water into my hands to splash my face, then set to work fixing my hair. I noted to myself that I should make a trip to wash up fully at some point today.

"Ah!" Peter scoffed. "So Bill's infamous ladder prevents bad dreams now, does it? See, that's it right there. It's your not-so-secret adventures with him that's really hurting me— no, *wounding* me emotionally. I think I'll be scarred for life, actually."

"Scars are fine," I chirped, and tugged him to the door. "They look tough. Let's go find those Mome Raths."

"Lead the way, Love."

Six

Dorothy

My head was pounding and I could hear the *tinking* sound of glass settling from its suspension in the air. I slowly raised my body from the ground and checked Toto, who, once free, exploded out from under me and looked around wildly.

I clambered to my feet and approached the front door to figure out where my house had been dropped. Hopefully it hadn't moved too terribly far away from the foundation. I was also hopeful that Aunt Em, Uncle Henry, and my cousins might emerge out of the cellar to receive me.

One of our cabinets had been knocked in front of the door, and it took all of my strength to slide it to the side enough for me to slip out. My eyes widened at what I saw before me, and I clutched my head, certain I had a concussion.

"This certainly isn't home… I, I don't even think this is Kansas anymore, Toto," I stammered breathlessly as I looked around at the tiny village I had been plopped in the midst of.

Every little round cottage was no more than three feet tall, each one painted a vibrant shade of blue and fuchsia. Spiraling from the center of the little town was a yellow brick courtyard that eventually turned into a little road, leading away from the houses on either side of the small village.

I stepped out the front door and scanned all around me. To my surprise, my house's exterior was not broken or buckled in any way as one might expect from a tornado tossing. The screen door was still missing and the windows were still busted, but the boarded white walls and blue trim remained in the exact same condition as they were in before the twister. The sky was a picture-perfect blue, and the sun shown happily down in the little clearing. Like the storm had never even happened.

A sudden onset of harsh and frantic barking around the side of the house alerted me that Toto had spotted something upsetting. My uneasy mind spun through all the horrible possibilities that could be awaiting me as I rounded the corner of my home.

"Toto… What is it?" I asked timidly, only to choke on the end of my question and crumple to my knees. I covered my mouth with a shaking hand trying to process what I was seeing.

Sticking out from the side of the house were two stockinged legs, mutilated at the kneecaps. The still pristine feet were covered by a pair of shimmering silver shoes that glittered in the sunlight.

I blinked back tears and swallowed down a lump of nausea, digesting the fact that my house had just landed on some poor woman and killed her. I plopped down entirely and buried my head against my knees for a moment.

"Ah!" I squealed as a jolt of raw energy surged through my body, and I looked up again to see that the silver slippers were no longer on the dead woman's feet.

Startled, I sprang up, scanning my surroundings for the thief. Who would come steal shoes off a corpse that was still warm? I wished that I had landed with some farm tool I could use for self defense. I thought about going back in my house to look for a kitchen knife, but was distracted as I began to see little heads slowly poking out from around and inside the tiny houses.

I took a step back towards my house, snapping my fingers to summon Toto closer in case we needed to make a mad dash for the door.

"Who's there?" I managed to call out.

My question was met by the sound of multiple indistinct voices muttering to each other. Then, a tiny man inched his way into the open from his hiding place behind a tree.

"Dead? Is she really dead?" The man asked, his unnaturally pitched voice trembling. I could only assume he meant the woman underneath my house. I nodded and swallowed hard.

Another small person came to stand behind the first. She fidgeted with her skirt, before finally asking, "And, the shoes truly went to you? You wear them now?"

"I beg your pardon?" I asked, appalled, and feeling more confused than ever. "I'm not wearing…" I trailed off, my eyes fluttering to look down at my own feet.

Sure enough, instead of my regular muddied farm shoes, my feet adorned the same dazzling silver slippers I had just seen on the crushed woman moments before.

"But, I swear I didn't take them. I mean, er, I don't know how…" I stammered fearfully. I gripped my head once more, trying to rationalize how the shoes could have gotten on to my feet without my knowledge. "What's happening?"

"She's dead!" The tiny man called out loudly, his voice laced with glee. "There is a new one who wears the shoes!"

Before the echoes of the man's giddy declaration had finished making its way through the clearing, countless more tiny people erupted into the open, each one of them either cheering or asking questions.

"Is she a Good witch?" A tiny woman asked her neighbor.

"Am I *what*?" I piped up, unsure as to why the term *witch* was being tossed in my direction.

"Look, she does wear the shoes!" Another man chimed in.

"The Wicked Witch of the East truly is dead!" The unified cheering grew into a crescendo as everyone joined in at once.

I was left standing over a foot taller than the bustling excitement growing around me, perplexed and bewildered. Toto, caught up in the excitement, began twirling and barking with the rest of the group.

The first tiny man gently tugged at my elbow. "Please, Miss. Are you a Good witch or Wicked witch?" His eyes were bright and hopeful.

"Oh, dear. I'm afraid I'm not a witch at all," I answered him honestly.

"But, you wear the slippers now," He countered, his smile never wavering. "So, you most certainly are a witch now, even if you weren't before.

You see, Miss, when a witch dies here, her powers transfer to whomever is responsible for her death. If the death occurs out of cold blood, you are forever Wicked. If it occurs out of sacrifice, you are Good. Your house falling on the Wicked Witch of the East seems to have been an accident. So then, do you choose to be a Good witch or a Wicked witch?"

"What a strange dream I must be having. Though normally I wake up as soon as I have realized I'm dreaming..." I trailed off and rubbed my temples. "Well, I suppose, if I have the choice, I don't want to be forever Wicked."

The little man stared imploringly and the whole village

seemed to be holding its breath.

"I... I choose Good," I answered more definitively this time.

"Hooray!" The man cheered, and the crowd resumed its parade of glee.

I crouched down a little to reduce the height difference. "Excuse me, sir. What is your name?" I asked the tiny man.

His eyes grew round with awe and he had a sharp intake of breath, as if being asked his name was some huge honor. "Boq Huckensmirf, ma'am."

"Nice to meet you, Boq," I said kindly. "I am called Dorothy back home, in Kansas. I don't believe I am in Kansas at all after the twister picked up my house. Could you please tell me where we have been dropped?" I gestured to me and Toto, who was still prancing in place, absorbed in all the surrounding enthusiasm.

"The very most west part of Oz. This is the Munchkin Village. For years, we have been plagued and tortured by the Wicked Witch of the East. We are ever so grateful for your 'dropping' as you put it."

The munchkin bit certainly explained the tiny people's short stature, but the rest was not so forthcoming. "Is Oz anywhere near Kansas? Perhaps Nebraska?" I tried hopefully.

"Who is Kansas Nebraska?" Boq asked, clearly baffled by the state names.

"Oh, dear. That was what I was afraid of." I shook my head and looked around at the budding forest surrounding the munchkin village. "How does one, um, I suppose... How would I leave Oz?"

"Oh, but you've only just arrived! We have been without proper protection from a Good witch for such a long time. Not since Glinda left for the North and was murdered by the Wicked Witch of the West all those years ago."

I furrowed my brows in confusion. "I'm sorry, did you say Wicked Witch of the West? I thought my house landed on the Wicked Witch of the East?"

"It did."

"Oh. But, I thought you said we were in the westernmost part of Oz?"

"Oh, yes. That is also correct," Boq nodded.

"So, why was the East witch tormenting munchkins in the West?" I prompted.

"Because Oz is in the East," Boq replied with a soft chuckle, indicating this was common knowledge.

"I'm sorry, Boq. It might be my hitting my head in the fall, but I am afraid I am still mighty confused. How many witches are there in this Oz place?"

"Forgive me, ma'am. I have forgotten that you are new to our world."

"World?" I gulped. Was I not even on Earth anymore? Just how big was that cyclone?

"You see, Miss, Oz is the most east from the signpost that sits in the center of our world as a whole. Everything is directionally based here. The Wicked Witch of the East got her name because she was infamous in all of Oz, not just the most eastern side of it.

Usually when we get someone new, they end up at the signpost, but that twister that brought you must have blown you off course due east.

So, you see, there was only one witch to worry about in this part of Oz, and she is dead and gone beneath your home. That is why you have liberated my people from her reign of terror," Boq explained cheerfully.

"So, what about this Wicked Witch of the West then? She

murders Good witches?" I inquired with a bewildered look to the sky to see if any witches were flying by on broomsticks. I was fresh out of houses to drop on witches.

"Well, she is actually fairly well-known in all directions as the most Wicked of witches, for she has killed the most— Good and Wicked. But, I believe West is the direction she started in when she first arrived," Boq paused thoughtfully to think if he had left anything out, then snapped his fingers. "Oh, and the western direction in our world is called Wonderland."

"She arrived here too? Like me?"

"Sort of. It was quite a while ago though."

"Oh. Will I have any luck in the southern or northern directions? I really just want to get back to Kansas."

"I'm afraid I have never left Oz myself. And I don't know for certain who this Kansas person is, but I do not believe you will find them in Oz," Boq conceded. "If you follow this Yellow Brick Road out of Munchkin Village that direction," he pointed west. "Then you should eventually find yourself at the signpost. It will be up to you where to search for Kansas from there."

"Thank you, Boq." I extended my hand, which was accepted with much surprise to the little munchkin man. "It is very kind of you to help me. I hope you enjoy your new freedom. I suppose I will have to leave my house here…" I looked over the place I had called home for half of my life. "Take care of it, please."

"Of course, ma'am. With great honor, we will protect the home of our savior, Dorothy the Good Witch of the East!" Boq's eyes were brimming with sincerity as he squeezed my hand. "Thank you. Best of luck to you."

"And to you. Toto!" I summoned my dog back from the center of on-going celebration.

He bounded over gleefully, tongue lolling and eyes bright and undaunted. "Alright, Boy. Let's see if we can't find this signpost."

But, before we walked away, the air was spliced by a screeching sound overhead.

"She knows!" The munchkins began wailing as they bolted back into their homes.

"What?" I looked around wildly to see some winged beasts flapping about in the increasingly darkening sky.

"The Wicked witch must want you. Run, Dorothy!" Boq cried out as he dove for cover.

I didn't need to be told twice. I quickly scooped up Toto and bolted away from the village down the Yellow Brick Road.

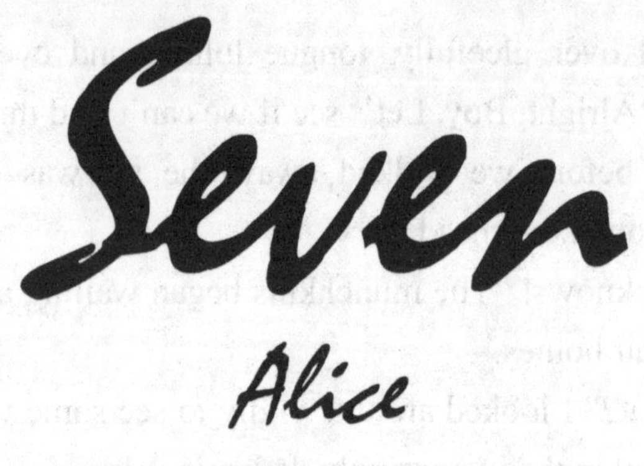

"Be careful, Love!" Peter's voice broke through my distracted thoughts that were torn between the horrible nightmare I'd awoken from earlier, and my quest to find a Mome Rath at Nonsense Falls. It was eerie to realize that Cheshire's strange warnings before bed had been right on target. I guess I didn't dream wisely like he had advised. Shivers of unease were actively being pushed away.

I was balancing on a log that reached across either side of Nonsense Falls. I had taken my shoes off and was walking barefoot, feeling the damp bark bend around my toes. I'd outgrown the shoes a while ago, but not so much that I couldn't make do. Most of the time, I was barefoot like Peter these days. There was a mist spraying around me, and little beadlets of water were collecting in my hair. "Any luck?" I called back to him, kneeling down to peer into a hole in the log.

"None over here," Peter's reply came from a short distance away, and I imagined him probably mostly ensconced in a bush.

"I don't think I see anything either. Maybe we ought to regroup and look somewhere else. How about— Ah!" I squealed, as a shiver of cold ran over me and my hand suddenly slipped on the moss-soaked bark. I teetered for a moment before losing my balance fully and slipping off the log towards the pool of water. "Peter!"

I was tumbling headfirst towards the water— the water that turned people insane if ingested. I braced myself for the hard contact the height of the fall would surely inflict, and closed my eyes. But, instead of plummeting into the bottom of the falls, I felt strong arms tighten around my waist and slow my descent. Peter had caught me at the last moment.

"I thought I said to be careful," He chided lightly as he sat me down on the ground. "You alright?"

"If I ever got to fly on my own, you wouldn't have to catch me," I grumbled, avoiding eye contact, instead choosing to glower at the falls.

"Oh, come now, Love. I'm always around to catch you. See, everything is fine. I saved you. Let's see where else we can check for Mome Raths. Maybe we can ask the Dodo for more detailed information." Peter, as usual, waved away my inquiries.

"How about Neverland?" I asked sharply, still glaring at the water. I felt strange. Frustrated without real cause or direction.

"Mome Raths don't live in Neverland, silly," Peter laughed awkwardly, but seemed to have picked up on my mood change. "Alice, are you sure you're alright? If you're embarrassed about falling, it really isn't a big deal."

"Right. Because you can fly and I can't."

"What?"

"Why won't you ever share the pixie dust? Afraid I'll fly off and leave you?"

Peter was quiet. I huffed and finally pulled my eyes away from the water to look at him, but when I saw the expression on his face, my anger seemed to melt away. His gaze was far away and he looked as if I had struck him across the face.

"The pixies have been stingy with dust as of late. I'd hate for you to run out and fall," He replied evenly, slouching back, but never looking away from me. We bickered some here and there, but I never was so confrontational with him. If anything, I was more afraid that he would be the one to fly off and not come back.

I swallowed hard and hung my head. "I'm sorry, Peter. I'm not sure what came over me. Of course I know you have your reasons."

"It's fine, Love. We all get cross sometimes. You did just have a near brush with losing your sanity, so it probably just rattled you or…" He paused and leaned in close to me.

"What?" I asked, inhaling sharply as he reached out and picked up my compass.

"Well, that's new!" His brows raised in surprise.

"What's new?" I snatched the compass from him to look at it. The arrow was slowly roving from south back to the northwest position it was normally at. I hadn't seen it do that since my first night in Wonderland when I'd realized no one from my world was coming to find me. Other than in my dream, that is.

My dream.

The compass had been activated. That's what the figure had told me in my dream, which would mean it was going to start taking effect. My face drained of color and I felt instantly ill with dread. The rocky clearing around the waterfall seemed to darken and shrink around me. I felt small and cold.

"What is it?" I felt the warmth of Peter's hand on my shoulder, bringing me back from the cusp of my own despair. "Did you swallow some water or something?"

I looked at him like he was a beacon of light shining warm in the cold darkness. He was calm in the brewing storm within me.

He made me feel happy when I was sad, safe when I was afraid, and cared for me when I was alone. He was *Good*. Then what was I? He was impulsive, reckless, and irresponsible. He rarely took anything seriously, and yet he was always there, keeping me safe. He was my friend. I weighed the option of telling him my dream against not telling him. The choice became abundantly clear.

"The dream I had, you know, the one this morning," I began quietly, and Peter nodded. "Well, there was this figure in it that tapped the compass and told me it was activated. Then it asked me where I would run. I had all of this anger and fear explode from within me and it killed you."

"Bloody hell," Peter sighed, his eyes wide, but he also nodded along. "So, you think whatever this compass is meant to do has finally started to take effect?"

"Yes," I replied solemnly. "And, whatever its going to do to me is bad, Peter. I don't want to hurt anyone, least of all, you."

"Of course you don't. I'm your *favorite* after all." Peter cracked a smile.

"You mean, you aren't afraid of me hurting you?" I perked up. I'd known it was the right thing to do to tell him what I had seen, but I had also been afraid that he would reject me for such vile thoughts. The world seemed to brighten, and the woods breathed a sigh of relief alongside me.

"Like I said this morning, I'm right here and I am just fine. I can't be mad over a dream. You like to bruise my ego here and there, but other than that, I'm good. We're a team, you and I. Two lost souls in a crazy world, having adventures along the way. Nothing has to change that if we don't let it." He leaned back, relaxed as ever.

"You're right," I smiled back at him, though I still felt apprehensive about what I could potentially be capable of.

"I'm always right!" He chirped cheekily and floated in the air, gripping my hands to pull me to my feet. "You've just have yet to accept that as a reality."

"And I never will," I clipped back, then clutched the compass to my chest. Images of Peter's lifeless eyes flashed before me, and I shook my head to banish the memories of the horrible nightmare. It had felt too real.

Had that figure been living inside the compass all this time? Was it magic? Would it possess me like a demon or ghost? It could be an illusion simply meant to intimidate me, or it could be a cursed fate I couldn't escape.

"Hey, Peter?"

"Yes, Love?" He grinned and looked so happy. Meanwhile, I could feel fear and unrest yawning open within.

"I'm not feeling in best of spirits right now. I'm sorry."

"I think I can find a way to fix that! Let's see… We could have a race? Though I'll obviously win and that won't make you feel better. We could just lay in the grass somewhere and strategize how to locate those Mome Raths. Seems harmless enough."

I shook my head slowly. "Actually, I was thinking perhaps I'd go for a walk to sort of clear my head, sort through my thoughts some."

"We could fly?" Peter offered, extending a hand. "Wherever you want."

I looked at my feet, which were squishing into the muddy ground. "I think I'd like to walk."

"Alright, we can walk. Shall we head back to your home?" He dropped to the ground and looked at me expectantly.

"No, I mean I think I'd like to go for a walk alone."

"Oh. You don't want me to come with you?" His face

crinkled with a mixture of concern and confusion. I couldn't blame him. Since we'd met those years ago, we had spent every single day together. We were inseparable, but now I needed to sort through something he couldn't be a part of, because it was within me, not some adventure he could dashingly storm through.

"Not this time. But I'll meet up with you later. Soon. Just head back by air, and I'll go on foot. You'll beat me there, but we will be heading to the same place and it'll give me time to…" I fished for a word I'd heard my mother use. "Time to process things. Sort my mood out."

"Promise you won't go falling off any cliffs or logs?" He forced a joke, though I could see his shoulders sag. "And promise you'll be right behind me then?"

"Absolutely!" I tried my best to look reassuring. Without thinking, I reached out and threw my arms around him, pulling him into a hug.

"Oh," The sound of surprise escaped him.

"I know this is confusing for you. It is for me too. But we will figure it out together, just like we always do. I just need to sort through a little on my own so I don't, er, you know, do something I'll regret." I released him and patted his shoulder. "Trust me?"

"Always," Peter's eyes flashed intensely before he nodded to me and lifted away to fly through the trees.

I sat in the quiet for a moment. The roaring of the waterfall became dull in my ears. There was something dark forming within me, but why now? I began to walk into the woods, not paying much mind to where I was going.

My mind dragged through images of long afternoons in the garden back home. I imagined running through the meadows, stretching far and wide. I thought of hot baths on cold night, and the picture books I'd look at before bed. Then I remembered the long rainy days when I was trapped inside. Inside a world where no one around understood me. How I'd longed to run through the rain those days, but, of course, Mother would never allow it. I would have been soaked and unkempt, and therefore, unacceptable.

I trudged forward, mindlessly putting one foot in front of another, delving deeper into my memories. The faintest ticks of the compass' twitching needle echoed in my ears. The outside of my skin felt cold and icy, but there was a heat building within. Just like in all my nightmares. Perhaps, if it came out when I was all alone, it would be over and done without hurting anyone.

But in order to let it out, I had to dig deeper and get to that fire. So I kept walking and thinking. Thinking about my past. How I had tried time and time again to get my family to listen to me, to spend time with me. I had pleaded for them to let me show them the world as I saw it, but they hadn't any time for my *wild imagination*. It wasn't proper. It wasn't practical. It didn't look good for Eleanor's respectability, or the family's. I had been an unwanted puzzle piece that simply didn't fit.

I didn't fit in the world of lavish parties, and societal restrictions, where… where… I stopped, and now was standing in some part of Wonderland I had never been before, staring at a row of perfectly white roses. The ticking grew stronger and I glared at the roses, feeling rage envelop me. I was in a bubble of heat and resentment.

"In a world where talking about these damned white roses were more important than finding me!" I finished the thought, my voice rising into a crescendo. My vision blurred in a cloud of blacks and red and the next thing I knew the white roses in front of me were dripping red.

"Hey! What have you done to her majesty's prized white roses?" A voice barked at me and I turned to see a humanoid playing card staring me down.

I looked down at my hands to see them stained in red. *Blood? No. Paint.* There was a bucket of paint on its side at my feet. I must have grabbed it when I'd blacked out. I'd painted the white petals red— the same red as the dress I'd insisted on wearing the day I ran away. I'd run away and found a friend in a world that understood me. I'd found The Hatter, Cheshire, Dodo, Bill, the Tweedles, and the March Hare. I'd found Peter Pan. I stumbled backwards, my mind seeming to break the surface of a deep murky water.

I looked around more consciously now. Somehow my feet had taken me to a part of Wonderland that Peter and I had decided was best to avoid. The Red Queen's castle. I was standing in the hedge maze outside the palace. Flamingos were flocking about, and as a cloud passed in front of the sun, a tall armored figure stepped out from around one of the hedges, which seemed to hiss and part in his path.

"She defiled the flowers, Sir Red Knight." The card, a Six of Spades, pointed a hand at me, the other one gripping a paint brush. He'd been painting an archway, and it must have been his bucket I had grabbed.

The Red Knight was a fitting name for this character. He was formidable in size, and his armor was crimson and iridescent. There was something cold and calculating about him, I could tell, even though his helmet remained obscuring his face, and it put me at unease.

I swallowed hard and cursed my blasted mindless feet for taking me here. I'd promised Peter I wouldn't be far behind him, and now, here I was in completely the wrong direction. He'd be cross with me for sure, when he found out. *If* he found out. Sweat began beading on my brow as I recalled why we avoided this part of Wonderland. The Red Queen was the one who chopped off heads.

"Did she now?" The Red Knight began walking towards me. I stared at him, paralyzed with uncertainty until he stood in front of me and reached his gauntlet forward to hold my head by my cheeks, and looked me over from head to toe. "And you did nothing to stop this filthy wild girl from defiling the Queen's prized white roses? What a shame."

A small whimper of fear escaped my lips and a chill ran down my spine.

Then, quick as lightning, he pulled his sword, and in one fluid sweeping motion, severed the head of the card, without ever even breaking eye contact with me. It rolled to the knight's feet and the headless body collapsed. I couldn't help it, I bit my tongue to try to stop it, but the screams flew uncontrollably from my mouth. I was terrified.

"Peter! Peter, help!" I screeched, rending my face from the gauntlet with such force that I fell backward.

I had only wanted to sort out what this compass would do. Did it bring me here? Was that its purpose… to bring me to the means of my own demise? The ticking sounded again, roaring thuds against my eardrums, thrumming in tandem with the blood and adrenaline now pumping through my veins.

The heat burned within me, turning my fear into malice. I felt braver, sturdier, more resolved as I rose to my feet and faced the knight. I wanted to hurt him for his brutality, but I had no weapons to fight with and with his armor, I wasn't going to be able to land a lucky hit.

Think, Alice. I pushed myself and an idea crossed my mind.

I'd run back from where I'd come. I dodged nimbly around the rose bushes and launched myself at the nearest hedge, hauling myself upward. It coiled and bobbed beneath me, clearly alive and greatly displeased that I was cheating the maze by climbing to a vantage point. Thankfully I was close to the exit. I dropped to my feet and headed there, hearing the heavy footsteps of the Red Knight and more card soldiers falling in hot pursuit.

I didn't let up on my mad dash for the falls. There was a dense patch of woodland that was covered in gorse and other thorny tendrils. I'd lose them in that and then they'd lose track of me in the misty woods and cliffs at the falls. I'd find somewhere to hide there among the rocks until they gave up and retreated.

Or you could lure the knight onto the log bridge and push him in. He'd sink like a stone in all that pompous armor. An intrusive thought pushed its way to the front of my mind and I shook it away, the ticking growing louder. Why would I even think that?

My lungs were burning, and my feet throbbed from the many thorns I had tread through. A quick glance over my shoulder told me my original plan had been correct, and I had lost the soldiers in the thicket. I slowed to a stop in the center of the log bridge to catch my breath.

"Alice! What the bloody hell has happened?" Peter glided down in front of me, looking alarmed and alert as he stared behind me. "Where were you? I heard you screaming. Why is that a normal occurrence for today?"

Trumpets sounded, echoing around the misty clearing. The tone was overwhelming and I clutched at my ears.

"That sounds like the Red Queen's card army. What are they doing out here in the forest?" Peter shot into the air for a better vantage point. "Alice, have you done anything to upset the Red

Queen?" He asked me as he landed back on the log.

"I might have accidentally changed some of her landscaping design…" I answered reluctantly, unsure of how to begin explaining how I had ended up in this situation.

"There she is!" A Three of Clubs pushed his way through the brush into the open.

"What?" I gasped. We'd lingered too long in the open.

"Surround her!" The Club bellowed.

"What did you do, Alice?" Peter queried warily.

"I threw red paint on her white roses," I admitted, clicking my jaw in frustration. "Then this Red Knight fellow grabbed me and decapitated some poor card… I thought I'd lose them in the woods and hide here but…"

Cards swarmed in, blocking off the escape route on either end of the log. We were trapped.

"All this because you painted some roses red?" Peter asked incredulously, his green eyes rolling. "Apparently you might as well have declared war on the castle. Bloody hell. Now what?" He groaned.

"Quick, give me some pixie dust," I hissed at him as I pawed his hip for his dust pouch.

"I don't have any more right now."

"What do you mean you don't have any?" I gasped, incredulous at the notion. "You are Peter Pan. You *always* have dust."

"Yeah, well, the fairies and I are in negotiation right now and I'm currently wearing the last of what I had," Peter explained tersely. "I told you earlier that they weren't being as forthcoming."

"Ugh," I groaned, and looked from one end of the log to the other as the cards closed in closer. My heart raced wildly. *Destroy them. Them or you. Them or Peter*. My mind pushed those dark thoughts to the front.

"The Red Knight wants the filthy girl alive or folded!" The Spade barked at us

"Folded?" I echoed fretfully.

"I don't know, but it doesn't sound pleasant," Peter muttered. He pulled his dagger from his side, behind his pouch, and tossed it from hand to hand. "If I can best pirates, I can take care of some cards."

"That pitiful knife won't do much good against this!"

"Peter! Look out, I cried out as the Red Knight charged forward through the cards, sword raised.

Peter whipped around and blocked the swing in the nick of time with his dagger, but was slowly being overpowered.

Push him. Trip him. Do what you must to protect and survive. The thoughts coursed through me like wildfire, and the heat began building.

"No, not so close to Peter!" I whispered to myself. Was this it? Was this where I'd hurt or kill my best friend?

My head was spinning, trying to think of a way out. The ticking of the infernal compass grew louder until it blocked out everything else around me. Everything seemed to move in slow motion for a moment. The cards were racing towards me, spears and maces and swords raised to fight. Peter was grinding his knife against the much larger blade of the Knights sword.

Do it. My inner voice spoke again, this time quieting the fear I felt about harming Peter. I looked at him and felt calm. I knew then that I would never hurt him, no matter what this damned compass ended up doing to me. He was too precious to me.

Do it.

And now I had to protect that. The red clouded over my gaze and the next thing I knew I was throwing myself against the hilt of the knight's sword to knock him backwards away from Peter. He stumbled, then slipped, falling from the log bridge towards the pool.

He will sink like a stone.

I smiled despite myself at my victory, but then his blasted gauntlet coiled around my ankle and pulled me down with him. I belly flopped against the trunk, clipping my chin before sliding off the slippery surface for the second time that day.

"Alice!" Peter shouted, the desperation in his voice raw, as if he were willing me to somehow float to safety on his words. For the first time in six years, I saw the sky darken in Wonderland, as storm clouds blew in from the east. Dark, rumbling clouds that tumbled over each other.

I saw movement in the shadows at the base of the falls, and a faint glimmer flicker in the distant trees. The hair on my arms rose. The Knight hit the water beneath me, but as his armor shuddered with the impact, it broke apart, revealing an empty suit. He wasn't real. Not physically real anyway, but the armor did in fact sink heavily below the water's surface. I was only a few seconds behind him.

At least I'd been brave when it counted. Perhaps that's all the compass had been; it had been challenging my fears and insecurities, but ultimately, activated to show me my own strength. I hadn't hurt Peter, I had saved him. It was a comforting thought as the pool of insanity rippled to welcome me into its depths.

Peter dove after me but we both knew he wouldn't reach me fast enough this time. "Hold your breath and don't swallow the water." His echoing advice was the last thing I heard before I sucked in my breath and splashed like a missile into the water.

The water was frigid as I sank far below the surface. Bubbles passed by my face as the scattered pieces of red armor sank rapidly beneath me. It was the only thing that kept me from becoming completely disoriented under the water, as I watched the bubbles rise towards the surface.

The fire that had burned so viscerally within me moments before was out, quelled by the shock of the water and the dazed realization that I had been responsible for the Red Knight's lost footing on the log. Even though he hadn't been a real physical person, I hadn't known that when I'd lunged for his sword. Was the courage unleashed in me dangerous or helpful? I'd helped Peter, but condemned someone else. I'd listened to the voice in my head telling me to protect at all costs, and I'd succeeded… But, was that right?

Had the cost been my own sanity and life? Was it selfish of me to even think that way when Peter was safe above the water? My nerves sparked and I felt frazzled. I couldn't push away the knowledge that I'd fallen into Nonsense Falls, and how if I swallowed any water here at such volume, I could lose my mind forever.

I kicked out hard with my feet. My lungs were bursting,

wanting air. How deep was I? My head was growing fuzzy until I was certain I was drowning, on the brink of death. Oddly enough, it made me miss my home. I missed my Mother, who though would often ignore me in lieu of Eleanor's company, had always comforted me when I was truly ailing.

For the first time, I allowed myself to ask what really might have happened when I didn't return that one night. I'd resented that they hadn't known where to find me, but I'd never really allowed myself to move past that feeling and consider whether they even *could* find me. Why would they have ever thought to look for a portal to another world inside an animal's burrow? They didn't think like I did.

Perhaps my harbored resentment was unjustified. Images of the other half of my nightmare flashed in my mind. I'd seen Eleanor looking so forlorn out the window at the meadows. What had happened to her? Did she blame herself for my reckless disappearance?

I pictured her helping look for me, at first annoyed, but then concerned when there was no sight of me anywhere. My father would have locked himself away, and my mother would have blamed Eleanor, telling her if she had paid more attention this would have never happened. A village search party would have been sent out, and when they couldn't find a trace of me, they'd eventually have to declare me dead. The world would have moved on without me with no closure for my family. They had been self-absorbed, lost in parties, pious society, and looking for a suitable husband for Eleanor, but I couldn't believe they'd ever wished me dead and gone.

Perhaps both sides were to blame. Or, perhaps it was all my fault. *I* caused all the hurt and grief when I'd given into my anger and hadn't continued to look for a way home. The thoughts dragged me down as I kept swimming for the surface with a new sense of determination.

I'd had my fun in Wonderland. If I survived this, I would have to search for a way home. Eleanor shouldn't have had to bear the guilt of my disappearance for so long. My parents surely would never be at peace until their youngest daughter was home safe and sound. I had been so selfish to stay so long, immersed in the magic and wonder. I had to get back home. Everyone would be so grateful, they'd ask what had happened and this time they would listen. It'd mean leaving behind all the friends I had ever known, but it wasn't the world I'd been born into, and I knew I needed to make things right. Then maybe I could even return… but something inside me told me it would be saying goodbye to Wonderland and everyone in it for good.

But, while it might not be the fun thing to do, it was surely the right thing to do. My vision shuttered, and my head pounded, everything inside me needing oxygen. I'd seen the darkness in Wonderland, and I didn't know I could unsee it. I just needed to not drown here and now. I had to survive.

Then, as if by a sign from the universe, two hands grabbed onto me and yanked me through the final stretch of water. Without thinking, when I broke the surface, I opened my mouth to suck in fresh air, forgetting that there was still water streaming from my drenched hair down my face, a waterfall of sweetness. Too late, I realized my mistake and spat out the water. Had I swallowed any?

I coughed and spluttered, weakly treading water to stay afloat. As my head started to clear with each intake of fresh air, I saw Peter staring intently at me. He was floating in the water beside me. It had been him who'd pulled me up when I'd almost puttered out.

"Thank you," I croaked hoarsely. "You dove in after me?"

He still was gripping firmly onto my arms. "Of course I did, Love. You can't go dying on me now. We haven't finished our adventures yet."

My heart ached. "Well…"

"We need to get out of this water though. Who knows if you can absorb any insanity from soaking in it or not. Plus you look a little worse for wear."

"Thanks a lot," I grumbled self consciously, pulling away from him to swim away. "Peter, I…" My voice trembled, but I grabbed on to the compass, hoping that since it was still there, it would lend me a little more courage. "I think I need to go home."

"Sure thing, Love. We can definitely cross off today as thoroughly, if not overly, exciting. I think we've earned ourselves a good do-nothing day tomorrow though. Kick back and just enjoy each other's company. I'd suggest with Caterpillar but… Well, you know how he is most days," Peter prattled off happily as he swam along behind me, like nothing dangerous had happened at all. Like I hadn't witnessed a beheading and nearly drowned, after almost basically killing someone else myself.

"No," I said a bit more firmly than I meant to. "I mean my real home. In the real world where I came from. Where I belong."

"What? But you—"

"I need to go, Peter. It's time to stop behaving so childishly and think of my family instead of myself. It's time to look for a way back." I swam to the edge of the pond and climbed onto a large rock.

But, when I turned around, Peter was no longer in the water or anywhere to be seen. Maybe the water I'd gotten in my mouth had made me hallucinate. Or… maybe I'd hurt him after all. The thought crushed my heart, and I blinked back tears. I shouldn't have been so aggressive in my delivery, but I was hurting too. It was an impossible decision to make and yet I'd made it.

If I'd caused some big upset with the Red Queen, then who knew when her anger would ebb. After her knight had fallen in the falls, I could only imagine she would want revenge, and I didn't know that I could survive that. If Wonderland wasn't going to be a safe place to play anymore, then it was apparent that growing up was going to catch up with me whether my body was young or not. My mind knew better now and I didn't know how to undo that. I'd robbed this place of its innocence. I'd hurt my favorite person by being too harsh, and I'd hurt myself by hurting him.

The light was dim, and the surrounding forest growled and cooed in eerie tones. I sat there hugging my knees. Everything had spoiled in the course of a day and it was all my fault. I had never felt so alone and scared as I did in that moment. I was a stupid child and I wanted to be home with my family where I was not going to always be out running danger. It was time I finally stopped being so reckless, and gave into being logical. I'd go back and have to grow up in a world of sanity. I had to admit, having less nonsense and a bit more straightforwardness didn't sound so bad. The only thing I would truly miss from my adventures would be Peter.

I heard a noise and turned, hopeful and expecting to see him. I jumped back, almost falling into the water again as a tall slender figure stepped out of the shadows. She was elegant and poised, the picture of sophistication.

What had frightened me was when I saw that her skin was sickly white, and her left eye was covered with an eye-patch. This was the Wicked Witch of the West Peter had warned me about on my first day in Wonderland. The witch gave me an unreadable smile as

I sat there, soaking wet, alone, and defenseless.

"Hello, Lovely. I don't believe we've met."

The witch did not cackle and she did not condemn me to hell. She did not put a curse on me, or try to frighten me in any way. Instead, she flicked her wrist and I was suddenly dry, my hair resting neatly over my shoulder, my dress like new, and my hair bow tied in two perfect loops. I stared blankly at her, wide eyed and in awe.

That was magic. Real impossible magic.

"My name is Avrilia," She introduced herself, sitting down and smoothing her long black frock that clung to her body. Seeing my obvious hesitation, she gave an awkward giggle. "Come now. Don't look at me like that. If I were going to hurt you, Lovely, I would have done so by now. I simply can't stand being wet, I figured you didn't fancy it much yourself. Stand up on your feet. That's right. Now, would you like to tell me your name, darling?" Her voice was sticky sweet like honey..

I swallowed hard, rising to my feet as she spoke. "Alice. My name is Alice," I answered finally. Peter had said she was a *Wicked* witch. And after my afternoon, it took everything in me to not tremble my way back into the pool of water beside us.

I could use some of that extra courage to get myself out of this situation. I wished Peter would come back, though I knew he had every right to have left to process what I'd said to him. Especially since I had just barked it at him in frustration with no explanation. From what I could tell, since he spent every day with me, I was his closest friend and most favorite person to spend time with too. Losing me would be just as hard on him as it was on me. Especially if he felt the same way about me as I did about him deep down inside. A different sort of fondness, new and unexplored. But instead of talking things through with him to make sure he didn't hate me,

I was sitting here staring at a Wicked witch, waiting for her to do something Wicked.

The pallid color of her skin was not as bad once you looked at it long enough. Honestly, the way Peter had described her, I had expected her to resemble a pale lizard and have scales, but her skin was smooth and completely devoid of reptile qualities. Her good-eye was a soft brown rimmed by a wide pool of white. Long black, hair cascaded from beneath a wide-brimmed pointed hat, pleating into a neat braid that rested over her shoulder. A few strands of the dark waves framed her delicate face. She was actually quite beautiful in her own way, and she looked to be around the same age as my sister when I'd left— early twenties

"That was quite a fall you took, Alice," Avrilia prompted. "What happened?"

"I was escaping the Card-guards," I answered honestly. It probably wouldn't serve me well to be dodgy with a witch of such infamy as to be referred to as the Wicked Witch of the West.

"Oh, yes, that pesky Red Queen and her henchmen. All they ever do is get under foot really." The pale witch waved her hand dismissively. "I've been wanting to find a way to rid Wonderland of her for eons now. It just seems to keep slipping my mind." She tapped a slender finger slowly against her temple rhythmically.

"Goodness," I breathed.

"Oh, come now. Don't look like that. Surely, you have heard of the terrifying Wicked witch lurking west of the signpost." Her eye flashed.

I nodded silently, tugging anxiously at my necklace.

"Then you know I am Wicked. I am not a Good witch." Avrilia's good eye locked onto my compass. "What does that word mean to you, Alice?"

"Wicked or Good?" I asked nervously.

"Both."

"Er, well, Wicked would indicate wanting to do harm to others… cruelty without reason. It's all the wrong actions. Good is, well, the opposite of that. You don't hurt others, and do the right thing," I answered candidly.

"Interesting. So, then, why didn't I just kill you if I am Wicked?" Avrilia smiled.

I stared blankly back at the witch. I hadn't the faintest idea of why she hadn't harmed me yet.

"Exactly. I'm afraid you have a very black and white view of morality, Alice. Which is interesting considering your current predicament. There are a lot of colors in between the two. Most might view me as a villain, but they rarely bother to find out my side of the story."

"How you became Wicked?" I blurted the question, then cursed inwardly. I didn't need to go poking her civility by bringing it up. Then again, maybe she just wanted someone to hear her story. I could understand that.

"Yes." Avrilia nodded thoughtfully. "Do you know how magic works in this world?"

"No, I'm afraid no one has ever explained it to me. I've not been around any magical people since I arrived."

"Is that so?" The witch smiled knowingly. "How interesting. Well, allow me to explain it to you in the simplest way. Those who use magic here are witches. You can be a Good witch or a Wicked witch, but the choice is left up to actions. I was gifted magic before that rule became readily apparent, but the one who gifted it to me is no longer around, and no one else has ever known how to intentionally transfer magic. Magic is transferred to one witch when another witch dies by their hand or direct action."

My heart was hammering in my chest and my mouth suddenly became dry. "So one becomes Wicked when they—"

"Kill someone?" Avrilia interrupted, quirking an eyebrow. "Yes, that is true. But, there are many reasons why our moral compasses can run wrong. Just like not all Good witches' morality points due north." She sat down next to me. "I became Wicked when I was trying to save my sister. I tried to protect her, but it ended up not helping save her after all. In my distress, I lashed out vengefully with magic. It bounced back, because witches cannot fight magic with magic here. It goes haywire. That's what took my eye and changed my skin."

"Oh." My eyes widened. If that knight had died when he'd been knocked off the log, would that have made me Wicked? I wasn't a witch though. "I'm sorry about your sister."

"In a place like this, it is much easier than you'd think to turn Wicked than it is to be Good. Only accidents leave it up to you," Avrilia continued on, with a brief nod to acknowledge my apology. Then, as if reading my previous questions lurking within my mind, she added, "anyone can become a Wicked witch if they kill in cold blood or malice. And anyone can become Good with an act of self sacrifice, though what little good that does if you're dead anyway."

"Oh dear…" I felt sick to my stomach at the thought. I'd come too close to dancing with the devil on that log. Like Avrilia, my intention had only been to protect, but I wasn't Wicked. I wanted to return home to be Good. Surely protecting others and putting them first was Good and not Wicked. Or, maybe I was looking at things too black and white again.

"It's a shame you've got that trinket around your neck." Avrilia broke into my thoughts casually. She tapped her own collarbone with that long prim finger of hers to indicate my compass. "The magic in it is going to weigh you down and hold you back. It will feed on your uncertainty."

"What?" I gasped, looking down at the compass, which was resting in a due west position currently. Did she know about the bursts of courage the compass had given me? Perhaps that meant too much courage was dangerous like I had feared. I bit my lip, trying to keep my mind from running away with me.

"Your compass is active, and it will affect you at random now. Or whenever whoever is in control of it decides to pull the strings," Avrilia explained, folding her hands demurely in her lap. "But, if you can leave here, everything resets. The magic disappears and you can go back to normal… Or perhaps a new normal. That is what I believe anyway."

"Without your sister?" I thought of Eleanor and my heart ached with guilt and homesickness once more. I thought of her ringless hand in my dream and truly hoped I hadn't ruined her life.

"She isn't dead, you know," Avrilia chuckled.

"What?" I tilted my head in confusion. "But, I thought you said…"

"I couldn't save her? Another gray area. You can lose people to more than just death," Avrilia explained, her voice thickly edged with bitterness. "No, I lost her to Wickedness in Oz. She was tricked by a so-called Good witch and lost herself along the way. She has no remorse, and I was chased out of Oz to the West, branded as a Wicked witch after acting hatefully with my magic for vengeance. Good or Wicked, titles can be deceiving depending on who decides them. I never saw Glinda as a Good witch after that. Not after everything she's helped create and be a part of. Fear creates its own form of unstoppable power and it tends to lend itself to darkness. If we don't fight it, it will fool us, betray us, and consume us for the worse."

Despite the heaviness of the conversation, it felt somewhat refreshing to be having a discussion with someone who wasn't insane— that I could tell anyway— and who had such a complicated past. She was direct and forthcoming, and she actually wanted to converse about more serious topics. Everyone in Wonderland was varying levels of bonkers, and Peter always kept things light and fun, which was nice, but I hadn't realized how much I needed to talk about the heavy side of things too. It was like being trapped in a cage of sunshine. At some point you need the rain too.

As I started to feel more at ease with the witch, the previously foreboding atmosphere had lifted and the surrounding foliage swayed gently in the breeze. Golden light dappled the ground, and an ethereal mist rolled off the surface of Nonsense Falls. The whole clearing seemed to sing with mystique.

"I take it you haven't found a way home?" I asked, a bittersweet spark of hope blooming in my chest. Perhaps if she had found a way, I could too.

"The easiest way used to be the second star to the left and straight on till morning. But that way was sealed quite some time ago. Since then, no one else has arrived at the signpost... Until you." She stared at me expectantly.

I realized what she was saying and shook my head. "I'm afraid I can't be of much help. I fell down a very peculiar rabbit hole. I had crawled into a burrow chasing after a rabbit and when I touched some glowing shards of glass, I fell down the hole. I'd felt like a shooting star though because it was coated in silver sparkles. Then, when I landed, I was on a path at the signpost. Everything before that disappeared, so I don't think my way of getting here is a means of getting out," I explained, while Avrilia nodded.

She bit her lip in contemplation. "Anything else?"

"At that point I met Cheshire and he convinced me to go West and—"

"You've been here since," Avrilia finished for me. "Right." Her delicate fingers coiled into a fist of frustration before relaxing once more. She adjusted her hat. "Well, I suppose there isn't much to be done then."

"I'm terribly sorry—"

"Except," She interrupted again, raising a single finger. The use of that one finger was so deliberate, it held a sort of emphatic power all in its own. "There is one thing. Glinda stores memories and illusions in these bubbles. She guards them at the Northern Gate. She closes the gate for the night around this time, and it takes quite a bit out of her from what I can tell."

"Bubbles?" I asked skeptically. "Seems awfully fragile for holding something so powerful."

"Exactly, Alice. But you see, I can't go to the Northern Gate without her being able to see my coming in one of her bubbles. She spies with them and she can see magic in it. The ways in and out of here are magic too. But, see this is where you might be able to help."

"Me?" I squeaked. Perhaps I had been too quick in assuming this woman wasn't insane. She'd completely lost me, and her one visible eye was blazing.

"You aren't magical, despite the compass. She won't have any suspicions of you."

Avrilia clasped her hands together and pulled them apart, the space between turning to a dark cloud, and then forming a dagger.

She offered me the weapon. "If you can damage her bubble, it might reveal the true way out of here when there is no one there to shield them from the world. Who knows, one of the bubbles might be a portal in its own right."

"With a knife?" My voice faltered and I swallowed hard, staring at the weapon. "I don't see why I need a knife to pop a bubble. Won't a stick do?"

"In case you need to fight back. She's powerful and you're a young girl without magic. You need a weapon."

"Oh, I don't think I can do anything like that…" If I harmed Glinda, wouldn't that make me Wicked? Unless it didn't count in self defense.

"Alice," Avrilia leaned in and spoke softly. "Do you truly want to go home? I heard you talking to your friend in the water."

"Yes, I want to go home," I said firmly, balling my fists until my nails were digging into the palm of my hand. "I have to."

"Then we will do what we must to make that happen. Then everything can reset for both of us." Avrilia smiled sweetly, and then her eye appeared to fixate onto the compass dangling around my neck once more.

She stretched her slender finger forward and tapped it with a strange sense of absent force that knocked me off balance a bit despite it only being her one finger. I was right that it held power of its own. I flinched as I recalled the whispers of the hooded figure in my nightmare. The face of the compass fractured a little, shallow cracks crawling across the glass, and Avrilia's composed face winced ever so slightly.

The arrow started spinning, and I felt an internal heat building within me. My brain felt like it was jumping in and out of warm water, submerging into anger and darkness and breaking the surface of clarity once more.

"What did you do to me?" I spluttered, jumping away from

the witch with doubt clawing its way up my spine.

"Nothing *to* you. I defected your compass so no one else can control it. It's going to help you."

"Control me?"

"Don't worry about it, that should be irrelevant now." Avrilia pursed her lips and her eye roved around the area, almost daring anyone to contradict her. "Whoever held its power doesn't anymore. It's free, albeit perhaps a little unpredictable, but free nonetheless.."

I only absorbed half of what Avrilia was telling me. I was burning, but differently than before. It felt more accessible and attuned to me rather than something latched onto me. The feeling of fogginess evaporated in the heat and I lost track of what felt like darkness and what felt like light. I hadn't any idea of what it was that was coursing through me, but I felt invincible. At that moment, I knew whatever I did, I could not be stopped. She must have freed the courage from its warped control!

Seeing the change in my demeanor, the witch stood a little taller. "How do you feel?"

"I feel heated inside," I fished thoughtfully for a description. "I feel capable of anything. I'm not afraid of anything."

Avrilia grinned. "Excellent." She handed me the dagger, and placed her hands on my shoulders. "Take this to the Northern Gate, and pop her bubble. Undo her secrets and veils. She holds captive memories that in the wrong hands can be twisted and controlled. They were never hers to have. They don't belong to her. Follow your compass, it'll show you what to do. Without her interference, we will have a much better chance of going home."

I felt something inside of me pulling me towards the north. I looked at the compass and saw it was still spinning wildly. I nodded and gripped the dagger at my side.

"I'll be here when you're done," Avrilia said, sitting down gracefully.

I started off slowly in the direction of the Northern Gate, feeling a strange desire to destroy overcome me, but faltered for a moment. "If she is Good, why did the Good witch trick your sister?" I asked Avrilia over my shoulder. This world seemed to have an inverted view or morality and I still didn't feel like I understood.

Avrilia hesitated thoughtfully before answering, "We all follow the means to achieve what we believe we need, regardless of our moral titles. You can't trust someone is Wicked or Good simply because of a word, but rather by what they choose to do with it."

I thought about it for a couple of heartbeats and decided the answer satisfied me. The burning in my body felt ready to erupt, needing some sort of outlet I didn't yet have. It made me feel hazy once more, but in a different way this time. Like I was fighting internally to settle into something. Red crept into the corners of my vision and I knew where to go. I turned back and started towards the gate to confront the Good witch for her Wicked actions.

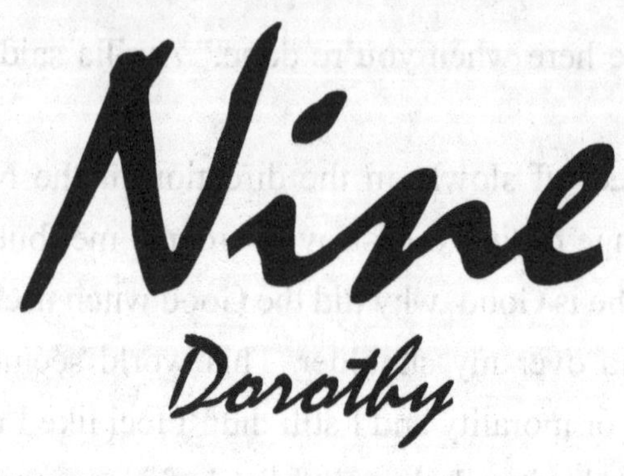

The feeling of pure terror continued to propel my feet forward, despite my lungs screaming for me to stop running. The shrieks of the monkeys had grown fainter, but I kept sprinting forward at full speed. I had to reach the signpost Boq had described to me, then perhaps I would truly be safe— or, at least, find out which direction I needed to go next. I was also feeling vaguely relieved that I hadn't managed to snap an ankle running in my new heeled footwear.

In an instant, the yellow bricks of the road fell away to dirt. Unable to slow my momentum, as soon as one of my crystal toe tips made contact with the dirt, Toto and I were shrouded in a brown haze as a strong wind whirled around us.

"Ack!" I squawked, tumbling to a stop and curling myself around Toto for the second time that day. I closed my eyes against the zipping dust particles. "Not again! I am not even in a house this time!" I wailed.

Then, just as fast as it had started, the cyclone ceased its angry swirling, leaving me and Toto in a crackling silence. The screaming monkeys were nowhere to be seen, or heard from. I slowly opened my eyes and set Toto on the ground. He sagged his head and collapsed, with a definitive plop, onto his side.

"I feel the same way, Buddy," I mumbled quietly to my poor little dog.

As I rose to my feet, I began to take in my surroundings once more. I was surrounded by woodland— a different type of forest in each direction. I turned around and saw I was now standing right in front of the aforementioned signpost I was to look for. *Weird.*

I inspected the post, seeing one picket-fence sign reading North, another West, an emerald patch covered the splinters in East, and the South read in a childish scrawl. I reached out and touched the East sign.

The sun was beginning to rapidly sink below the treetops, warning of nightfall, and leaving me in darkness— the kind of darkness that appeared to echo. Yellow eyes, of various shapes and sizes, were popping up all around me, and anxiety began tumbling in my stomach once more.

"Need some assistance?"

I whirled around at the sound of a voice cutting through the reverberating night. Blinking rapidly, my eyes adjusted to the dark enough to make out a tall sturdy blob standing a few feet in front of me.

"Where did you come from?" I gasped, taking a step back.

The blob then reached into, what I could only assume was a pocket of some sort, and pulled out some sort of shimmering golden dust. Sprinkling the dust over his head, the glowing flecks illuminated the blob and a small radius around him. That is, I could now see it was a *him.*

He had a mop of disheveled auburn hair and bright green eyes. He was in a short white tunic of sorts— the kind that had the criss-cross at the neck—rolled up at the sleeves to reveal muscular forearms, and a pair of brown pants, torn about the knees. His feet were bare. Overall, he had a sort of wild feeling to him.

"Just like this," The boy said and lifted off the ground, grinning like it was some sort of parlor trick and he was waiting for my reaction.

But, I was tired and surly. I had already squished a woman with my house, met tiny rejoicing munchkins, became a witch with magically infused shoes, and escaped a flock of flying monkeys— all before being teleported in a dust devil to the signpost, which had previously been nowhere in sight. I didn't feel like acting astonished at the flying boy in front of me now. As long as he wasn't dangerous, I didn't see the need to get all excited again just yet— especially if he wanted me to.

"Are you a witch too, then?" I asked lamely, as I plopped myself back down on the ground.

The boy, still glowing, frowned and plunked down in front of me. "I am most certainly not a witch. Witches are girls, which I can assure you I am not."

"A thousand pardons, *Sir*," I emphasized his gender sarcastically, and propped my face in my hand. "Go on then, how do you fly if you are not a witch?"

"I use pixie dust," The boy sniffed, then with a twinkle in his eye, he added, "which, of course, comes from *fairies*." He leaned on the word, obviously still trying to conjure a reaction.

"Oh," I sighed. "That must make you fairy-adjacent then?" I smiled tersely at the boy.

"No, it does not." He sagged down with an irritated huff. "What about you, then? You're a witch? I've never heard of you."

"Well, you haven't even properly introduced yourself, let

alone asked me for my name. How would you even know then if you'd heard of me?" I pandered wickedly, shooting an eyebrow up inquisitively.

"Fine, I am Peter Pan. Who, pray tell, do I have this very special honor of speaking with?" The boy called Peter shot to his feet, and gave a tiny bow as he spoke.

"You have the special honor of speaking to Dorothy Gale. My home was plucked from Kansas in a horrible twister and dropped me directly on some woman, who, upon her death, apparently decided to magically imbue my feet with her shoes. That is who I am, and why I am here."

"So, you did kill the Wicked Witch of the East then?" Peter perked up once more.

"No. My house did," I retorted, folding my arms crossly across my chest.

"I beg your pardon. Does that make you killer adjacent?" He grinned cheekily.

"No, it does not," I snipped, and got back to my feet. "It was an accident. The munchkins agreed and allowed me to choose to be Good or Wicked. I sound positively insane even discussing this with you. So, if you'll excuse me, I am trying to escape some very vicious creatures and find a way back home."

"Didn't you say your house was dropped that way?" Peter pointed East.

"Not my house. That can't be home anymore. I need to get back to Kansas, to my aunt and uncle— to my family. They are all I have. That is where home is," I explained and reexamined the signpost. I had to steady my nerves as a piercing wave of homesickness and anxiety rolled over my body. "North looks the most normal. Perhaps I should just head that way," I mumbled to myself as I analyzed the different writing, squinting in the darkness.

Peter looked at my shoes, then back at my face and gave me a thoughtful smile. "I'm afraid I never shared the same sentiment with my family. Though, I do know someone who does. She is trying to get home too, and as luck would have it, I think she is just about ready to figure it out. There is really magnificent tea there too."

"Really?" I turned hopefully towards Peter. "Who is she? Where can I find her?"

"If you head West, you'll find her sooner or later. Her name is Alice."

"Alice? Well, I suppose she is the only lead I've got at this point," I sighed and looked at the western sign. It looked very nonsensical. "And you're certain she is where I am from?"

My question was met with silence. I turned away from the sign to see that the glowing boy had vanished, and I was again all alone with my dog.

The surrounding wheat whistled in a sudden breeze, causing goosebumps to ripple over my skin. I bit my lip nervously and rubbed my hands up and down my arms. A nice cup of warm tea didn't sound too bad in that moment.

"It looks like this is our best shot, Toto. I guess we are going West."

Ten

Alice

Something inside of me knew where Glinda was. I could feel my raging energy and desires being pulled towards her life force. I was like a magnet, negatively charged, being drawn towards my positive. Avrilia had given me a dagger to use as a weapon and the rest was up to me.

I half stumbled towards the Northern Gate, feeling dizzy and disoriented despite the rage boiling in my stomach. Perhaps it was the water from the falls. On any other day, the sensation would have frightened me, but I was not afraid. I was exhilarated, propelled towards a cause.

Heeding Peter's initial warnings of the ambiguous North, I had always just stayed away from it. After all, there had been plenty in Wonderland to keep me busy without venturing in any other directions. North had sounded particularly daunting before, but now I felt my curious nature gnawing at the opportunity to see what it was truly all about.

I knew my newfound bravery had to be due to the compass. I also knew that the witch's touch had done something to free it. I figured it must be something to do with courage. The invincible feeling I felt as the arrow spun around and around was not something

I wanted to go without ever again. It was simply intoxicating.

I neared the border from the West to the North and picked up my feet carefully. She was close, so close I could practically taste it. A new start. It was all only a few moments away. All I had to do was one little jab…

A single dewdrop of doubt pooled in my mind as to how I was supposed to best a powerful witch with just a knife if she did choose to attack. I reflected that Avrilia had assured me there was a certain time when Glinda would be weak from closing the Northern Gate, and I should have the upper hand, and the element of surprise.

Glinda had never met me, and she had no reason to assume a young girl would be carrying a knife and was planning to hurt her. Most importantly, I had yet to be doused in magic of my own so there was no way for her to see me clearly. Even the compass had been altered so she might not be able to pick up on its magic either. My thoughts whirled in my head, filling it up with gusts of chaos.

This was by far the most reckless and impulsive thing I had done yet. Up until now I had just wandered about freely, and sometimes trouble found me. This time I was looking for trouble. I could feel myself being propelled into compulsion by the guilt-driven need to return home, but if everything would reset and I'd make amends for my disappearance, then I had to go with it. And, I'd agreed to help a witch, so I didn't think I could very well not follow through. Though I didn't think she would necessarily hurt me if I failed, I didn't want to risk it either.

Follow the compass and it will show you what to do. I reminded myself that if fear was some sort of agent of darkness, surely having a courage compass brimming with tenacity would aid me as I needed. I just had to see it through and not be held back by fear.

I steadied myself as I saw the glow of the gate. This was my first time being on the edge of North and I had to swallow back my curiosity over what was being guarded behind the gate. It was do-or-die time. I peered through the branches to check the height of the sun in the sky. It was setting, which meant that Glinda would begin closing the gate at any moment now. Then, I would strike.

My eyes dropped from the sky to land on the infamous Northern Gate, and I was not disappointed by what I saw. The bars and pillars were shimmering marble, like they had been carved straight from a star. It reminded me vaguely of how I remembered the rabbit hole I'd tumbled down. Perhaps that white rabbit had been a creature of the North and used some of its magic or some such.

Light poured from the gate, bathing the small glade in silver light. Squinting my eyes, I swore I could see tiny glittering particles floating in the air around the magnificent gate. There was a thick gray mist rolling around on the inside of the gate, obscuring whatever was on the other side. The fog pooled at the base of the entrance and spilled out onto the ground, like a waterfall of swirling clouds.

Floating in front of the magnificent gate were the bubbles I had been sent to reclaim. They were glittering, transparent orbs hovering in the air, flickering images faintly appearing and disappearing again. Memories and thoughts locked in a prism.

And, in front of everything else, was the tall figure I knew had to be Glinda. She was radiant. Every bit of her appeared to glow like an angel, and I wondered why someone like her would be as dangerous as Avrilia said. But, if she was what was keeping me here, I would have to take away her hold. Was it impulsive? Maybe. But, the pull of the compass and the burning heat in my core urged me forward.

Trust the compass. Follow it. I coached myself resolutely, shoving away any doubt trying to penetrate my sense of purpose.

Even Peter had made it seem like the northern area was a type of danger to be taken seriously and it was best to keep one's distance. I suppose I should have attributed that to *whom* it was that made it dangerous rather than *what*. I would be doing this world a favor. It was a logic I could follow, and I was choosing to.

The moment had arrived and my thoughts quieted, centering on one single purpose. I seemed to float silently and slowly forward. I felt as though I was not in my own body, but rather was some sort of detached essence, floating alongside my physical body. It was like I was in a trance. I was absorbed in the heat, magnetized towards my outlet. Everything else was a haze.

It was not until my knife made contact with her bubble that I realized I had actually struck her. To my surprise, the bubble didn't just pop and drop the witch to the ground. Instead it crunched and fractured like glass. I stood there with my hand still on the knife's handle, the blade embedded in the bubble.

Glinda whipped around and stared at me in horror. "What have you done?" She gasped, her eyes were fearful.

I took a step back, doubt freely pooling in my chest again. There was a conflict of the raging heat and the coolness of my own fear, battling for control of my body. Avrilia had told me to follow my compass and it was screaming at me to stop fighting it. After all, it was unfiltered courage I was feeling, right? Then the emotional fever took hold once more and I lifted my chin.

"I am taking away your control of these memories. I am restoring them to their owners so they can't be twisted anymore," I said, and twisted the knife. More cracks spread through the bubble.

"No! Stop, you don't understand. I am not what you think I am."

"I think you're a Good witch who has chosen to do Wicked things," I replied stiffly, blindly reciting the information I had been given. Crimson was leaking into my vision again as I spoke. "And, this control you've obtained by doing so, is no longer your concern."

I yanked the knife free and the bubble shattered in a burst, sending glistening fractals in all directions. I threw my arms up to cover my face from the shrapnel before looking to see what would happen next.

Glinda made a choking gurgling sound and sank to her knees. "I won't be able to protect you for interfering, Alice."

"You know me?" The sound of my name from this strangers' lips slapped me across the face.

"It won't matter now. You've destroyed it. He will just find another way now," Glinda gasped, clutching at the ground. "He will have another plan."

"Who will? What have I destroyed?" I asked, feeling like I was free falling in the rabbit hole once more. "I destroyed your hold over the memories and thoughts," I insisted.

"You've destroyed the memories themselves. The connections will likely be gone with me, and he will hate you for it, and he will target you," Glinda whispered before collapsing fully, her body still and lifeless.

In the same instance, I looked around the glade to see the remaining bubbles shatter, sending down a hailstorm of glass. The fog that was leaking out from behind the closed gate sucked itself back behind the bars where it spiraled like a misty, ethereal tornado, unreachable. I had destroyed it all.

A small part of me felt horrified as I realized I had just killed her. I killed this woman and I hadn't even bothered to find out what would happen when I popped the bubble. It seemed like I would just be waking the world from a dream, not killing its keeper. Either Avrilia had been terribly wrong or I had let that Wicked witch manipulate the hell out of me.

But, for the third time, my morality was seemingly swallowed up by the heat. I felt hollow and numb; the only glimmer of feeling remaining in me was charred.

I stared at the body and realized there was a cut on Glinda's arm, but instead of blood, the same material that made up the Northern Gate was spilling out as dust. I looked at the knife in my hand and crouched next to the body. Morbid curiosity rolled over me like a tidal wave.

I rolled Glinda on to her back, seeing more little wounds bleeding silver dust. Taking a deep breath I plunged the knife into her chest, cutting it open with the same ease as tearing fabric.
I still felt nothing. What was wrong with me? I was cutting someone open! I should be feeling *something*. Or, rather, I simply shouldn't be cutting someone open at all, and yet I couldn't stop.

Stop it! Stop following the compass. Its betraying you, stupid girl! I shouted at my own mind, but it was like my self control and inhibitions were being held captive somewhere unreachable. Instead, my unfiltered, curious nature was going off without supervision.

I leaned over her and peered in awe at what I was seeing. This woman was little more than a scarecrow that appeared to be filled with something like stardust instead of straw. Sitting where her heart should have been was a chunk of sparkling silver glass, not unlike the shards I'd seen years ago. I pulled it free and held it in my hand, staring at it in disbelief. Glinda wasn't an actual human witch. She was the shell of something.

My mind was rolling. Why had I pulled her heart out? It was as if my body was acting of its own accord and my mind was a fuzzy step behind with its realizations, vibrating with an infectious numbness. I felt perfectly mechanical as I took in the chaos I just created in a matter of moments. My compass was whirling. It had a vice hold over me.

You killed her— whatever she was. That horrifying thought clanged through my body like a bullet loosed from a gun.

I looked at the glass heart again. It began to glow in my hands and I could not look away. The dust in the body lifted and swirled around me, obscuring me in light. I suddenly felt a bolt of energy surge through me, so fiercely that my hands released the heart and I dropped to my knees, gasping.

The dust had dissipated and the heart was a dull lifeless gray now, more like a piece of tin than glass. I certainly felt different, and, in an instant, I knew what had happened.

Pulsing with an edge of delighted insanity, I reached a hand out to the side and pointed my finger at Glinda's body. With a sudden crackle, lightning erupted from my finger and fried the remains of the body until there were not even ashes left, just scorched earth.

I had absorbed Glinda's magic. With a twisted smile, I laughed and twirled in a circle, dancing on the shattered memories. I felt so powerful and inhuman. I was beast and angel all rolled up into one. The compass whirled and I spun in tandem with the needle.

Then, I stopped dead in my tracks as I saw Peter behind me. Something about his presence seemed to stop the spinning compass, and bring me back to reality where Goodness took hold once more.

His face was grim but he did not appear afraid. His eyes looked me up and down— my disheveled hair, the knife still in my hand, my still-bare feet crunching the remains of the bubbles, and lastly the glowing compass around my neck. The arrow was pointing due south, then it slowly began twitching to a more standard position at west again.

Peter gave me a lifeless laugh. "Well, I think we finally know what kind of compass it is."

"Courage to do the impossible?" I suggested hopefully, though something in that theory now felt broken and left me feeling an overwhelming shadow of shameful corruption enveloping me.

Peter shook his head, and approached me, standing close as he took the compass in his hand. "Alice, this is undoubtedly a moral compass and even though it looks a bit roughed up, it is definitely active. It can change your morality forever now." He looked at the patch of burnt earth and the glass littered clearing. "Like making you kill her. I think you're a Wicked witch now."

~*~

"What the bloody hell was that?" I demanded crossly as I confronted Avrilia back at Nonsense Falls.

Peter had flown me back to meet the witch, though he hadn't spoken the whole way. He probably was trying to ignore the fact that I'd just killed a Good witch and taken her power.

"Not only do I not see how any of this helps me get home, but you tricked me into killing some woman!"

"Was she though?" Peter mused with a shrug, speaking for the first time since finding me at the gate. He was standing behind me, hand on his dagger, still skeptical of Avrilia's friendly disposition. I, however, was not feeling quite so cautious.

"She wasn't?" Avrilia fixed us with a hard stare, her one brown eye boring into mine. "She wasn't actually a real woman?"

"Well... She was a witch, right? I suppose your body must go through curious changes when it is full of magic. Regardless, I am responsible for her *demise*," I pressed emphatically.

Avrilia paused thoughtfully, biting her lip in concentration. Her fingers tapped rhythmically on the boulder she was leaning against. "This just proves my theory."

"What?" I asked, taking a step back. "This wasn't something you shared with me *before* sending me there."

"She was just a husk wasn't she?" Avrilia demanded, looking wildly back and forth from me to Peter, and not acknowledging my accusations of withholding information.

"Once she was dead, sure," Peter offered, seeming to take a more keen and active interest in the conversation. "Lovely little Alice here cut her open and all this silver sparkly stuff came out. Her heart appeared to be a chunk of it." He swiveled his finger in lazy circles around his chest.

"I think it transferred her power to me when I held it. Which, by the way, makes me a Wicked witch now?" I added, though as more of a question I desperately needed to be answered. Anxious thoughts turned my stomach, and stoked a fire within once more.

"If she wasn't really human then maybe you aren't Wicked. Maybe it was coming in contact with the heart. Like, some sort of raw magic. You're only Wicked if you kill another *person*, I think," Peter mumbled mostly to himself, muling over his own thoughts as he started pacing and pivoting in the air. He was trying to rationally excuse what I had just done.

I waved him off, that increasingly familiar flame building. "But, this doesn't negate the fact that I feel very upset about this whole thing. Why did I cut her open in the first place? It was barbaric. So barbaric I can't even hardly stomach the words on my tongue. Furthermore, all of her bubbles popped when Glinda died. She told me that all of the connections were destroyed, and she couldn't protect me."

"It is a shame that the bubbles were all destroyed along with her. But, I must say, I think you did everyone a favor by getting rid of Glinda. She is just a pawn in a bigger game." The pale witch's tone was edged with hidden knowledge.

For a moment, I was taken aback by Avrilia's nonchalant manner regarding Glinda's death, but it was quickly replaced by a quiet seething rage.

"What do you mean it is a shame to lose the bubbles? I thought that was the whole point of sending me on this reckless escapade! I thought it was supposed to help us find a way home! To fix things and to stop them before they got worse." My voice grew in volume as I spoke. "What kind of game is this? Furthermore, *whose* game are we even playing?"

Avrilia straightened up and folded her arms across her chest, clearly not appreciating my rise in temper. "It was for the greater good of getting us all home. All of us who have been doomed to an eternity of hiding, or being consumed by the very shadows we try to conceal ourselves in. All those who have found themselves lost in this world." Her eye flashed as she looked from me sharply to Peter, and back.

"That didn't answer my question," I sniffed at the witch, lifting my chin to meet her intense gaze, equally unflinching. A single *tick* sounded in my head but then I pushed it down to a dull echo, until I didn't hardly hear it at all.

"Since the Second Star was sealed, we have all been trapped here. Someone with an awful lot of power would be the only one capable of pulling off such a feat." Avrilia's silky sweet voice hardened to something icy and cold. The wide brim of her pointed hat cast a menacing shadow across her face. "If there is a puppet master at play with the witches here, as I suspect, then he needs to be stopped."

"Who?" Peter, who had been quietly observing the last bit of our exchange while floating in the air, dropped down to his feet. His face wore an uncharacteristic expression of concern.

Avrilia flashed him a knowing look. Some sort of unspoken meaning seemed to pass between them, hanging in the air. Being the odd one out, my annoyance grew even more, causing my broken compass to spin once more.

"Don't all tell me at once," I snapped the rolling storm of my temper harder and harder to swallow down..

"The Wizard of Oz," Avrilia answered somberly. She caught Peter's eye and tilted her head at me. "He likes to collect little witches over in East."

I couldn't help but scoff. "You mean the *Wonderful* Wizard? That's the only way I've heard him mentioned before. Why would someone as highly regarded as him be puppeteering witches?"

"It's complicated," Peter shrugged off my question. "He has been wonderful to some, I guess. Mostly just to himself."

"Well, haven't I spent today being told that no one is all good or all bad? What am I supposed to believe here?" I demanded, taking a step towards Peter.

Peter flitted in the air once more, his eyes troubled and far away. "You can't believe anyone. Even those who are supposed to be there for you can wind up your worst enemy. Everything is a trick with him, and I don't like getting this close to anything to do with him. And you should steer clear too!" And, with an agitated huff, he took off, flying through the woods until he was no longer visible.

"What does that even mean?" Frustration boiled over in the pit of my stomach as I watched him leave. It wasn't the first time he'd flown away when conversations took a serious turn he didn't feel like discussing. What had otherwise been a fairly carefree adventure to a magical world of nonsense had suddenly been enveloped in shadows so dark, I couldn't see straight anymore. "Peter!"

"Alice, there is more to his—" Avrilia started, resting a hand on my shoulder.

"No!" I bit, shrugging the pale hand off me. "You sent me to *pop a bubble*, and instead I ended up slicing open some woman who may or may not be Good. You tricked me!" I rounded on Avrilia, who took a step back.

"Alice, I understand that this is confusing. But, there is a history here that is very morally complicated. And, Peter doesn't even know everything— " Avrilia began, obviously trying to remain composed.

"Killing is wrong!" I cried. I felt the flame of boiling annoyance churning into something bigger within me. My sense of manners in polite conversation were entirely out the window.
"Even if it saves others?" She retorted, her lips forming a thing line. "One life to save countless held against their will?"

"It is still a life."

"She wasn't even human anymore! You saw that for yourself. I was hopeful that the bubbles would still be usable, that was never a lie. But, I can't undo that now and I think we've uncovered some pertinent information this way. It was a means to an end, Alice," Avrilia tried to explain, but the boiling feeling in my stomach was growing, sending waves of hot energy into my arms and legs until I thought I would burst.

And then, I did.

Before I could register what was happening, a ring of fire burst forth with my body as the epicenter. Flames coiled around bushes, flashing brightly across the surface of Nonsense Falls in a blinding light. Then came a wave of sparkling lightning— just like the one I had turned on Glinda's body.

I raised a shaking hand, pointing it at the pale witch, who had managed to dodge my blast of power. My lips curled. I was so desperately tired of being some irrelevant little girl to be left out, ignored, and controlled. I envisioned burning this woman to a crisp, and this time I didn't mind the ramping up of malice as I knew now that my compass was twisting me.

Give in. It's cursed you and it's broken. You are broken. There is no going back now, so just give in.

A hand grabbed onto my arm and yanked me away from Avrilia. Everything had been happening in slow motion, and I was suddenly snapped back into real time as I fell backwards onto the ground.

"You'll find more answers at the Red Castle." A crackling sound announced the departure of Avrilia back into the shadows of Wonderland as her voice echoed away.

"No! I… I didn't mean to! I don't know what happened?" I babbled helplessly, scrambling to my feet. Shame doused me.

"Wow. Going for two witches in one day? That really snowballed out of control fast, didn't it?" Peter's voice sounded once more behind me, and I knew he had to have been the one who pulled me back from edge of no return. "I saw the light of the fire and came back to make sure you were alright. Good thing too. If you'd actually landed a blow on her like that, it would have come back at you."

I turned and faced him, tears welling in my eyes. "I don't know what happened," I whispered, my voice catching in my throat.

Peter looked at my crumpling face and dropped to the ground

from where he had been floating. He shifted awkwardly from foot to foot before taking a tentative step forward, then another until he was close enough to wrap his arms around me.

I buried my face into his shoulder and let the tears spill down my cheeks. It was a tender moment and it felt so nice to feel comfort in his arms.

"It's the compass," Peter said quietly after a moment had passed and we had separated once more. He lifted the compass to eye level. "It was activated somehow, and I don't know why Avrilia cracked the compass. But it's spinning out of control now."

I looked at the compass to see the arrow no longer fixed south. Instead it was spinning endlessly in circles. "What does it mean?" I looked at Peter with round, frightened eyes.

"I think it is worse now. Before your morality could be changed… now it is just unstable," Peter answered somberly.

"Well, I don't want it!" I shouted and pulled the chain over my head. With all the strength I could muster, I threw it into the rippling waters of Nonsense Falls.

"I'm afraid you and I both know it doesn't work like that, Love," Peter replied, pointing at my neck.

"Ugh." I looked down with a sigh to see the compass had rematerialized around my neck once more. "So, I am just stuck this way?"

"Afraid so," Peter shrugged and smiled at me. "But, on the plus side, you have all of the power from Glinda. She was very powerful. You'll certainly be a force to be reckoned with so long as you're here. I'd watch your temper though. I think it will pick up on your emotions and use them."

"Oh, bother." I sank under the weight of it all. "I am trapped here as a Wicked witch, responsible for death and mayhem. I don't know how you've shown up twice, after my killing and almost killing someone, and seem fine with everything."

"To be fair, when we first met, I told you that you get used to death and dismemberment around here. I wasn't actually joking. I don't think you're some evil person now just because you got twisted into lashing out at a couple witches today. One was some weird pseudo person— that seems better left alone— and the other was because of your compass reacting. It just happened. I guess you'll be getting more used to it too, since you're a Wicked witch now. Just don't go using your magic on me without permission," Peter chirped nonchalantly. "We can adjust and still have fun. This will be the new norm and we will find a way to make it work."

For a moment, I felt comforted that he would accept me still so willingly, despite his obvious mistrust of witches. He reached out and wiped away a tear rolling down my cheek.

"I don't like it when you cry." His gentle touch and words put me at ease.

Then a thought struck me. "Unless…" I started, wiping the remainder of my face with my hand.

"What?" Peter fixed me with a tense, uneasy gaze, though the thoughts behind the green were unreadable.

"Well, this whole mess started with me trying to get home. I was so afraid something bad would happen and it did. If I leave Wonderland— leave this whole place— I will reset." The words and ideas tumbled over each other in race to be spoken. "I'm Wicked here, but the Good thing to do is set things right at home. Then I will be normal again. The bubbles were just one idea. There has to be more ways."

"You really want to leave?" Peter's voice was quiet, his eyes on the ground.

"I think I have to. Will you help me, Peter? You're the only one I can truly trust," I pleaded, taking his hand in mine and giving it a small squeeze.

Peter looked at our interlocked hands for a moment before closing his eyes tight shut. Heaving a long sigh he squeezed my hand back. "I'll do my best to fix this," He promised.

"Thank you, Peter!" I untethered my hand from his so I could throw my arms around his neck in a grateful embrace. "Where should we start? What was it Avrilia was saying about the Red Castle?"

Peter whisked an arm around my waist and lifted us both into the air. "I think we start by going home and then get a fresh start tomorrow. You might not have realized it but it's the middle of the night."

"Oh," I looked around and realized I hadn't even registered that I had launched my attack at Glinda at sunset, so obviously now it was late. "I suppose you have a point. Do you have to go back to South?" I added quietly.

"I'll stay the night here," Peter replied, his grip tightening ever so slightly on me. "Can't seem to leave you unsupervised without you trying to take out witches."

I jabbed his side with my elbow, and he laughed.

"What? Too soon for jokes?"

"Way too soon." I smiled despite myself, feeling peaceful and calm as I flew with Peter through a moonlit Wonderland. "If I never hurt another soul because of this wretched necklace, it'll be too soon."

Something in my words felt void and hollow, but I willed them with all my might to be true.

My dreams were filled with images of the day before, and I woke up multiple times until I gave up on sleeping altogether and instead slipped outside to pace about the clearing outside my little cabin. I'd left my too-small shoes behind at Nonsense Falls, and my naked feet were tired, dirty, and cut up from all the chaos they'd raced through.

I curled and uncurled my toes in the dew covered forest floor as dawn was transitioning into full morning. The coolness was refreshing and grounding. I looked up at Peter, who, worried about ambushes in the night, had opted to sleep outside to awake at the first sound of trouble. He was sleeping on his back on a wide branch, one arm dangling over the edge, and the other shielding his eyes from the growing light.

He looked so peaceful and serene. Since growing older, he had outgrown the clothes I had originally met him in, and had swiped some clothing from a pirate ship in Wonderland. But, being Peter, the clothes were quickly as torn and stained up as his old clothes had been. There hadn't been any girl clothes for me to change to, and all of the pirates clothes were far too big for me.

I walked over to where his shoulder was roughly eye level

and looked at his arm. The sleeves of his once-white shirt were tattered and pushed up above his elbows, but even through the fabric I could see the impressive muscle that was underneath. Something inside me fluttered, and I had the sudden urge to run a finger down the length of his arm.

My eyes roved to his face, and I bit my lip. He really was so very handsome to look at. Everything in me wanted to be closer to him. Had Eleanor felt this for her betrothed? Could she have felt such feelings when he hadn't been so strong and wild as Peter was? Certainly she had never seen him shirtless while swimming or seen him wield a blade with such youthful courage and excitement burning in his eyes. She had never counted the little scars on his torso and arms when he wasn't paying attention, I'd bet too. Why did those things draw me to Peter like they did? Perhaps my fondness for him was changing into something…

"Well, hello, Love."

I'd been so lost in my own mind that I hadn't realized that Peter's green eyes had fluttered open, and were now staring sleepily down at me. He quirked an eyebrow and flashed me a crooked grin.

"Are you watching me sle—"

"No!" My eyes widened and, panicking, I shoved him off the branch.

"Oof." The sound puffed from his mouth as he hit the ground, not being able to switch to flying fast enough. "I was going to say it was nice to wake up and start the day here with you, but now I'm not so sure that's the case."

I brought my hands up to my face and dragged them down, willing my scarlet cheeks to stop flushing with embarrassment. Without saying anything further to defend myself, I marched back into my cabin and splashed my face with cold water.

"The compass probably just scrambled your brain. And your lack of sleep," I consoled myself, as I prepared to go back outside and interact with Peter. "If he brings it up again, just blame it on that."

I took a deep breath to steady my pounding heart, and exited the cabin. Peter was laying on his back in the center of the clearing, hands tucked behind his head lazily.

"What's the plan, Love? Apart from shoving poor Peter from trees, that is," He asked as I plopped down next him, and gave me a wink.

I scowled at him and rolled my eyes. "Avrilia said we would find more answers to things at the Red Castle so, I suppose we ought to go there."

"Can I interest you with a nice do-nothing day instead? We can cloud watch." Peter smiled happily and gestured above us at the sky.

"I know it is a frightful place to go and—"

"It's not about fear, Love. I'm not afraid to go there, I just don't really fancy it," Peter interrupted curtly.

"Well, I *am* afraid to go, so I would really appreciate you coming along with me." I hugged my knees as images of the Red Knight beheading the Card-guard wormed their way into my thoughts and turned my stomach.

"We don't really *need* answers though. We can just lay low and go about our lives."

"As tempting as ignoring everything that happened yesterday is, I'm afraid I can't just pretend like it didn't happen. I already was afraid of what the compass would do to me when I thought it was for courage. That's why I went to pop Glinda's bubble in the first place," I countered, folding my arms, and drumming my fingers on my forearms.

"You mean when one witch convinced you that something bad was going to happen to you so you would go kill the other witch who had turned her sister Wicked? So, we're just trusting her now?" Peter sat up on his elbow to stare at me skeptically.

"Well, what choice do I have, Peter?" I snapped and got to my feet. "The compass isn't for courage, its for morality and I did bad things when it went off. I'm a witch just like either of them now. I have magic, no idea how to use it, and who knows what horrible things I could be capable of the next time it spins out of control?"

"You're not an evil person, Love." Peter floated to his feet. "I'm sure even your Wicked isn't going to be as bad as others. Look, you're concerned about just the idea of it. Most Wickeds aren't like that. You're a Good person, Alice."

"I have to reset myself. I can't live with the guilt. I can't go on and hurt people I care about like nothing is wrong. Can't you understand that?"

Peter dropped his head and looked at his feet, but didn't answer.

"I just need more answers. And storming a castle— that has Peter Pan written all over it. Can't we just make this a signature Alice and Peter adventure? We'd have had to do it eventually anyway to have explored all of Wonderland like we said we would."

"Using my love of adventure against me now?" Peter brought his hand to his chest, feigning like I had wounded him. "Maybe you *are* Wicked. But, when you put it like that, how can I turn down an adventure with you?"

I let out a little trill of happiness. "Thank you, Peter."

He shook his head and smiled, "You know how to work me too well, Love. Come on then," He held out his arm to invite me in for flying.

My heart thudded a little as his arms closed around me and I leaned in against the firmness of his chest. After my little embarrassment earlier, it was all I could do to not immediately turn thirty shades of red. Instead I embraced the closeness and how calming and reassuring Peter's presence was. I hadn't even realized how much having him by my side had come to mean to me until he almost wasn't willing to go to the castle with me. I cozied myself into the embrace to be comfortable for the flight over, and I could have sworn I heard Peter's heart rate pick up a little too.

"Peter, are you nervous about something?" I asked innocently, but looked at him slyly. Payback for earlier.

He swallowed and cleared his throat. "Of course not. I have heard that Queen of Hearts has a lot of magical books. Books on everything really. Maybe one of them has an answer that Avrilia was talking about looking for."

"I have seldom enjoyed reading books," I sighed, remembering my picture books on the shelf in my old bedroom. "My sister was more of the reader. But, I'll try anything!"

The wind whistled through my long hair as we rose above the trees. Peter hovered for a moment, as if waiting for my approval to proceed. He looked at me, his face inches from mine. There was a softness in his expression, but his eyes were rolling storms of green, covering what he was truly feeling behind them.

I smiled at him reassuringly. "Alright. Let's go!"

~*~

Peter and I landed at the end of the maze of hedges leading to the Red Queen's castle, where I'd witness the beheading. We entered the maze slowly, deciding flying would be too conspicuous. We just needed to sneak into the castle and go from there.

We had successfully managed to navigate a good share of the maze thus far without running into any Card-guards, and I was feeling optimistic in our mission. I had never made it this far before. After all, my last visit with throwing paint on the roses, had resulted in orders for my execution— or a folding at the very least.

"So, are we just going to sneak in and find a library?" I

whispered to Peter.

"I guess we had better try—" Peter's answer was cut short as we suddenly felt spear tips poke at our backs.

"Halt! Turn around slowly and state your business," Barked a Card-guard.
Peter and I obeyed, slowly rotating to look at a run of clubs facing us.

"Er, we were simply…" I attempted lamely, shooting Peter a sidelong glance that pleaded for help.

"I don't think the Queen would be very pleased by this," He chimed in, folding his arms across his chest. "I believe all of the guards had orders to go track down Alice."

"Peter!" I gasped in shock. He couldn't possibly be turning me over to save himself, could he? My stomach dropped and I could feel my emotions tugging at the arrow of my compass. He wouldn't do anything so terrible, surely.

"In fact," Peter continued, without missing a beat. "Last I heard, she was seen at Nonsense Falls. Why you would be looking for her here at the castle is beyond me. If I were you, I would hurry and find her before the Queen has your heads!"

"Oh," I sighed in relief. "Indeed. If you go now, we promise we won't say a word to her majesty," I added, clasping my hands together and smiling.

The cards looked at each other, their faces turning from skepticism to uncertainty. They slowly lowered their weapons and a Seven of Clubs stepped forward.

"You won't tell her majesty, you said?" It asked quietly.

"Believe me, Seven. May I call you Seven? Telling the Queen about this is the very last thing we would want to do," Peter grinned, and was even so bold as to throw an arm over the card's shoulder, escorting him away as he spoke.

"Halt! In the name of the Queen!" The same Three of Diamonds that had been at the bridge came into the courtyard in front of us. Recognizing us, he led the charge towards the entrance to the maze.

"What?" The Seven gasped, looking horrified at Peter's arm around his neck. "You mean you're them?"

Peter sighed and rolled his eyes. Quick as lightning his grip around the card tightened. He used his free arm to sweep under the guard's feet, lifting them towards the head to fold the card in half. With the Seven incapacitated, he lifted into the air and pulled a small dagger from his waist.

"So close. You couldn't have waited five minutes before showing up?" Peter asked the charging cards before nose diving in their direction.

"Peter!" The squeal escaped my lips as his shadow zoomed over my head. "We should just run into the maze and lose them."

Acting independently of its owner, Peter's shadow gave me thumbs up to communicate that everything was fine. My anxious hands flew to my mouth as I watched. Back home I seldom fought with anyone verbally, let alone physically. I mostly just grumbled to myself.

Sure enough, Peter aimed true and, with his dagger fully extended, he tore straight through the advancing cards. He was so... Heroic. Diving into battle like that. I felt an odd tingling in my toes as I watched.

The cards shrieked in terror as their centers ripped, before falling flat and incapacitated like regular playing cards once more, though it seemed they weren't dead. The corners of my lips twitched behind my fingers at the sound. Peter pinned them to the ground with his knife, then retrieved another one he'd had concealed, flicking it skillfully with ease through his fingers into his palms.

Time ticked like a clock in my mind, pulsing adrenaline. The compass was spinning wildly. I felt heat course through me, but it'd come on so fast this time, I hadn't had time to question it or will it away.

Hearing the commotion, more cards of every suit and color were pouring into the courtyard. Peter and I were surrounded and grossly outnumbered. Yet, strangely, despite the whirling compass, I felt an icy hot calm fall over me. It felt as though something had disconnected in my brain, detaching me from my northern morality. My hands fell from my mouth back down to my side, electricity sparking off my finger tips.

"Uh..." Peter groaned, hovering in the air and eying his advancing adversaries. "I'm all for trying impossible things, but I am not currently liking our odds so much here. I think you might have been onto something with that retreating idea of yours, Alice."

"Or," I began. Red rimmed my vision as I walked forward calmly, confidently. I raised a hand and extended it in front of me, watching as the sparks morphed together in a ball of rolling lightning in my palm. Flicking my wrist, I released the orb from my hand and watched in satisfaction as it obliterated half the cards in the courtyard.

"Whoa," Peter let out a puff of air and looked at me. "That is definitely a different plan."

"We could go get what we came here for," I finished, smiling mischievously at Peter.

He grinned back at me and narrowed his eyes.

"I never knew you to be a scrapper, Love." He gave me an impressed nod. "Ladies first then, I believe it goes."

"Don't mind if I do!" I chirped and skipped forward. I felt oddly giddy, like there was something at home with the newfound chaos. I recognized it as the same feeling I'd had while dancing around Glinda's ashes, only this time I didn't feel nearly so frightened. Summoning another orb into my hand, I raced forward, Peter sweeping in next to me with his dagger. We really did make a good team.

"Guards! What are you doing? I told you I wanted her *head*!" A shrill and angry voice reverberated against the stone courtyard and marble pillars.

I halted in my tracks and scanned the overlooking balconies. My eyes locked on a figure I knew had to be the infamous Red Queen. Her raven black hair was pinned up in a disheveled bun behind her ornate crown. Even at such a distance, my skin pricked at her steely gaze from two infinitely black irises.

I lifted my chin and sprinted into the castle, calling over my shoulder to Peter that I would be back. I paused in a grand foyer, decorated from head to toe in red and black checkers, to gather myself. Golden hearts and spades twirled around one of the banisters of a large staircase, while diamonds and clubs spiraled around the other. A large portrait of the Queen hung on the wall at the top of the stairs. I noticed immediately that in the portrait, the Queen's eyes were green and her hair was perfectly arranged.

The sound of clapping rended my eyes from the portrait to see the actual Queen, who was leaning on the banister, once more fixing me with her blackened gaze. Her smile curled into the most unnerving grin I'd seen in Wonderland yet. It was the face of the Wicked.

"Well done, Alice. You've stormed the castle."

Twelve
Dorothy

By the time I had walked for what felt like a good mile, with only the iridescent glimmer from my silver slippers to light my way, my eyes were fully adjusted to the shadowy absence of light.

I observed a tree, residing right in the middle of the path, and slumped against it. As I did, a flurry of little creatures erupted from behind me, squeaking and honking. I gasped when I realized that they were little creatures, made up entirely of faces and legs, scurrying away.

"Sorry!" I called after them. "What is this place, Toto?" I asked my dog, who responded by resting his head on his paws. "Yeah, I have no idea either. Are you tired? Me neither. I suppose this is probably all a dream anyway. Do you get sleepy in a dream? I guess you wouldn't know. You probably just dream of chasing Miss Arroyo around. Can't say I blame you. Horrible, wicked girl. I'm glad you tore her dress and scratched her. You should have chewed on those Mary Jane shoes she was wearing. You could have snapped those buttons off with one—" I stopped short when I caught a glance at the shape of the silver slippers on my feet. Mary Janes with a little snap button on the strap. They were identical to Miss Arroyo's shoes, only with a distinct abundance of shimmering gems. "Why would…" I didn't complete the thought. This had to be a dream after all.

I looked around me, defeated. Perhaps I should have chosen a different direction after all. There were no guarantees that Alice would be able to help me. In any case, she was probably just as lost as me if she was still here.

At some point during my walk, I had stumbled through some sort of thicket, and tripped over tendrils before I could make them out. I knew I had to be coated in dirt, and there were probably various sprouts of wheat and sticks protruding from my hair. I closed my eyes for a moment.

Then, a deranged laugh rang out from the distance. My eyes popped open and I looked around me to see a glint of light deep within the forest. The glint stretched and contracted, stretched and contracted, until finally it expanded in a blast of light, revealing a long table covered with teapots and cups. Then, like a light switch, it was dark again, the air quiet and still.

I was breathing hard, my back pressed firmly against the tree trunk. Another flick of the switch re-lit the world, only this time it brought the table closer. Lights off, more faint laughter. Lights on, and it was only ten feet from where I was sitting. I waited to see if it was going to move again. When everything appeared to be staying as it was, with no more strange flickers, I rose to my feet and slowly approached, taking my first steps from the path since the crossroad.

Trying to ignore the tiny branches that snagged around my ankles, I picked my way through the brush. Toto's steps followed hesitantly behind me, crawling and craning to avoid the sticks that were much larger to a creature of his size than mine.

I could see more with each step, until it was no more than a foot in front of me. I realized now that the elaborate tea table was resting on a grass carpet, and had no ceiling or any walls around it. Piled around the dishware were colorful cookies and decadent little sandwiches. At the center of it all, was an exceedingly large and sparkling tea pot.

I took a step onto the perfectly pristine grass, and just as I did so, the lid of the gigantic tea pot popped off. A tiny mouse, in an equally tiny purple coat and hat, jumped out and scurried around the table. I squawked in surprise and turned to retreat to the path only to find in dismay that it was no longer there.

Instead I was staring at a small white picket fence, and a plethora of multicolored shrubs. I had apparently been teleported to somewhere new entirely. Everything about this place felt very disjointed, like each area almost existed entirely separate from everything else.

"Oh no," I breathed, trying to swallow the panic rising in my stomach. I slowly turned back around to the table as a small mechanical tinking of music began playing.

Then, like a time-bomb, two figures exploded from a nearby cottage— which I only just noticed was beyond the dining table— singing loudly and dancing up to their places at the grand tea party.

One wore a rather large top hat with some sort of fraction stitched on the side, and had oversized Victorian boots on his feet. His waistcoat and trousers were a pale blue that offset his pastel pink shirt. He appeared to be an older man with crow's feet around his eyes, slightly flabby cheeks, and a mess of curly gray hair peeking out from beneath his hat.

The second tea party attendee made my mouth drop as I identified that he was, in fact, a large brown hare wearing a violet jacket, embroidered with green and white flowers down the lapels.

I stood frozen as the two cackled and crowed to each other,

pouring tea in their cups, hats, bowls, and even their sleeves. The little mouse appeared to be a guest as well as she reappeared with her own tiny cup and saucer, rolling on her back in a fit of laughter.

As a farm dog, Toto had never been fond of mice, so it only made sense that his instincts would kick in and he'd spring out from behind me, barking frantically. Though, I really wish he hadn't announced us.

The three stopped laughing and stared at me. I waved awkwardly, but they continued to stare, the hare still pouring tea into an overflowing cup, his ears overly erect.

I took a step back. "Sorry, I didn't mean…" I trailed off as the two looked at each other from the corners of their eyes and grinned.

"Could this be a new guest?" The man asked, his voice carrying a sort of sing-song lilt.

"I think she could just be the most important guest of all," the hare responded, his voice high with a lisp because of his two enormous front teeth.

Once the ice was broken, Toto ceased his barking and raced forward, aggression forgotten, tail wagging, jumping into a chair.

"Toto," I shouted, advancing towards the table, unsure of whether these people— or whatever— were safe company or not.

The little mouse scurried up to Toto with a small bit of cheese in her paw. She offered it up to his snout, rubbing his nose as he accepted the treat.

"Good doggy," She cooed in a tiny, high pitched voice. "Cheese for whiskers, whiskers for snouts, snouts for a mouse," She rambled to herself as she skipped away.

I reached the side of the chair Toto had leapt into, and was about to pick him up, when a loud clattering drew my attention back to the strange man and the hare. They had both leapt onto the table and were clambering towards me, stepping on saucers and kicking cups to the side.

Before I could react, they each linked an arm in mine and sat me down in the chair adjacent to my dog. Then, they both took a seat beside me, eyes wide, and faces in their palms.

"Pray tell, do you prefer tea or crumpets?" The hare asked, offering up a platter with crumpets and tea cups of different colors and sizes.

"Well—" I tried but was cut off by the man in the top hat.

"Nonsense. She will want biscuits and lemonade!" He crowed, leaping back onto the table and doing a little jig. He leaned in close and placed his hand beside his mouth in an attempted discrete motion. "We don't have biscuits or lemonade so you can have tea and crumpets." He thrust a cup into my hand.

"Very well," I agreed weakly.

I took a tentative sip of the tea. Its flavor was one that I couldn't place as it swirled around my mouth in a torrent blend. I swallowed and watched as the hare dumped an entire cup of sugar into his cup, then threw both cups over his shoulder, whistling nonchalantly.

"Have some more!" The man topped off my cup again.

I complied, feeling that the tea was taking the edge off some of my suddenly-realized hunger and thirst. I took a sip, then a gulp, then two gulps. Each taste was more refreshing than the last. The man kept topping off my cup. Then suddenly he slammed the tea pot down on the table, shattering it. I stiffened.

"Candy or lemons?!" The man shouted, leaping up and choosing a new seat to sit at down the table. He slouched dramatically in it, kicking his giant boots up onto the table, twiddling thumbs clasped in his lap. "Lemons or narwhals? Oh, the choices to be made."

"I don't think I belong here," I said, once more feeling ill at ease. "I should be going. Toto, come!"

"Ah, but what is belonging?" The hare queried. "Indeed. Is nonsense really something one 'belongs' to?" The man replied thoughtfully.

I shook my head. "No. I am quite certain, however, that it is possible that I belong in a world of sense. So much sense, in fact, it makes you all look very nonsensical."

The hare gasped, pausing from his frantic sorting of tea cups. "The Hatter is the wisest…   He is the very best there is. How could you think… why, you are, you are…" He rambled and then flung a silver cup in front of me. "Why, you're nothing but a silver cupper!"

The Hatter gave a cheery laugh. "She's a silver cupper, indeed! Well placed. The March Hare is very good at assigning cuppers."

"Alright then, I am content with a silver cup," I played along amicably.

"Silver cuppers usually are," The Hatter responded, in a tone as if I were the biggest simpleton he'd ever met.

"I'd be fine with any cup. However, I would much rather be taking my tea iced, in a diner, back home in Kansas with my aunt and uncle. Thank you very much." With that, I stood.
As I did so, my brain felt fuzzy, like it was swimming in shapes and colors. I shook my head and beckoned Toto to follow me. This time he complied, abandoning the mouse to join me.

"Miss, before you go…" The Hatter approached me, with a silly saunter.

I sighed. "Is it my shoes you want, is that it? I'd give them to you, and let you face the horrid flying things that also want them, but unfortunately they seem to be cemented to my feet," I glanced at the shoes then lifted my chin and pointed to the gate in the fence. "And my feet are going that way."

Toto ran and threw himself against the gate, barking three times.

"Your shoes?" The Hatter questioned.

"Yes. These damned slippers that are on my feet. Apparently some group of munchkins think that they are a good thing, but all they've done is get me chased and lost. I tried to remove them twice already. Oh, and apparently I am some kind of witch because of whom my house decided to fall on. Yes, the whole thing is very unlucky, and nonsensical. I'll be going now. Thank you for the tea."

Tea. There was a yellow, oblong tea pot right on the edge of the table. It was good, so good. Perhaps I could have one more sip.

Seeming to see my longing look at the tea pot, the hare swiped it off the table and tossed it to the Hatter, who promptly offered it to me, his eyebrows quirked and eyes twinkling. I tentatively reached for it, only to start as it began whistling.

The tea inside began to bubble until it was splashing out of the tea spout. And then, it just exploded in my hands, sending little fragments of glass different directions.

The Hatter ducked and gave a startled *ah-hoo*! A cookie fell from the hare's mouth, mid-chew. Somehow my hands had remained miraculously unscathed from both the glass and the hot liquid. My silver shoes glowed.

"You defiled the teapot!" The hare cried out.

I certainly wasn't making a very good impression with this talking animal.

"Filed! De-filed. Pot of tea," He stammered, hopping in circles while tugging on his long ears.

"I didn't mean... that is, I don't know how..." I tried to defend myself, but I was too confused by what had just happened that my words fell flat.

"Oh dear, that was my grandmother's teapot," the Hatter said, taking off his top hat to reveal another teapot balanced on his balding head. His fluffy eyebrows rolled across his face and a shrill giggle escaped from his lips. "You know, I do believe you defiled my grandmother's teapot. Silly little Mome Rath."

"Your grandmother's?" I felt a little guilty, but then the Hatter kept talking.

"Whose?"

"Yours," I snapped impatiently. I didn't know what had possessed me to keep trying to talk to this man. "Never mind."

The Hatter covered his eyes with one hand, and cupped his left ear with the other. "You don't suppose it's the shoes?" He whispered, pointing to my feet.

I had a sick feeling in my stomach about those shoes. "What about my shoes? I didn't even put them on my feet to begin with! You see, there was this tornado in Kansas, and my house somehow..." I gulped. I was wearing a dead woman's shoes and just defiled a grandmother's teapot. I stared down at my feet.

"They're lovely," the Hatter cooed with a smile.

"Well," I said, resolving to leave once more. "This has been wonderful. Goodbye."

"Oh, but won't you have some tea?"

"No, it seems perhaps it might be safer for our teapots if she goes," The hare insisted. He wiggled his nose at me and twitched his ears, his eyes bright and twinkling, though not at all unwelcoming. "Have a nice night then," He said sincerely, and I believed him.

"You too." I opened the gate for Toto and we wandered back

onto a red dirt path together. "It's night already?" I heard the Hatter say behind me.

"I do believe it's been night all along. I think it's actually morning," The Hare responded, and the two burst into laughter once more.

I stumbled away from the area as fast as I could and resigned myself to wander through the forest until we'd left their laughter behind us.

Thirteen

Alice

"**I** take it you are the Queen then?" I ventured, suddenly feeling small and conspicuous in the large palace as I stared up at the intimidating woman above me. "The… The Queen of Hearts?"

The Queen gave a shrill, shrieking laugh, throwing her head back emphatically before immediately sobering once more. "Who, her?" She pointed to the portrait. "No." With a snap of her fingers she set the portrait ablaze.

"But… I don't understand. You are not the Queen of Hearts then?" I stammered. I knew everyone in Wonderland was varying levels of mad, but that portrait *had* to be the woman standing in front me.

My eyes locked on the green in the portrait before flames curled the painting into charred ashes. Her use of magic was also surprising to me, and I had to remind myself that Peter had told me that the Red Queen was in fact a Wicked witch too. A very important detail to remember, indeed. And, probably something we should have weighed more heavily before coming here. Damn my impulsive nature!

Everyone had always made the Red Queen sound like a nuisance to avoid for risk of getting decapitated rather than anyone with formidable magical powers to wield. Perhaps that was why Avrilia had said she hadn't gotten around to getting rid of her yet. She would have to take her by force, though judging by the slouching figure gripping the banister, I would have thought Avrilia could overpower her easily.

My mind spun with various theories. Perhaps Avrilia was working with the Queen. Either that, or she had been lying in her nonchalant demeanor regarding getting around to killing her at some point. Maybe Peter had been right to say we shouldn't trust her advice.

"I got rid of *her* a long time ago," The Queen's voice broke through my thoughts. She took a few clumsy steps down the stairs towards me.

I raised my arms defensively, but faltered a moment later when The Queen chortled.

"Come now. I am sure you know neither of us can just fling magic directly at each other willy nilly, without the risk of unfortunate repercussions. So, settle down."

Despite her crazed appearance, her words made sense. I lowered my arms slightly, but took a step back just in case. I wondered how she knew my name and that I had magical abilities too. News certainly had traveled fast considering no one else had been around save for Avrilia, causing me to doubt her honesty once more.

"What do you mean you got rid of her?" I queried nervously. "Was she your sister?"

"That pitiful creature?" The Queen scoffed, continuing her slow descent of the checkered steps. "No, my sister was far superior to that wretched woman." Her lip curled in disgust, then her expression brightened suddenly.

I pursed my lips thoughtfully. "I don't think she looked pitiful. She looked kind," I pressed, my curiosity wanting to know the difference between the two Queens— besides the eyes.

She clasped her hands together and leaned forward like she was telling a story to a child. "She was weak. When her sister, The White Queen, died she couldn't bear the grief. They built Wonderland together. Did you know that? A marvelous, beautiful creation of two sisters' boundless imaginations. Of course, Wonderland was mostly her doing, not her sister's. The White Queen was more of a helper in this land. She used it to escape the rigidity. An escape to a world of splendorous nonsense, where things didn't need to make sense. And then, you think it such a brilliant idea to paint her beautiful white roses red!" She gestured wildly with her hands at images only visible to herself, and promptly slid down the remainder of the banister, her red skirt fluttering around her suspended feet.

Slapping her feet to the ground, she dismounted with a sense of precision she had not displayed while walking earlier. I took another step back as she approached closer, backing myself into a wall that was covered in various shaped mirrors.

"So, she searched for a way to separate her grief from herself so she could be free of the torment. She spent long hours practicing magic that hadn't ever been tried before. Do you know what happened?"

"I don't believe I have enough information to answer that accurately," I replied shakily, clutching at my compass. I looked around for a weapon but couldn't find any in the empty foyer.

"She succeeded!" The Queen squealed in delight, pacing back and forth in front of me. She paused and whipped her head around to look at me, her black irises even more unsettling up close. "She created me."

"Is that why your eye color changed?" I asked, feeling like I was finally making sense of this woman's rambling. "You pulled it all from yourself?"

"Wrong!" The Queen snapped, and twirled her fingers in a circular motion while making a tsk sound. "You haven't been listening!"

The next thing I knew, I was being pressed flat against the wall of mirrors by a magically altered banister post. The Queen had obviously made it come to life to attack me. A clever loophole.

"That was The Queen of Hearts!" She pointed wildly at the smoldering portrait. "I am the Red Queen!" Her voice pitched with insanity. "*We are not the same.*"

"Alright, I'm—" I started to apologize but my mouth was suddenly being covered by the ribbon that had been holding my hair back moments before.

"We are two different people. She split herself in two and I was her other half! All the Good stayed inside her, while everything else," she pulled a face and pointed to herself. "Everything else is inside me. And, of course, she didn't truly want to have any fun. She didn't appreciate the nonsense anymore. She certainly didn't like *my* nonsense. No, she didn't think any of my creative adjustments to Wonderland were amusing at all."

All I could do was widen my eyes in surprise. I was being bombarded with information, though I doubted any of it were the answers I needed to solve my situation. I could do with answers on who was puppeteering witches, or with how to get home— though the former wasn't really relevant to me if the latter was achieved.

"She especially didn't like creating a water source that makes everyone who drinks it insane. Oh, I thought it was all great fun! She kept trying to undo my nonsense, but I got the madness to run so deep that the very core of Wonderland is just as topsy turvy as me. Even some of its most esteemed occupants. They made great unknowing test subjects— Like the King of Hearts and the Hatter. I am part of its creator after all, so there is no way to undo it!" The Queen twirled about blissfully, clearly envisioning the chaos she had caused. Had that been how I'd looked to Peter when he'd found me at the Northern Gate?

"Whrrr hppnmed mmm hr," I mumbled through my gag.

The Queen raced up to me and cupped her hand to her ear emphatically to my mouth. "What's that? What became of The Queen of Hearts?" She asked giddily. "Well you see, one of my earlier creations was a special looking glass. It acted as a portal of sorts normally, but I fixed it. It took some time, but I made a little deal with an outside source and I made it a wonderful trap. You see, I made it so that instead of transporting her, it would trap her within the glass. Portals weren't working right anymore at this point anyways. Then, can you guess what happened next?"

I shook my head. My heart was pounding, and my head reeled with the new information I was gathering from this insane woman's story. Clearly, Avrilia must have been bluffing when she talked of getting rid of the Red Queen. One must have to be exceptionally powerful to create an entire world, and then pull oneself apart, and then tamper with the world beyond repair of the other creator.

"With her trapped in the glass, I broke it!" The Queen threw her head back and stretched her arms out wide. All of the mirrors on the wall behind me burst into a cloud of shards, showering the foyer in broken fragments. "And, she died. I *killed* her."

I closed my eyes against the blast, trying to figure out how to take control of my restraints. The lightning had come easily in the moment, but this appeared much harder. I winced as multiple falling shards nicked my arms.

"You have to be careful though," The Red Queen continued on. She wagged her finger as she spoke, ramping up in excitement again. "There was only the one looking glass and if you plant the shards in the ground, you can grow new mirrors. I ordered the guards to dispose of all the glass properly, but the buffoons somehow dropped some pieces along the way. It's alright though because the portals only take you back to the castle now, so even if one did grow back—which takes a very long time— you'd have to know to break the glass and step through to get to the maze. I made the maze too, by the way. It always changes."

I had so many questions, my inquisitive nature momentarily obscuring my mission's purpose, and as if reading my mind, the Queen twitched a finger, sending my ribbon back to my hair.

"Any questions?" She cooed at me, swaying back and forth like a small child.

Question after question tumbled around in my mind, but only one made it out of my mouth. "What killed your sister?"

The Red Queen who had been swishing about, stopped dead and looked at me. "What?"

"What killed your sister?" I repeated my question, unsure of how this mad woman was going to react. My curiosity was acting on its own without my intuition again.

"It was a conglomerate of effort," She sniffed with a deep frown souring her face. "But, ultimately, it was all *his* doing."

Was this the same mysterious *him* Glinda had alluded to?

"Whose doing?" Peter's voice echoed around the foyer as he floated in. "Looks like you've got yourself in a bit of a bind here, Alice," He added, taking note of my current hostage situation with the Queen. "Probably should have reminded you she had magic, shouldn't I? Blast, and you're bleeding."

"You!" The Red Queen released her hold on me and rounded on Peter, practically spitting out the words. "*You* killed her! You killed the White Queen!"

"*What?*" Peter and I gasped in shocked unison.

"Peter, what is she talking about?" I demanded, getting up from where I had fallen to my knees, ignoring the pieces of glass impaling in my skin.

"I don't know!" Peter spluttered. "I didn't kill anybody. I have never killed anybody. Maimed maybe, but never killed. It isn't really my thing. Furthermore, I never even met the White Queen! She's been missing my whole life here."

"Oh, you met her once, and that's all it took for you to kill her!" The Red Queen snapped viciously. "Everything was fine, more or less, before you arrived."

Peter, still floating in the air, looked at me with a confused expression and slowly brought his hand to his head, twirling it in the universal gesture for insanity.

This, however, did not go over well with the Queen. With a violent screech of fury she began to glow red. Her black eyes burned like hot coals.

"You know how fighting with magic can have unfortunate results?" The voice that came from the queen boomed like a monster. "Well, I'll admit I had to do some fighting to get The Queen of Hearts into that looking glass."

"Huh?" Peter asked. Having missed her whole explanation, he had to have been terribly confused by this reference. He looked at me inquisitively, pointing to the witch. "Isn't she…?"

I shook my head. "I'll have to explain later." I was more concerned about the fact that the queen's body was beginning to alter shape to match her new monstrous voice.

"I don't think it should count when you're technically fighting yourself. Nevertheless, the rebound gave me a very unique ability, and I call it the Jabberwock." The banister shot forward, once more, pinning me by my waist to the wall.

"Uh oh," Peter groaned, coming to land beside me. He brought a hand thoughtfully to his chin.

"What is a Jabberwock?" But I didn't need a verbal answer to my question, because I could see very plainly what it was as I watched the Queen transform.

Her glowing skin became dappled with scales, and, in a rather frightening display, large fangs sprung from her mouth. Her head swiveled rapidly back and forth as her neck stretched and elongated. Matching the new sizeably long neck, her body morphed and grew into that of a beast, complete with two wings protruding from her lumpy, ridged back.

With the sudden increase of size, the red dress the Queen had been wearing tore away from the monster's body, revealing more scaly bulk beneath. Her deformed body doubled over, slamming two enormous feet into the floor, splintering it from the impact. Sharp claws erupted from where curled knuckles had been moments before.

My eyes traveled from the feet back up to the Queen's face. However, there was no human face to be found anymore. I was staring into the same black eyes I had seen before but this time they were bulging above the muzzle of a beast. Long black and red tendrils hung from either side of the long snout.

I gaped in horror as I took in the horrible beast in front of me. There was no more Queen, but instead a terrible dragon-like monster. It was a creature of nightmares.

"Uh, Peter, I think it is about time to get out of here!" I called, frantically pulling at the bewitched banister that had me pinned. Blood was running down my arms and legs, and droplets scattered about on the floor, flicking from my struggles.

Peter rushed over and tried his hardest to pull it off me, but it wouldn't yield. By then, the Jabberwock creature had fully formed and was zoning in on Peter with hateful eyes of malice.

"Watch out!" I shouted as the beast lumbered towards us.

Peter zipped out of reach of the snapping jaws just in the nick of time. "Look, lady, I don't know what you're going on about. I had nothing to do with the White Queen's death. I don't think I was even born yet. I've barely even been to Wonderland more than a handful of times before Alice showed up. I only followed her in from the signpost when she first got here."

"You did what?" I squawked.

"Oh, don't be so surprised, Love."

But, the Jabberwock was not listening. It appeared to be just as mad at the Queen as it lifted into the air by its mutilated wings and took off after Peter.

"Alice, I know this is all new to you, but do you think you could try to magic a way out of this just this once? I didn't exactly have plans to be eaten by a weird monster-Queen today, but it would be a bit unfair to just leave you all tied up. So, can you work with me here a little?" Peter shouted to me as he darted around the foyer.

"I don't really know. I seem to have lost connection with it," I tried to think of a solution. Running straight for the Queen without a proper battle plan had been in rather poor judgment on my part. To be fair, I didn't realize that she was also a formidable witch. And, that bloody compass made me so damn compulsive.

To both mine and Peter's surprise, the Jabberwock opened

its mouth to shoot out a stream of flames at Peter.

"It breathes fire too? I guess a Jabberwock is just a weird name for an ugly dragon. I hate to say it, Love… But, maybe you ought to tap into that compass of yours. It seems to get things going," Peter offered, flitting overhead. He stopped suddenly and started moving backwards. "Blast!"

"What are you doing?" I called up to him.

"It isn't me. It is this blasted shadow. He's trying to run away. Coward!" Peter shouted at his shadow, which was in fact pulling him towards the door. "We can't just leave her!"

"Yes, I would much prefer if you did not leave me trapped here, Peter's Shadow," I agreed heavily, still trying in vain to remove my restraints. Splintered wood was collecting beneath my bloodied nails as I frantically clawed at the banister.

"So, where are we at with that whole compass deal?" Peter asked, seeming to have gotten his shadow back under control in time to avoid a collision with the Jabberwock. It was like watching a cat chase after a fly.

"I don't know. The compass makes me do bad things! I can't hit her with magic anyway," I answered lamely. I closed my eyes and thought hard for a moment. "Of course! I am an idiot," I sighed as the obvious solution finally came to light.

"I wouldn't say that, but if you could get a bit of a move on with whatever you're thinking because I believe I am going to run out of dust here shortly…" He trailed off, his green eyes suddenly stretching wide. Then, he fell to the ground with a thud. He propped himself up on his elbows and coughed, the wind driven from his body.

The Jabberwock didn't miss a beat and was hovering over him. "You were smart to keep your distance from me for so long,

Boy. Now, I can finally avenge my sister."

"Again," Peter gasped, still trying to get his breath back. "I have no idea what you are talking about. I didn't kill your bloody sister, Witch."

I didn't want to rely on the compass to jump-start my plan, but it seemed it was the only way that I could save Peter. I closed my eyes and clutched at my compass, focusing all my fearful energy on it. I felt the internal heat build up and I knew the arrow was spinning. Taking a deep breath, I opened my eyes to see the familiar red bleeding around the edges of my vision.

Moving as fast as I could, I placed my hands on the banister, setting it ablaze until it crumbled away, leaving me unscathed. Then, still keeping at speed, I shot a blast of lightening at the ceiling, sending large chunks of rubble cascading down on the Jabberwock. I paused for a moment, seeing that it had succeeded in pinning her down under the pile of stones, then proceeded forward, knowing it wouldn't contain her for long.

"Peter, your dagger! Quick!" I called out, breaking into a run towards the two. The calm certainty of destruction had claimed me with vicious precision once more.

"I don't think a little poke from this will do much but, alright," Peter conceded, and tossed me his dagger. "After yesterday, I won't doubt the damage you can do with a knife."

"Thanks!" I said, catching the knife without breaking my stride. I winced as the blade slipped in my hand, slicing my palm.

Peter clamored to his feet and stepped back from the debris, which had begun to rumble. "You got a plan here, Alice? Because, I think she's coming back for more," He cautioned.

As if in response to his words, the Jabberwock's head and egregiously long neck erupted from the pile of rubble with a loud, angry screech. I leaned into the sway of the compass, allowing it to pull me forward, like it had when I'd faced Glinda.

"Right on cue," I said to myself. I took the hilt of the dagger in one hand, and the tip of the blade in the other and pulled, a similar motion to what I had seen Avrilia do to create the knife earlier. True to form, the blade elongated into a sword.

I cleared the remaining distance between me and the monster, dropping to my hip and sliding across the floor as the monster thrust her head at me with gaping jaws. My offensive charge caught the monster off guard, making her vulnerable. In the same fluid movement, as I slid under her outstretched neck, I lifted my sword in an arch, slicing deep into the Jabberwock's neck.

The beast let out a choking, gurgling sound and blood began pouring out the wound splattering against the ground. The Jabberwock's head fell to the ground with deep labored breathing. She fixed her burning black eyes on me.

"You are a fool, Girl," She coughed in the same unearthly bellowing voice. "He will destroy you. Just like—" Her warning was cut short by a fit of coughs as she choked on her own blood, before her head pulled to the side, black eyes, cold and sightless.

I got to my feet, trying not to slip in the pool of blood. My body was speckled with collateral splatter mixed with my blood from my own wounds, but it didn't bother me. This death hadn't bothered me. I felt the sudden pulse of energy course through my body as I took on the power of the second witch I had killed.

"That was bloody fantastic, Alice!" Peter cheered, fully recovered from his fall. He raced up to me and grabbed onto my arms in excitement. "Are you alright? You've always been curious, but a bit timid with your follow through. But, wow! Color me impressed. I had no idea you were such a gutsy fighter!"

"I'm fine, and neither did I," I laughed, looking over the deceased Jabberwock's body in amazement. I looked up at Peter and smiled. "It was the compass, really. I just knew I had to save you no matter the cost. Who else would I have fun with around here if you got eaten by a mad dragon-creature?"

Peter stared back at me for a moment, his gaze intense. I could feel his fingers tighten and loosen rhythmically around my arms. He smiled back, suddenly pulling me in closer and clearing the gap between our faces to kiss me.

My heart pounded like a hammer and my stomach felt like it was fighting to contain a million butterflies. I felt energy run through my veins like lightning, but this time I knew it wasn't from the compass or any witch-magic. I closed my eyes and leaned into the kiss.

"Why did you…?" The words were barely spoken through my shock.

"I wanted to, so I just did." Peter replied with a happy shrug.

"You kissed me," I breathed, biting my lip as we pulled apart, utterly stunned.

"What?" Peter laughed, taking a step back and stuffing his hands in his pockets. "That wasn't a kiss, I gave you a thimble," He corrected.

I blinked at him, raising an eyebrow inquisitively at his nonsense.

"No, a thimble is what we just did there," he gestured between me and him. "And, a kiss is a small little thing that goes on your finger," He lifted a finger and mimed placing something on the tip.

"Who told you that?" I couldn't help but laugh, another wave of affection tumbling through my chest at his innocence.

"No one. It doesn't matter," Peter mumbled awkwardly. I could see color rising in his cheeks.

"You've just got it switched around. A thimble," I said, taking his hand in mine, goes on your finger to keep it from getting pricked while sewing."

Peter looked at our hands then back up at me, his eyes twinkling with mischief. "And a kiss?" I smiled and tilted my face up to his. I kissed him back and pulled away. "Just like that."

"And why is it that people kiss?" Peter asked me, tilting his head to the side.

"Well, I believe one does it when they are fond of the other person," I tried, then looked down at my hands. "Are we fond of each other then?" I asked quietly.

Peter opened his mouth to reply, but was cut short as a slew of Card-guards raced into the room. They stared in awe at the defeated Jabberwock beast.

"You have slain the Jabberwock? The Red Queen is no more?" A King of Diamonds queried for the group. I nodded slowly.

"Then we hail you, the one called Alice, as our new Queen of Wonderland!" The card called out and the rest of the cards erupted in cheers.

I looked around me and lifted my chin. "Um, very good." I tried to use a commanding tone. Remembering the original purpose of coming here, I realized I could just use the library now to get my answers without a problem. "As you were then. Oh! And do something about this mess. Please," I added, and turned to Peter. "Right, shall we look for that library then?"

Something faltered in his expression for a moment but he shrugged it off as quick as it came. "Right. The library." He gestured to the doorway. "I suppose we will both be walking. After you,

Queen Alice."

"Oh, hush. You needn't mock," I scolded as we left the foyer and entered a long hallway.

"What? That is your title now. That carries some weight to it. I don't think you have much to fear now that you're in control. Even those in the East would think twice about coming after someone who killed two witches in the accelerated span of a single day." I looked at Peter, knowing what he said was true.

"Well you needn't call me that. I don't plan on staying for a lengthy reign as queen. I said, clutching at my compass. I'd pushed the Red Knight. I'd killed Card-guards. I just killed the Red Queen. I didn't want to lose myself so quickly and not be able to escape before fully succumbing to the Wickedness of the cursed compass. I needed to remember what was driving me home, and that was the opposite of how I had gotten my newfound title. I must hold onto who I was. "Just Alice will do."

Fourteen
Dorothy

Not too far into our walk, the trees started changing shapes, becoming shorter and rounder until they disappeared altogether, and in their place, only mushrooms of various sizes remained. Their caps flashed with a timed illumination, and were covered with tiny, glowing bugs that were having some sort of marching instruction. The March Hare had been right about it actually being morning because, the sun was casting strands of light through the treetops.

I thought I could make out smoke shapes, like square, triangles, and stars, billowing out in the distance but convinced myself that I must have been imagining it, along with the rest of what I was seeing. After all, I was standing in what appeared to be a forest of fungi. I paused on the bank of a stream to read a posted sign.

"This way to Nonsense Falls," I read aloud. "Hmm. Well, I definitely think we should avoid that direction entirely," I added to Toto, hopping gingerly across some slippery stepping stones.

Toto looked skeptically across the stream before dutifully plodding along behind me. With us both safely across the water, I surveyed our surroundings. I hadn't a clue which way I ought to go to find this Alice girl. I was standing in a forest of mushrooms about to despair when I caught sight of the same smoke letters I had seen earlier.

"I suppose we had best give it a try. I don't suppose it will be any stranger than what we just walked away from," I said, resolving myself to trek through the mushrooms towards the smoke.

I was, however, quite wrong in my previous assessment that what I would find would be less strange than a tea party with Hatters, hares, and mice. As my eyes trailed along the puffs down to their owner, I stood staring agape at a large brilliantly colored blue butterfly sitting atop a flat mushroom head.

In one of his many hands, he clutched at a tube, which he brought to his lips to inhale from. Lips. He had the face of a human man, though it was the same vibrant hues as the rest of him. His expression was dull and crinkled with vague annoyance.

I closed my mouth and cleared my throat. "Ahem." The butterfly-man did not respond. Instead, he continued to lazily puff letters into the sky. Toto approached the creature and sniffed at the tube it was holding. Then, with some intuition I had been lacking, he clamped his teeth around it, holding it firmly in his mouth.

Once the stream of smoke had been interrupted, the butterfly-man scoffed and brought the tube up to his eye to inspect.

"Explain yourself!" He barked suddenly, still staring down his tube.

"Oh!" I started. "Hello… Sir?" I tried, unsure of how to address the creature.

"Caterpillar," He answered gruffly, swiveling his face in my direction.

"Oh."

"Oh? What is confusing?" The butterfly barked. His face crinkled into deeper lines of crankiness.   "Well, you are a butterfly."

"And?"

"Well, you are a butterfly, not a caterpillar."

"Of course, I am not a caterpillar. It is my name," Caterpillar explained slowly, like I was impeccably dense.

"But, you were a caterpillar before you became a butterfly. I just wouldn't have assumed what you were once would be your name now since it isn't what you are now," I rambled, running over the confusing sentence once more in my mind to confirm it did in fact make sense.

The butterfly sighed, using a leg to shoo Toto away from his tube. He inhaled deeply and blew smoke rings in my direction.

"Er…" I tried to find my train of thought once more.

"Who are you?" Caterpillar drawled.

"Me?"

"Who else?"

"I am Dorothy."

"Not what. I asked who."

"No, that is who I am. I mean, that is my name. Dorothy."

"Indeed."

"I am a human, I suppose."

"You *suppose*?" The butterfly quirked an eyebrow, leaning on the oh sound of the word *suppose* long enough to blow more smoke at me, this time shaped as rings.

"Well, no. I definitely am. Although, apparently I am also a witch in these parts," I laughed lamely, trying to ease up the surly atmosphere.

"But, why would I call you by *what* you are rather than *who* you are?"

"Oh. I see your point, Caterpillar. Names are important. It is nice to meet you." I nodded and worked up a smile.

Caterpillar sniffed. "I'm sure it is." Then he returned to puffing random shapes into the sky.

"Well, I was hoping you might be able to help me. I am trying to find my way…" I trailed off at the sound of a dry laugh from the butterfly.

He shook his head. "I don't care about your direction. Go bother the Cheshire Cat about that. Names are superior information. As is who one is. It tells you a great deal. I am far too busy to worry about such nonsense as directions."

I bit down the retort that he was a butterfly, so, clearly, he must have had some idea of direction when he was flying about. Instead, I folded my arms across my chest in annoyance. "Doing?"

"Exactly."

"Pardon?"

"Doing. Now go," Caterpillar waved me away. "You look terrible."

"Well!" I couldn't help but gasp in offense. "How I look isn't a name or a who."

"Looks are most definitely part of who one is. Just as a name is."

I shook my head and began to walk away crossly. Toto huffed at the butterfly, hot on my heels. In one final attempt, I looked back over my shoulder.

"Well, we will have to find someone else to help us find her," I said loudly to my dog.

In an instant, the butterfly dropped the pipe and fluttered into the air. I blinked and he was hovering right in front of my face.

"Who?" His eyes were as round as the moon, more like a moth staring into a flame than a butterfly.

"I suppose you'd like her name then after all?" I smirked.

"Who are you searching for? Not where, *who*."

"Alice," I answered.

The butterfly's eyes got even bigger and his eyebrows raised nearly to the top of his strange face. Then, to my surprise, a twitch in his lips gave way to grin as Caterpillar began chuckling. Then the chuckle turned into a loud cackle. He shook his head from side to side and propelled himself higher into the air.

"What's so funny?" I called after him, rising on my tip toes for maximum height.

"One way you might find her, the other you won't. Direction is dicey. Remember *who* not *what*! *Which* who is very important. You've been asking the wrong questions."

"What?" I shouted in vain. The butterfly had vanished and Toto and I were once more all alone. Insects chirped around us.

"I thought he was only interested in names, but he sure had a lot of questions involving whats," I grumbled as I continued on my way through the mushrooms.

"Whats can pertain to whos if you know how to ask."

"Ack!" I squawked at the sound of the butterfly behind me. But, by the time I whirled around he was back to smoking his pipe, expression dull and cranky once more. I decided it best not to disturb him again.

"No one makes any sense here. Nor are they any help whatsoever," I groused to myself as we walked away. Eventually the mushrooms slowly gave way to regular flora again. I scrambled over large tree roots of varying colors, and weaved around dense thorn patches. I paused next to a cluster of reflective stones to take in my appearance.

I grimaced. Caterpillar had been correct in his assessment. I did look terrible. As I had imagined from my terrible night, I had twigs and wheat sticking every which way in my curly brown hair. It was still tangled and wind swept from the twister, and no doubt the second dust devil, with more hair out of my braids then in them.

I gingerly picked the debris from my hair and used my fingers to comb through the tumbleweed of strands as best as I could. Using the rocks as a mirror, I managed to tame it back into two neat braids once more.

"That's better, I think," I said to myself, feeling the slightest bit more refreshed. "No need to look completely crazed. Not that everyone else isn't entirely insane already."

Toto looked at his reflection and tilted his head to the side before vigorously licking his matted fur.

"Guess you feel the same, huh?" I laughed, leaning on my outstretched hand against the crystal stones. "I just wish we could figure out where this Alice lives around here. Then maybe we could get back home." Did I ever know an Alice back home, and this was some subconscious trick trying to help me remember her?

I felt a sudden surge of energy course through my body as a bright light pulsed through my hand. I stared at the light in awe bringing my hands in front of my face. Then the light lifted from my fingertips, taking the form of an orb, and floating up to the crystal stones.

To my surprise, the orb passed straight through the stone illuminating a hedge maze as it went. I leaned to the side to confirm that there was in fact no such hedge physically behind the rocks.

"What in the world…" I breathed and stretched my hand out to touch the stones. Once my fingers made contact with the surface it cracked like broken glass, shattering into countless pieces and falling to the ground. Left in its place was an open pass-through into the maze— like some sort of gateway.

Toto looked up at me and wagged his tail. Then, with a yip, he took off at a run through the passageway and into the maze. I hesitated for a moment in my amazement before clambering in after him.

To my immediate dismay, I watched as the hedges spindled and crawled, creating a new wall, and separating me from my dog. With a gust of wind and the sound of rustling behind me, I knew the same thing had just cut me off from the stone passageway.

"Toto!" I screamed, and bolted down the new pathway to my right, further into the maze.

Fifteen

Alice

It had been months since I had inadvertently seized control of Wonderland. I'd moved into The Red Castle, and spent what time Peter hadn't wormed into monopolizing on searching for answers in the grand library in the palace.

In that time, the compass had gone off several times, resulting in the casualties of many Card-guards. Each incident made me colder, more accustomed to using force, and more fixated on returning home to undo it's cursed power of my morality. It was a horrible cycle.

I had earned a reputation around Wonderland for being brutal now, and part of me was horrified by the notion, while the other half that was claimed by the compass felt proud of my infamy. Each passing day made it easier to give into that darker half, and only Peter seemed immune.

More often than not, it would simply be a matter of the internal rage boiling over in a random magical burst. But, I was ashamed to admit, my temper had allowed me to take mortifying actions on occasion of my own volition. I was plagued by nightmares at first, then slowly, as the death and dismemberment became more regular occurrences, the nightmares came less and less.

I was standing in one of the grand upstairs hallways, staring out the floor to ceiling window that overlooked the hedge maze when Peter came whistling up to me. He stayed in Wonderland most days and nights now.

"Afternoon, Love." He placed his hands on my shoulders from behind and gave them a small squeeze. "What are we looking at?"

"Prison," I grunted, but turned to smile at him anyway.

Peter made a tsk sound and twirled me around whimsically, lifting me into the air with him for a moment before setting me down again. "Now why would you go and say a thing like that?"

I raised my eyebrows, then rubbed at the fatigue in my eyes from reading so much that day already. I had always detested reading books without any pictures or interesting conversation in them. It seemed like a cruel joke the universe— whichever one I might be currently residing in— was enjoying playing on me, because all of the books I had read in the library thus far were entirely informational, and not entertaining in the slightest.

I sighed wistfully. If only Eleanor could see me now, she would have nothing to say other than teasing since I constantly vocalized my dislike of her books for the very same reason. Though I hadn't had another vivid nightmare about my sister alone and miserable, I still felt compelled to do Good by everyone back home. This thought of my sister alone was enough to will myself to open another book.

The Queen of Hearts had apparently been some sort of academic once upon a time, because her library was overflowing with books of information on all things Wonderland, and even a few on things in Oz and Neverland as well. She must have really enjoyed research before she lost her mind.

There were also some damaged diaries and books on more normal topics too. I had found a rather scandalous one behind her pillow. Although, I had even perused that one in case it had any hidden answers I was missing.

I was feeling anxious and impatient. The compass drank in all my uncertainty and toggled the arrow, and my emotions with it. I was completely exhausted and frustrated beyond belief. Avrilia had sent me here for answers that didn't exist! She also broke my compass, and I hadn't killed anyone before she cracked it.

"You need a break," Peter commented from where he was leaning against the wall. "You'll lose that pretty face of yours if you keep up all that scowling. Why don't we go have an adventure?"

I slouched against the wall in front of him and weighed his offer, stretching forward a hand to squeeze his. He grinned wickedly and tugged me into his arms, looking smugly down at me.

I let out a squeal of surprise followed by a short laugh. "Is this you saying you're taking me out regardless of my answer?"

"It's like you know me," He joked, leaning in a little closer until I couldn't take it, and leaned up to meet his lips to mine. No matter how bad everything felt, moments like these with Peter still gave me butterflies and made me want to melt into him. Apparently this was some side effect of physical attraction, or so I had learned from that book in the bedroom.

Peter and I had grown closer and closer in the several years that I had been in Wonderland and something had certainly shifted in our friendship since we'd first met merely seven years ago. That much was undeniable. Still, I could not truly be sure what feelings I had towards him— with no one sane to discuss the matter with— nor if he had any special admiration for me beyond mutual attraction. It could just as easily be because I was the only human female around his age in any direction. We couldn't escape biology. Though, I really didn't like entertaining that thought for too long.

We never verbally addressed the matter. The closest we had ever come was after defeating the Red Queen. But, even then, we had never finished the conversation before I'd really lost myself in finding those damned answers I'd been told about.

I wished I could ask Eleanor. Being so much older than me, she had already started having young suitors calling after her affections. Was it terrible of me to be torn between a boy and my family? Or was this simply a cruel part of growing older? I'd have been turning nineteen soon in the real world, so maybe there were things the mind could not escape regardless of how young the body stayed.

"Let's go for a swim," Peter pulled me back into the moment, letting go of me and strolling for the staircase. "Anywhere but Nonsense Falls— you pick the place!"

I watched him go and felt my chest ache. This back and forth of wanting to leave and wanting to stay was eating me alive. I knew what I should do, so the sooner I got on with it, the sooner I could leave all the torment behind me. I'd heal. Who knew if I'd even remember any of this once I reset… That thought alone caused another wave of pain I had to swallow down. I needed answers now.

"Actually," I piped up, racing down the stairs to catch up to Peter. "I have an idea of an adventure."

"What's that Love?" Peter's face brightened and his eyes gleamed with excitement.

I blinked my big blue eyes at him, trying my best to bat my lashes attractively. "How would you like to storm another castle?"

"One isn't enough?" Peter laughed. "I don't know if we have it in us to face another Jabberwock."

"I'd like to pay Avrilia a visit. We can go in peace." I smiled, holding up my hands in an unarmed gesture.

"Why do you want to go seek a Wicked witch out?" Peter wrinkled his nose in disdain.

"Hey, *I'm* a Wicked witch, you know. You seek me out plenty!" I feigned offense, and bumped his shoulder playfully with my own as we neared the exit to the courtyard.

"Well, you're not like the other Wickeds." Peter shoved his hands in his pockets.

I rolled my eyes. Peter seemed to have a selective memory for my inadvertent Wicked deeds that were starting to stack up. "If she was out for blood, she would have launched some sort of attack by now. You know, I heard she had winged monkeys for minions. That sounds dreadfully frightful. But she hasn't ever used them on us. I guess she controls them with this hat of hers."

"And you still want to waltz up to her castle?"

"You go after pirates," I countered, pursing my lips skeptically. "What's the difference?"

"Magic, Love," Peter sighed. "Pirates are different because they aren't magical."

"I have magic too!" I couldn't help but gasp at his one-sidedness.

"Alright, fine. If it gets us out and about, we can go pay the *Wicked Witch of the West* a friendly visit, and hope it stays that way," Peter conceded, waving his hands in defeat. "But, I'd like the record to show that I think this is a bad idea for an adventure, and I'd like you to promise at some point you will go cloud watching with me on a nice do-nothing day like I've been suggesting forever."

He poked me in my ticklish rib as we halted in the courtyard and I laughed. "You strike a hard bargain, Mr. Pan, but you have yourself a deal." I stuck my hand out for a shake.

He reached forward and gave my hand a single shake, then lifted me into his arms and shot off into the air. Wind whistled by my face, and reminded me of how much I enjoyed flight with Peter. I liked to think Wickedness couldn't reach me up here.

We passed by the shifting cottage of the Hatter, zipping into place near the Fungi Forest, and I spotted two bouncing pin dots I knew were the Tweedles. Smoke shapes puffed up from the Fungi Forest, and it looked like Dodo and Bill were visiting with Caterpillar. Everything felt magical and peaceful from up here, nothing like the darkness that had followed me since my compass activated.

The two other castles of Wonderland gleamed on the horizon, one white and the other obsidian. Peter lowered up down as we neared and clicked his tongue thoughtfully.

"Which do you suppose is hers?" He asked emphatically then chuckled at his own joke. "You sure you don't want to explore the castle that isn't currently occupied?"

"Nice try," I teased and pointed towards the ominous castle. "Let's land and walk up so we seem peaceful."

"We *are* peaceful," Peter commented as we neared the ground just a little ways off from the obsidian palace. It was lodged into the side of a rocky cliff of equally black rock and I wondered if Avrilia had made herself. I also wondered how she had cohabitation in Wonderland with the mad queen for so long. Then, I supposed the flying monkey army was probably much more intimidating than the playing cards.

Peter and I walked on in silence, Peter's eyes shifting around every so often like he expected an ambush from behind every boulder and crevice. To my surprise when the entrance to the castle came into view, I saw the tall slender figure of Avrilia waiting for us. Flanking her on either side were two of the infamous winged monkeys.

They looked like normal chimps of some variety, but they had long fangs that protrude from their top and bottom jaws. Their wings were webbed and black, reminding me of bat wings. Long tails coiled through the air like snakes. A chill ran down my spine but I squared my shoulders and kept walking forward.

Confidence.

"Hello, Lovely. I was hoping it was you I saw approaching," Avrilia greeted me politely. "Though you are lucky I realized before my monkeys got the wrong idea."

"A pleasure as always, Avrilia," Peter chirped casually from beside me.

I, however, didn't feel like exchanging pleasantries. "May we come inside?"

Avrilia's one good eye sized me up before she smiled sweetly and dipped her head. "Of course."

She led the way into her palace, which was equally as elegant as the witch herself. The black rock was rich and shiny, like the absence of space where a star once would have resided. Everything was primarily decorated in black and white— which I found to be vaguely ironic given her morality lessons— with the occasional pop of green here and there.

As she opened the door to a sitting room, she looked at my tattered dress. "That is practically falling off of you, my dear," She commented coolly.

"Well, I don't have anything else to wear," I replied curtly, folding my arms self consciously across my body.

"You didn't wear the Red Queen's wardrobe?"

"That's a bit morbid, don't you think?" I countered, wondering why my attire was the focus of conversation.

Avrilia nodded slowly, then her gaze flicked to Peter, who was watching our every move, and back. "So instead of making new clothes, you opted to wear an old dress worn to threads. It's one step away from being see-through and tearing off your body."

"Well, I—" I blustered, feeling even more self conscious. Did I really look that bad? My eyes too flicked to Peter and then down at my dress.

Avrilia gave a knowing laugh, then waved her hand around my body. "There are other ways to seduce a man, you know."

"What?" I balked, turning beet red at the idea of seducing anyone.

Avrilia's wave had replaced my dress with one of indigo blue and silver. "To bring out your eyes." She smiled coyly at me.

The dress fit my body snugly in all the right places, framing my figure flatteringly, then fanning out into a flowing skirt, with a slit up to my knees. On my feet were slightly heeled matching shoes. My hair was pulled up to the crown of head, still tied by my trusty black hair ribbon, and left a waterfall of blonde cascading from the bow. Two wisps framed my face on either side.

I could see myself in a mirror that was placed over the small fireplace, and gawked at my appearance. I looked regal, elegant and… attractive. Womanly even. I blushed even deeper.

Peter's eyes widened behind me and he looked away running his hand through his hair casually. "I don't know what *seduce* means, but I mean, I don't *not* like the new look." He grinned that charming crooked smile and shrugged.

"Thank you…" I mumbled. "I think."

"No, no. You're welcome." Peter nodded his approval and

then waved me forward. "Carry on. I believe we have some clouds to watch."

"Right, thank you, Avrilia." I turned back to the witch, who had taken a seat in a plush black chair. "But, a new dress wasn't why I came here."

"I would imagine not." Avrilia nodded slowly, her eyes calculating as she looked from me to Peter. "Did you find the answers at the Red Castle?"

"No, and see that's the problem that brings me here today." I chose a seat across from her.

"Oh?" She crossed her legs and folded her hands in her lap delicately. This time, her hat was resting on the end table that resided between us against the wall. Her hair was also flowing freely from her head in beautiful dark waves, rather than being secured in a braid.

"The Queen only mentioned a mysterious *him* once before she died and it really didn't give any information," I explained. "Then, I've scoured about half of her blasted library and can't find anything on going home. So, you see, I'd like for you to just tell me what you sent me there to find out in the first place."

"I'm afraid I can't do that, Lovely." Avrilia shook her head sadly. But, I felt something start brewing within me at her response, as my hopes faltered.

"What do you mean? If you told me to find answers at the Red Castle, surely you knew what you were sending me there for. Unless you were just tricking me again," I growled.

"No tricks." Avrilia looked to be forcibly refraining from rolling her eyes which only further fanned my annoyance. I *hated* being patronized. "I had sent you there for answers because I knew the Queen had been allowing Glinda access to Wonderland when it had previously been protected. If she had a relationship with Glinda, I thought she might have more information on what had happened to her and who was responsible."

I stared at the witch for a moment, trying to keep from shaking. I knew my compass was beginning to spin, but I had placed so much hope of clarity on this woman and now she couldn't help me.

Peter came to stand beside my chair, and rested a hand on my shoulder lightly. "Easy there, Love," He cautioned gently.

Avrilia watched the exchange and pointed one of those prim fingers at her neck. "Trouble with the trinket?"

I jumped from irritated to seething and as the compass encouraged thoughts of snapping this woman's fingers off, I looked closely at the pallid hand. Had that been the pale hand in my nightmare months ago that activated my compass? Even if it hadn't been in the dream, Avrilia had done something to it later that day in person and ever since then I had gone completely off the rails.

Images of every egregious deed by my hands that had happened in the months to come flashed in my mind and red curled into my vision. I shook Peter off and bolted to my feet.

"What did you do to it?" I snarled at her, grasping the necklace for emphasis.

"I told you before, I broke it so whoever had activated it wouldn't be able to control it from a distance. I imagine it was probably—"

"You!" I interrupted. I could hardly see straight past the pulsing red in my eyes. "You did this to me. Made me unstable. I've *killed* because of *you*. Fix it!"

"I can't fix it, Alice. Magical trinkets aren't my—" Avrilia started to explain, trying to maintain composure, but I cut her off again.

"You have to! And you have to get me home!" My voice was sliding from a shout into a shriek. "You are my last hope of making this right!"

Avrilia kept calm and shook her head. "I can't." Her words were clipped.

Hearing her say that she had no answers on how to get me home, nor could she undo the compasses hold, something in me snapped. Panic and despair rolled through me, tugging me down like an undertow, and the compass took complete hold of me. My eyes locked onto the hat resting on the table and I snatched it up and placed it atop my head.

"What are you—" Avrilia rose abruptly to her feet, fear sparking in her brown eye. "You don't know what that is."

"Don't I?" I smiled cruelly and lifted my arms. Heeding my call, several flying monkeys burst into the room, circling chaotically overhead. "I've done my research."

"Alice?" Peter queried from behind me. "What's your plan here, Love?"

"Destroy." The single word left my lips and the monkeys descended on the witch in an instant. I materialized a knife that resembled the very one I had cut Glinda open with and tossed it slowly from hand to hand.

The cacophony of shrieks from the monkeys tearing into Avrilia, and the witch's gurgling screams sounded like music in my ears.

"Stop," I commanded, and approached the blood soaked floor where Avrilia lay bleeding as the monkeys parted obediently for their master. They had ripped her throat out.

Compelled by the darkness tumbling within me, I lunged

forward and plunged the knife into her chest at her heart. The ends of my blonde hair were crimson with the hot, sticky blood that also stained my hands. The witch was dead.

"Alice!" Peter pulled me away from the corpse and shook me. "Look at me, Alice. This isn't you!"

I locked eyes with him at the same time as a jolt of fresh magic raced through my body. Instantly, it was like I had been in a fever dream and someone had doused me in ice water. I looked around me in a daze, shaking uncontrollably.

"What...? I didn't. I couldn't... I never really wanted to," I stammered at a loss for words. When my eyes fell on the maimed remains of Avrilia, I collapsed to my knees. This was by far the most horrific thing I had ever, or could ever do again.

Bile rose in my throat. I would fight with everything I could to resist the evil of the compass. I couldn't let it ever get a hold of me like this again until I got home and got rid of the darkness for good. Sobs ravaged my body.

I dropped my bloodied hands to the ground and leaned my head into them as I wailed in grief and horror.

"I... I'm Wicked. I killed them all. I am the Wicked Witch of the West now," I whimpered to myself pitifully, certain Peter had probably run for the hills for good. How could he stand by me after this? "I'm a monster."

But then he kneeled down beside me and pulled me into his arms. "No, you're Alice. You just forgot for a moment. Bloody compass. We can worry about that later. We didn't know it could sink its claws so deep. We'll be careful. Let's get back home and we can go count some clouds."

"Okay..." I sniffled miserably, and he lifted into the air to fly us back to the castle. I sobbed the whole way.

Sixteen

Alice

I pursed my lips thoughtfully as I closed one book and reached for a new one out of the pile I had beside me. Peter had made me promise to still enjoy the world around me as I searched for a way home.

I had agreed, but still tried to have a few books with me at all times just in case. It had been our compromise since that horrible day over a year ago at the obsidian castle.

I'd stayed isolated from everyone other than Peter since then, afraid of losing control again. Thankfully, my unwavering commitment to fighting the compass had allowed me to return mostly to normal with only random spasms of magical release.

I spent more casual time with Peter at first, since after reaching a dead end with Avrilia, I had despaired and lost all direction for finding a way home, until I slowly started looking through books again. I also could now control the flying monkeys without the hat since I'd done it the one time, and they remained my minions. I had them bring over all of Avrilia's research collection and added it to the slowly shrinking stacks of books I had looked through.

I couldn't bring myself to ever go back to the place where I'd succumbed fully to the Wickedness within me. Peter had tried to explain it away as the Wickedness was only a magical charm in the compass, and not me, but I knew it was different. It was picking up on my desires, secrets, and anger. Peter had countered on why it didn't affect other Wicked behaviors and only focused on violence, to which I had argued that the other things must not be as prominent desires. He hadn't had any further objections, but simply decided we'd agree to disagree.

After Avrilia's death, and defeating the Red Queen, I might be in control of everything West of the signpost, but I knew what was really in control, and it was dangling around my neck, feeding off my darkness. As soon as I returned home, all this nonsense and Wickedness would disappear. It simply had to. I had to believe that if I was ever going to be myself again, or return to my family. I might lose some friends, but I was older now and life would be different back home. And if it gave me the chance to leave the horrors of this place behind me, I had to take it, no matter the cost.

"Peter?" I asked lazily, setting the book down again. We were both lying in a field of flowers, just across the border between Neverland and Wonderland on the South side. I did not care for the flowers in Wonderland. They were rude, and Peter had just barely been able to convince me not to set fire to them altogether. Instead, I sealed their beds behind a magical door in the Red Castle.

Peter rolled onto his side to face me and stretched a hand forward to pull a piece of grass from my hair. "Yes, Alice?"

Even I had to admit that there was a lot of bliss in these moments. There had been a long gap in any attempt at getting home, and it seemed like Peter viewed it as such an impossible task that I would never actually leave. Especially on our lazy days like this. I'd recovered from the brunt of the incident with Avrilia, but I wouldn't truly be able to heal until I left this world behind. I just wasn't always so sure Peter understood that.

"I still want to go home, you know," I reminded him gently, tucking my hands delicately under the side of my face and letting out a short sigh.

"Now why would you still want to do a thing like that, Love?" Peter asked, rolling back over onto his back. It was always the same response from him when I brought up leaving, and I felt annoyed with his dismissive behavior.

I wished I could ask Eleanor for help sorting out this growing older nonsense. It was so much more involved than how I had described it to Peter on my second night in this world. Already, small things had changed as I got older. I had swapped out wearing dresses for the most part, choosing instead to wear trousers and a blouse after learning how to craft clothing from scratch. It was more practical attire for my endeavors. Flying around with Peter so often was my first inclination that a dress was no longer a very modest option.

I had kept my ribbon from home though, and had decided to keep the hairstyle Avrilia picked for me, pulled up and tied at the crown of my head. Peter's initial reaction to it also hadn't exactly deterred me from switching up my appearance. It made me a bit more aware of how I looked, and for some reason I wanted him to like it.

Perhaps I only liked Peter because he was the only one in Wonderland around my age. I had given up trying to convince Peter to take me to explore Neverland, the Lost Boys sounded woefully childish, and I found myself wanting more mature company despite myself. But, something inside me told me that my attraction to Peter ran deeper than coincidence.

I sat up and pulled my knees to my chest. Selfishly, I hoped

Peter was dismissive of my search because he did not want me to leave. Sometimes, I just wished he would tell me to stay. But, then what? Silly girlish thoughts I could no more control than the spinning rage inside.

Peter had closed his eyes. How could he be so relaxed all the time? With a sly smile, I reached out a finger and sent a small zap of energy to his nose.

"Hey!" He sat up abruptly and glared at me. "I thought we had an understanding about using magic on me. Big no-no, Love."

I flopped back down in the grass and Peter looked down at me. "I'm serious, Peter. I do not want to be crazy anymore, and I am tired of being Wicked. I am just ready to go back," I explained, my blue eyes boring into his moss green ones. "I need one of these books to tell me something useful! Will you help me read some? They are terribly dull."

His scowl flickered into a grin and he leaned over me. He lowered himself until his face hovered just an inch over mine. "Why would you want to leave all of this?" He asked softly.

When I just stared back at him without answering, he closed the gap between us, pressing his lips against mine. We never talked about the kisses when they happened, and instead just carried on about our business as usual. I knew the whole situation would have been terribly inappropriate back home. But, I wasn't home yet, so I kissed him back.

That was something I was glad for in this place. I could not deny that I got butterflies in my stomach every time we kissed. There was definitely something statically charged between us. There always had been, since we first met. Was this a sort of *relationship*?

But, having no one to discuss the sensation with, I never felt confident broaching the topic. Shockingly, that was something even

I was not brave enough to do despite the compass's control of my inhibitions. What if it was all just madness of my own making? But, then why did he kiss me if he didn't have any sort of fond sentiments towards me?

Peter pulled back, still grinning, and sat up. "That didn't change your mind, did it?" He asked me hopefully.

I smiled and shook my head. "*You* aren't the problem in the first place."

He let out a long sigh. "Alright, which book this time?" He surrendered.

I rolled over and tossed a random book at him. "Try this one."

"Alright, but I am going to try to find some way to make this entertaining," Peter grumbled. "I am going to pick a random page and see what it says!" He declared after thinking for a moment.

"Whatever gets you reading," I laughed and went back to my own book. There was a relaxing symphony of birds chirping and insects buzzing floating in the air. Everything was so calm.

"Say, Alice… I think I might have actually found something interesting in here," Peter piped up after a couple minutes had passed in the stillness.

I couldn't help but roll my eyes. There was no way that I could have been searching endlessly for something new to try, and Peter just happened upon an option by looking up a random page. No one was that lucky.

"Peter, I highly doubt—" I started, but was swiftly interrupted as Peter thrust the open book into my face. "These slippers!" He pointed to a drawing of silver shoes.

They had rounded toes, a heel, and little button snaps to fasten a strap. The illustration showed them to be made of some sort of shimmering silver material. There were arrows pointing to various notes scribbled about the shoes. My eyes scanned over the page, seeing there was a tear down the length of the page after the note, *these shoes get their magical properties from their composition of—* and another note below it that had once stated the shoe's creator. Parts of their abilities were also torn away.

"I vaguely remember something about these shoes!" Peter explained, lifting into the air to hover over my shoulder as I continued to read the page. "I believe these belong to the Wicked Witch of the East."

"What makes these shoes so special? And what makes you think that The Wicked Witch of the East would part with them?" I asked, letting the book rest in my lap. I turned to look at Peter.

"These are very special shoes! Last I remember, they let you teleport. And, I don't think she would much care to part with them. They still teleport though."

"Lots of things allow me to teleport. The glass rocks over by the Fungi Forest teleport to the maze, and the chess board teleports to Room of Reflect. The doors in the hallway teleport all over Wonderland," I countered skeptically.

"Yes, but these shoes teleport beyond each direction. I think they have a real shot of teleporting out of this world altogether." Peter puffed out his chest proudly as he spoke. "And you thought finding the answer would be hard. Now that we've answered it, maybe we can go see if we can walk between some raindrops."

"You really think so?" I ignored everything after hearing the part about teleporting out of this world. "Well then, I suppose it is worth a shot! It can't be worse than the whole flying monkey minions we released during our last venture. Those creatures are quite terrible. I really should have left that silly hat at Avrilia's castle alone." I shivered at the memory.

I hopped to my feet, shrinking the rest of my books down so they could fit in my pocket, leaving the book with the shoes out and open. One of the advantages to having read so many books now was that I had been able to learn quite a bit of magical skills that didn't require tapping into the compass for power.

"Well, there is a small caveat," Peter cautioned. "Bear with me here, but I don't think you'll like how we go about getting the slippers, and you'll probably just want to call the whole thing off."

"Why? How do we get them?" I quirked an eyebrow.

"The shoes are enchanted to their owner. They stay on their feet until the owner is killed. Then, they transfer to whoever is responsible for the previous owner's death," He explained, gesturing broadly and emphatically as he did.

"So, you're saying I have to kill *another* witch to get these shoes that may or may not be able to teleport me home?" I sank back down onto the grassy glade. "Peter, you know I don't like the whole killing thing. I can't go through that again. I could never kill someone on my own."

"But you have—" Peter argued, but I stopped him with a wave of my hand.

"No, that wasn't me. It was the compass kicking in. Glinda, you said yourself, wasn't even human anymore. Never mind the fact that I did not know popping her bubble would kill her. Avrilia messed with my compass, which made my morality go all cattywampus, which then led to my overreacting with the monkeys. Might I also add that I did not consciously know what I was really doing there." I took a breath before continuing. "And lastly, the Red Queen was insane, turned into a monster, and tried to kill you for reasons unknown to either of us."

"Sounds like you're finally starting to understand what I've been saying about the separation between the compass and you! Well, if you don't want to kill the Wicked Witch of the East, which I know for a fact, you do not, I guess you'll be staying here a bit longer," Peter chirped, floating downward like a feather until he landed softly in the grass beside me once more. "What shall we do?"

"I suppose you're right," I sighed. "Besides, I haven't had any quarrel with this Wicked Witch of the East. And, the title of Wicked can be awfully misleading," I sniffed, plopping my cheek against my fist as I looked over the page on the slippers once more, seeing a small space on the corner that listed the owners. "Looks like there have only ever been two owners too. That makes me think these shoes aren't so easy to get."

"Fascinating, I'm sure," Peter commented, closely inspecting the tip of his finger.

The first name had been smudged out. I tried to use magic to reverse the smudge but to no avail. Curious that the name would be enchanted to stay hidden. Apparently the Red Queen wanted to keep that identity concealed for some reason. The next name on the list read *Emmaline -Wicked*.

"Emmaline is the name of the Wicked Witch of East," I read aloud.

"Ah. I wonder what happens if the witch is killed by a man," Peter mused lazily. "Best to not think too hard on that one actually."

"I think you're getting too technical," I laughed. "Or maybe that is why the top name is smudged out. I just wish I could find something." Frustration burned in my chest.

Despite Peter's universally calming presence, the toggle of the compass was making me fill with rage. I tried to bite it down but I could see the red creeping into my vision. With a sudden outcry of fury, I shot a fireball at a nearby tree. Watching it engulfed in flames made me feel a little better. I felt like the compass was taking more and more of a hold over me the longer I stayed. I was always on the verge of burning someone to a crisp, stabbing them, or some other form of brutal murder. I really did try my best to control it, but the anger would always be stronger than me. It did not help that I had always had a penchant for impatience.

Peter floated upside down, his head in front of mine. "You're absolutely insane. You do know that, right?" He laughed. "And, I think it might be oddly attractive or some such nonsense."

"Don't be silly. I—" I stopped short of my banter as my eyes caught a glimpse of movement on the page in my lap.

A new name was appearing at the end of the list. My eyes widened as I watched the enchanted page write with an invisible pen, carefully crafting each letter. I clutched the book so hard in my hands that the binding was creasing, and I kept reading the name over and over again.

Being the most recent witch in a long time, I knew of all the current and previous witches if nothing else by their titles. Honestly, there hadn't been a terribly large amount that I could gather. Glinda, Avrilia, The Red and White Queens, Emmaline, and myself. There had been a record, which is no doubt how all the witches seemed to know me before I knew them. The newest witch at the end of the list was not a familiar name and what was even more surprising was that the page had just finished transcribing the title *Good* next to her name. How could she be *Good* if she had to kill the previous witch for the shoes? It wasn't fair!

Furthermore, I knew for a fact there had not been a Good witch since The White Queen— and perhaps the Queen of Hearts at one time— which meant she was not from Wonderland, or even

Neverland or Oz. With the gates sealed, I was certain there was no way she could have come from the North. Though with Good powers, perhaps she could have opened from the inside, but I felt that would have stirred something in the world to have it open after how abruptly everything had closed itself off when Glinda died. So, this new witch had to have come from the same place as me, and she had the shoes. Possessiveness clawed at my mind. *My* ticket home was on *her* feet.

Feeling the fury build within me, I flung the book as hard as I could. I heard it make contact with another small nearby tree, snapping the spine from the impact.

Peter, who had fortunately ducked out of my blind throw, was looking very cross. "Bloody hell, Alice! You nearly took off my head! Granted I know you are used to being in the Red Castle, but that doesn't mean you need to get any ideas about decapitating me with a bloody book," He muttered.

I turned and looked at him, feeling the water-blue irises of my eyes boiling. The grass and flowers shuddered as the ground began to vibrate with my anger. "She has my shoes, Peter."

"*Your* shoes? I thought you weren't going to go—" Peter blustered.

"And she is from where I am from. That is where everyone comes from one way or another. I can't let her use them!" I barked, interrupting him, still trying to remain calm so I would not cause an entire earthquake altogether.

Peter's eyebrows shot up. "Who?" He asked in surprise, retrieving the assaulted book.

A sense of purpose seethed within my spinning idle rage. Maybe, I would have to give into the Wicked just one more time. I could justify just one more time. I would do whatever it took to go home, even if it meant giving into the monster a final time to end it all.

I rose to my feet and started trekking back into Wonderland, and tossed the answer back over my shoulder as Peter followed me. "Dorothy. Dorothy Gale."

Seventeen

Alice

"How exactly do you expect to find this girl?" Peter asked as we made our way to the castle. "I have zero plans to venture East."

"I don't know," I muttered, keeping my eyes fixed straight ahead. I twirled my compass around in my hand and lifted my chin. "But, I'll think of something."

"Let's say you do find her… Then what?"

"I'll do what I have to."

"And what does that mean?"

I stopped and sighed. The Red Castle was visible through the trees. I was tired of the mindless noise. Peter's denial, Cheshire's riddles, the flower's jibes, Caterpillar's judgments, the Hatter's nonsense, and my own inner voice begging me to fight the compass. All of these things were constantly shouting over each other in my brain, vying to be the loudest voice. I was sick of the noise.

Would it be so terrible to give in the compass? It had helped save Peter from the Jabberwock. Avrilia had told me something that first day we met about how fear could be very powerful, and I was afraid. I was afraid of being broken forever. If I could just turn that fear into anger and let it loose, instead of swallowing it down, just maybe I could escape it all.

"Got an answer for me, Love?" Peter pressed, hovering in front of my face, blocking the way forward. "You've got that look on your face."

I stared at him, unflinching. "I'll do what I have to in order to get those shoes," I answered coldly, and stepped around him to continue on towards the castle.

"You're not Wicked, you know. Not really," He called after me.

"I'm the Wickedest Witch west of the signpost!" I shouted back without turning around.

Peter mumbled something I couldn't quite discern, and then followed along behind me. We walked in silence until we reached the castle.

"I can see a great deal when I enlarge. Perhaps we can send for the Tweedles," I mused aloud as I marched up the steps to my room.

"Seems a bit excessive. Why do you need to go after the shoes anyway? You live in a castle right now. I don't know why that isn't bloody good enough," Peter commented, trudging along behind me. He looked contemplative, usually a state of mind restricted to mischief when it came to him.

"It's not about that stuff. It's about doing what's right and what is right for me. I don't have a future here, Peter. It's been blacked out."

"You never worried about a future before," Peter argued, and I balled my hands into fists.

"I hadn't *murdered* anyone before. Now, are you going to be helpful or not?" I asked as I pushed my way into my bedroom. It was a beautiful room with a chandelier casting a glowing yellow light down on the golden walls and canopy surrounding the large crimson bed.

"Haven't decided yet, Love," Peter chirped, cheeky as ever. When he saw me whip around to glare at him he sighed. "I told you back when you first started on this path that I'd do what I could to fix the situation, didn't I?"

"I suppose," I nodded begrudgingly. "You just also happen to have that look on your face like you do when you're about to do something stupid, poorly thought through, and reckless."

"So, my expression must never change since I do those things on a rather constant basis!" Peter crowed and jumped on the bed, still standing. He snatched a decorative pillow and brandished it at me like a sword.

"What in the world are you doing now?" I tried to suppress the smile fighting to spread across my lips.

"If it's a fight you want, I'm happy to oblige in a duel of pillows." He wiggled his eyebrows at me.

"Peter, I can't play games right now. I am trying to strategize to find that girl."

"But isn't life just one big game?"

"Nice try," I rolled my eyes then stiffened as I felt the impact of the pillow against my back. I turned around slowly.

"It has a way of making you play along, now doesn't it?" Peter beamed at me, arm still outstretched from his throw.

"I don't think you want to play with me right now," I cautioned, speaking through the teeth of a forced smile. All I could think about was Dorothy, the magical shoes, and how all my torment was nearly at an end. "I might break the rules."

"I haven't set any rules, other than it has to do with pillows," Peter countered, spreading his arms wide in an invitation to strike back. "Go ahead."

Biting my lip for a moment in contemplation, I arched an eyebrow and smiled wickedly. "As you wish."

I raised my hands and set each pillow in the room on fire, including the one Peter was gripping.

"Bloody hell," He swore, dropping it to the floor where it smoldered.

"I win. Game over." I crinkled my nose with mock smugness, then went to look for one of tactician books I had left lying about somewhere up here.

Peter sniffed. "There is a difference between bending the rules and just breaking the game."

"Don't play games with witches then," I quipped back.

"I don't mind the crazies, it keeps things interesting, but you don't have to be an outright spoilsport. If you'd pulled such a stunt in Neverland we would have tied you up in the forest and sent the Lost Boys on a scavenger hunt to find you. First one to locate you would win."

"Well, you have my blessing to go play hide and seek with the Lost Boys now if you wish, but I really need to focus on…" I trailed off, pausing my ambient rummaging about in the large ornate chest at the end of my bed. "That's it!"

"It's a scavenger hunt not hide and seek. It's different," Peter grumbled to himself, plopping to a sitting position on the bed. He clasped his hands together in front of him. "And, I'm afraid the boys are otherwise engaged at this time, so you're stuck with me."

"I'm a fool for not thinking of it immediately."

"What?"

"What is the point of having minions if you don't make good use of them. I'll send the monkeys to go search for her and bring her back to me!"

"I thought you didn't like using the monkeys?"

"Means to an end, dear Peter. Besides, they are bound to follow my instructions which makes them basically harmless."

"Is that what it does?"

"Of course. We'll find Dorothy and then I'm going to get those shoes."

"Maybe we should think this through a little more. Perhaps over a cup of tea?"

"Are you trying to rattle my sensibilities?" I squinted at him and raised an eyebrow.

"Maybe." He shrugged honestly.

"This is good, Peter! I'm just playing Queen and taking command of my pawns. I'm so close to fixing everything."

"*Everything?*" Peter leaned on the word heavily, insinuating I was leaving something out.

But, all I could think about was achieving my goal. Nothing else mattered. I pushed open the white windowed doors that opened up to a small balcony. I once recalled trying to tell Peter about the romantic scene between Romeo and Juliet at her balcony, but he'd been more interested in hearing about the family feud than the romance. He couldn't understand how they could die so easily, and lost interest with anything to do with their storyline.

However, this wasn't Romeo and Juliet. It was closer akin to Macbeth, if anything. In any case, this wasn't Shakespeare at all. It was my life and, unlike Lady Macbeth, I would get the damn spot off my own hands. I had to.

Stepping out onto the ledge, I gripped the railing and summoned my monkeys. They came swarming, the sunlight casting ominous shadows of their wings against the castle. "Come my minions, and find the witch in the East who wears the silver shoes.

Bring her to me alive and as quickly as possible."

The monkeys screeched, a great cacophony of chaos, then turned spread out, disappearing into the distance. I turned and smiled at Peter, who was pacing through the air, his eyes clouded in thought.

"I think I'll just go ahead and pop by the Tweedles to see if they have any of thc biscuits made up. You know, just in case, since it's getting dark. I'll be back in a jiff," He said in a hurry, darting for the window.

"You're helping now?" I asked hopefully.

His shadow beneath him shrugged as he paused just past the balcony. "I promised I'd fix this. Can't break a promise that important." Then he zipped off until he dove through the trees and vanished.

I let out a long sigh and sat on the bed. I held my compass and closed my eyes for a moment, allowing all the images of every Wicked deed to swallow me up. A pointed storm raged within me, a storm I'd have to unleash again, just one more time. I opened my eyes and rose, leaving my room, plodding down the stairs, and I exited into the mad garden and materialized a knife into my hand, twirling it back and forth, staring at the blade as I walked into the thick of Wonderland.

A smile curled my lips when I thought of my looming victory against the compass. The sun set, dropping the world into a darkness that mirrored my state of mind. I tapped the tip of the knife rhythmically. "And now, I wait."

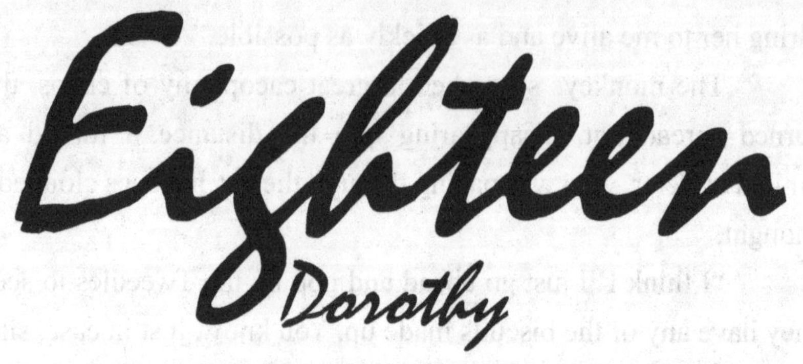

Twisted tendrils stretched and coiled on either side of me as I ran through the maze. I swatted them away as they tried to grab onto my arms.

"Toto! Toto, where are you?" I held my breath, listening for any sign of my dog.

I could hear faint barking in the distance and tried to pinpoint the sound. The maze shifted to reveal an open checkered area with various statues that looked to be life sized chess pieces. Some were tipped over, and others were chipped and scuffed. As I approached the board, I realized that it was made of light and dark pieces of glass. I peered into the glass, seeing it reflect everything back at me, except for my own reflection.

"This should give me a better vantage point," I assured myself, searching for a standing knight. Spotting one, I clambered up on the body of the horse to peer over the tops of the hedges. "Toto! Toto!" I called as loudly as I could.

It was a short lived attempt as the horse suddenly came to life and bucked me off. I hit the glass with a thud and groaned. Of course, the chess pieces were alive. Sitting up to glare at the Knight piece, I faltered.

"I could have sworn you were on that side of the board a moment ago," I said, approaching the horse. I twirled around, taking in my surroundings. Everything felt very disoriented, and my sense of direction was completely messed up since the world felt completely inverted.

"You seem lost," A voice spoke out.

I turned around gratefully, looking for who the voice belonged to. "Yes, I am."

"Such a shame," Another voice chimed in.

"Who is speaking?" I asked, looking around warily. "Friend or foe?" I laughed lamely.

"Well that would depend on which side you are on. If you are on that side, I am afraid you are a foe," The first voice spoke again.

"Then I am not on that side," I tried hopefully.

"If you're on that side then you are our foe," The second voice retorted. "You must pick a side and live with it. You can't be a friend to both sides and win the game."

"Win the game?" Then it clicked. I looked above to see the towering chess pieces were all looking at me.

"So, which side are you playing for?" The light rook asked. "This one or that one?"

"It looks like you were already in the middle of a match," I tried. "I don't think I can play."

"We can't reset until someone establishes the rules and finishes the game, on one side, or the other," A knocked over pawn called out from the side of the board. "I have been laying here for ages. But the Queen hasn't finished the game. She left part way through on that side. It is always a lot easier to abandon the game when you play for that side."

"I don't mean to be rude, but I am trying to find my dog. We got separated in the maze when it changed, and I really need to find him."

"Weren't you listening?" The dark king piece barked at me. "We can't reset until the game is finished."

"I understand, but I don't even belong here. And, I really need to find my dog," I said, backing away towards a new entrance back into the maze.

"You won't find your dog on this side," A toppled bishop laughed.

"Well, yes, I know. He is somewhere else in the maze." I turned around and began to walk away, then something caught my eye. "Has the sun always set to the east around these parts?" I asked hopefully.

"On this side," The knight answered behind me.

I had a sinking feeling in my stomach. "You keep saying 'this side' and 'that side.' What do you mean by that exactly?"

"We are talking about different sides of the board, of course!" The light king piece chuckled.

"Oh, of course," I sighed with relief.

"Yes. There is the world on this side of the glass and the world on the other side of glass," The light queen explained softly.

I closed my eyes tight and turned back around to rejoin the chess pieces. "I am in a world within the other world I was already in?"

"This chessboard portal puts you into a small world of reflection. It was one of The Red Queen's additions to Wonderland. She used it as a sort of dungeon."

"How good of a dungeon can it be if you can get out just by playing the game of chess?" I scoffed.

"Oh, but this isn't just a game of chess. You see, the Red Queen was very mad indeed. She made this game of chess have very special rules, so you have to establish the rules first to win the game."

"What are the rules then?"

"We can't tell you the rules. That is the first rule," Another pawn chirped.

"Why did you throw me in this dungeon?" I demanded crossly, rounding on the knight piece.

It shook its head. "It wasn't me. You must have offended the knight piece on the other side." "Great. So, I have to play a game to which I have no rules in order to get out of a reflection-jail. This is all such nonsense!" I huffed angrily.

The chess pieces exchanged glances before the light queen spoke up once more. "We are only permitted to tell you that you must establish the rules to play the game, win, and leave," She said emphatically. "Think about it."

"Yes, well how can I establish the rules for a game I have never played?"

The pieces all nodded energetically. I thought about the question I had just posed. There was no probable way for me to guess how the game was to be played. It would take eons anyway. But, what if it was a game that had never been played?

"Has this game I am about to play ever been played by anyone else?" I asked the pieces as an idea began to form in my mind.

The pieces looked at one another and shook their heads. "We are only permitted to tell you that you must establish the rules to play the game, win, and leave," They echoed the light queen's words in unison.

"Establish the rules… Establish the rules…" I mulled over the piece of information they kept leaning on.

"The only way I can think to establish the rules to game I am about to play that has never been played before by anyone else, is if I establish my own rules to my own game," I reasoned aloud, looking up to see the chess pieces blinking at me encouragingly.

"We are only permitted to tell you that you must establish the rules to play the game, win, and leave," They all said once more.

"Alright. What are my own rules then?" I thought for a moment. Everything had been utter nonsense in this place. Everyone was insane here. Mad tea parties with hatters and hares, rude smoking butterflies, and mentions of mad queens. I suppose I ought to think of some creative outcome that was unique to me. Well, unique to me if I was mad.

My mind wandered to my Uncle Henry and a strange little fact he had told me once while we played chess on one of my first nights on the farm. My heart ached at the thought of him and I knew I had to find Alice and find a way to get back home. I smiled, knowing I had my rules.

"I am the game master," I said in a commanding tone. "I have the power to make you into special pieces. Rule number one is that this is a single-player game, played by the game master. Rule number two is that to get out of the glass, we have to create a very special formation with the pieces. Rule number three is that I can banish any extra pieces to the edge of the board. Rule four is that the color of pieces does not matter. Rule five is that I must move all the pieces on the board once. Oh, and rule number six is about the changing pieces into special pieces. Best to keep it simple and direct. It will be fastest this way. Everyone understand?"

The chess pieces nodded.

"Right. The formation we need to make is to have eight queen pieces on the board that can move in all directions like a traditional queen piece. We have to place all eight queens so that none can attack each other."

I quickly counted ten chess pieces left standing on the board. I walked around and tapped two pons, pointing to the sidelines to indicate they had been banished. The pawns toppled and rolled away to the edge of the board.

"Okay, now, remaining pieces, I, the game master, turn you all into special pieces that are all queen pieces." To my surprise, the pieces left on the board actually morphed into queen figurines. I ran out the eight coordinates in my mind, envisioning the board.

"Queen one to A8. Queen two, B3. Queen three C1. Queen four to D6. Queens five, six, seven, and eight respectively, E2, F5, G6, and H4," I finished happily.

"I am terribly sorry, but I am not in the right place," One queen called out. "I can be attacked here." Her body went rigid and she toppled to her side, rolling off the board.

"What?" I ran over to where the queen had been positioned. "No, I placed you on G6. That is where you should go…" I trailed off, realizing there was another queen diagonal to me. "G7. Oh no. I lost? I'm stuck here?" I sucked in breath and fell to my knees. I couldn't stand being trapped with no way out. I couldn't swallow my fear any longer.

Panic pounded in my chest, and tears began to pour down my cheeks, dripping onto the glass. As I peered through, I saw two brown eyes staring back.

"Toto!" I gasped, only to start sobbing as I placed my hand against the glass. "I am sorry, Boy. I'm afraid I have gotten myself stuck down here. I tried to do that fancy Queen trick that Uncle

Henry showed me. I messed it up, Toto. I messed it up. I don't know why I picked that one. I wasn't thinking clearly. I am so sorry. I'm so sorry, Toto." I hung my head.

"Ahem," One of the pieces cleared its throat behind me.

Sniffling uncontrollably, I looked up at the piece. "Yes?"

"Per the established rules, rule five states that all pieces on the board must be moved once, before the game ends," The piece said gently.

"I know. There were ten pieces on the board. I sent two away, leaving eight on the board and I messed it up. All of the pieces have been moved."

"I believe you miscounted your pieces, Miss. I was neither banished, nor moved into place," The queen pressed.

Her words sent a jolt of tumultious hope surging through my spine, and I counted the pieces on the board again. My heart jumped as I realized even with the defeated queen, there were still eight queens on the board.

"There is still one move?" I asked hopefully, wiping the tears from my face..

The queen smiled at me. "I have yet to be placed on the board."

"G7. Uh, queen nine, move to G7," I commanded, scooting myself to the middle of the board.

The final queen slid into place with a click. All eight remaining queens began glowing until the whole area flashed with a light so bright I had to cover my eyes. When I looked back, the pieces were all normal chess pieces again, each back in their places on their own sides of the board.

"You reset!" I cheered. I looked through the glass at Toto. He started pawing at the glass. I frowned, feeling the cold solid surface against my hand. "How do I get back through? I won. I can get out now right?"

"Dive in," One of the knights answered.

Dive into solid glass? That did not sound the slightest bit logical. And yet, here I was, in a world of nonsense. What good was logic here? I sighed, and hopped to my feet.

Approaching the knight, I gave a small bow. "May I?"

"You may." The horse dipped his head in compliance, and I climbed up onto his back.

With a deep breath I looked at the center of the board and dove off the Knight's back. Sure enough, my arms pushed right through the glass as if it were air. I landed softly, still sitting on the board, but this time on the right side of the glass.

Toto wagged his tail and gave a triumphant bark before racing to jump in my lap. I held him close for a moment and buried my face in his fur as he licked at my ear, we both looked up at the sound of leaves crinkling. The hedge to one side of us crawled away to reveal a new entrance— or rather exit. Still holding Toto in my arms, I got to my feet and passed through the opening to find myself in a large stone courtyard of a castle.

"Well, Toto. Looks like our luck might be finally changing," I whispered to my dog. "Let's look for Alice. Maybe they have some more of that tea."

Nineteen

Dorothy

I noticed various burn marks scoring the red and white checkered cobblestone, and couldn't help but wonder what had caused them. Strewn here and there were what looked to be pieces of shredded playing cards.

"Looks like someone lost a game of cards here," I said nervously to Toto, who wound around my legs with a whine.

He gave the air a few sniffs and trotted off towards the castle, tail and head held high. He paused at the large door and looked back at me, as if to ask if I were going to follow him.

"Alright, I guess you must know something I don't. Lead the way," I sighed and trailed after my dog. In all fairness, he'd had a wonderful sense of intuition in this place so far.

We entered the palace and stood in a large foyer with a winding staircase. I observed a wall of framed mirrors that looked to have been shattered at one point and then messily pieced back together. At the top of the stairway was a mostly burned portrait of what appeared to once have been a woman. The painting had curled away from its ornate golden frame, leaving only a small flap of what had once been there.

"I don't care for this place." Despite the fact that I whispered, my remark echoed around the large room. "I think it might be dangerous, Toto."

But, my dog kept plodding along, completely undeterred by the evidence of potential foul-play. He approached the next doorway and threw his paws against it with a small, demanding yip.

"Toto, hush! I know you are on a mission, but we don't know if whoever lives here is friendly or not. I heard things about a mad queen," I cautioned my dog, pausing as I caught a glimpse of my reflection in the mirror.

My head reeled for a moment as I fixated on my reflection. My eyes widened as each individual shard refracted back a different image of me, each reflection acting independently of the others.

One was clutching her stomach in a fit of laughter, while another was skipping in circles. There was one that was napping while the one next to her was looking at an imaginary watch. Some of the reflections saw me in different versions of my gingham dress, and in various hairstyles. I clutched my head and took a step back, squinting my eyes tightly shut. When I opened them again, the reflection was normal once more.

"What...?" I breathed, stretching out a hand towards the glass. As my fingers made contact with the mirror, I caught a faint glimmer coming off my silver shoes. The glass shook in its assorted frames, shard by shard falling free and back onto the ground.

With a sharp intake of a breath, I raced over to Toto and opened the door, closing it firmly behind me as I heard the final crescendo of the glass pouring off the wall. I guess there was no hiding our presence at this point. I was looking for someone to help me, after all. But, there was still something telling me, this castle was not a safe place to be.

There could still be a chance that Alice had ended up here

though, right? I consoled myself as Toto and I continued on down a long hallway filled with doors. I scrunched up my face as I noted that there were different shaped doors resting at various heights on the wall, and one on the ceiling.

"I suppose we just start trying doors," I suggested, opening the first door to my right. "Ack!" I squealed. I quickly slammed it closed again as I saw it led to the edge of a crumbling wall.

With a shaking hand I tried the door to my left. It yielded to reveal another door. With a puff of annoyance, I opened the second door, and stepped through, only to find myself further down the same hallway I had just been in. Toto had paused halfway through, leaving his hind end at the beginning of the hallway, and his head poking out halfway through.

"What is this nonsense?" I grumbled. "I don't know why I am even surprised anymore. This strange place clearly has no room for physics or logic."

Once Toto cleared the doorway I closed the door and started back towards where I had left off. It made sense to keep on a steady pattern. I couldn't bring myself to abandon all common sense, after all.

"Alright," I pointed to the right door. "That is a cliff, or some such," I pointed to the left. "And, that one is a door within a door that takes you to another door. Let's see what's next." I approached the next door, which was particularly small, and turned the knob.

It yielded and revealed a garden with beautiful and large flowers of all sorts. I wondered if this was some portion of hedge-maze. Not wishing to get lost again, I opted that it would be wise to close that door.

"Look, another weed!" A voice heckled.

"I beg your pardon?" I asked, poking my head back inside. I

was trying to discern whether a flower had truly spoken or not.

"Indeed! We haven't got room for any stupider looking flowers here," A violet scoffed.

"I am not a flower, I am a person," I corrected the flora.

"Oh, just like that other one," Snipped the violet. "She is quite foolish too. She had such woeful petals that were wilting about her, much like you."

"Violet, you needn't be so rude. That is why we have been planted here in the first place," A red rose chided, while a cluster of daisy's nodded emphatically. "You never know if you'll have insulted another Wicked witch."

I looked at myself and realized the petals they were referring to must be my dress. If that were true, then they were certainly talking about another person.

"I am not Wicked. I chose to be Good or something," I interjected briskly. "I'm mighty sorry to interrupt, but who are you talking about with petals like mine?" I asked, trying to quell the hope that was bubbling in my chest.

"She called herself an Alice, but I believe her genus is a person like you," The rose answered politely.

"Really? I am actually looking for her right now. Could you tell me if I am heading in the right direction?" My mouth was stretching beyond its limits into an enormous grin. Someone was finally being helpful! Trust it to be a flower, but I couldn't complain.

"I would steer clear of the Wicked Witch of the West, if I were you," A tiger lily piped up quietly. I frowned and nodded.

"Yes, I have no intention of bumping into anyone Wicked if I can help it. But, am I headed the right way? Is Alice around here?" I asked again.

The flowers all looked at each other for a moment, each one

shrugging in turn, until the rose finally turned back towards me, and nodded.

"If you find one of these doors leads to the library, she spends a lot of time in there."

Everything inside me lit up like the Fourth of July. I felt truly giddy. An uncharacteristic trill of excited laughter escaped from my lips, causing me to cover my mouth in surprise. I cleared my throat and smiled around my hand, dipping my head in farewell before closing the door. Turning back towards the hallway, I looked down at my dog.

Toto ran in a circle, barking twice. Wagging his tail, he pranced up to the next door and lifted his front paw to point.

"That's right, Toto," I cooed, stooping to rub him on the head as I approached. "We just need to open all of the doors until we find the library. Then, we wait for Alice to show up."

~*~

It took a few tries, but eventually I found a door that took me to a library. Being in a world of nonsense around every corner, I didn't know what I expected out of a library here. However, whatever my expectation had been, it certainly didn't meet up to what I was seeing before me.

Spiral bookshelves wound their way from the floor to the globe ceiling, covered in books that were organized in beautiful spectrums of color on each spine. A winding staircase hugged the sides of the shelves, so readers could reach the varying levels. The floor was a golden marble that reflected the faint glimmer of my silver shoes with each step I took.

Though I hadn't climbed any stairs, the library appeared

to be on a second level. There was a large window that opened up to a short balcony that overlooked the landscape. Certainly an exceptional addition to such a beautiful and pensive space.

I made my way to the nearest staircase, and, for the first time since arriving in this strange place, I was able to appreciate the beauty of it. True, most of what I had experienced so far had been riddled with terror or frustration, but something about this magnificent library was making me see things a little differently.

While the accidental house-murder of a Wicked witch had taken priority at the time, the munchkin village really was quite amazing. The homes reminded me vaguely of Scandinavian architecture mixed with a little bit of Tolkein's hobbit lore. Something about drawing it back to home felt comforting.

The company at the tea party had been strange, but I had never seen so many beautiful teacups and teapots. Plus that tea had been so satisfying— more satisfying than any tea I had from home. It certainly sated any hunger or thirst I'd previously felt— and should be feeling now.

Though, I hadn't much to say of the butterfly's interaction, it did sort of push me in the right direction. The chess pieces had been helpful enough. And, I had held a conversation with wild flowers.

"Perhaps what I have been judging as nonsense has just been magic," I mused aloud to Toto as we continued our ascent up the stairs. "Have I detached so far from my sense of wonder that I haven't realized it till now?"

Toto responded with a small yip. I took it as his agreement to my assessment and sighed. Perhaps I just needed to embrace where I was. Maybe it was a dream, maybe it wasn't. But, either way, I was experiencing it, and I might well take a breath.

I scanned the varying odd book titles as I passed. These

included delights like, *What to Wonder in Wonderland, Keep Your Head: Staying on the Red Queen's Good Side, If You're Wicked and You Know It*, and *Who Is Afraid of The Madness*. The last one reminded me of the film,*Who's Afraid of Virginia Woolf*, from back home. It had just been released earlier in the summer, and I had wanted to see it with Uncle Henry.

Snuffing down my sadness at the thought of my family, I reached for the *What to Wonder in Wonderland* book and flipped to the index.

"Look, Toto," I called to my dog, squatting down to show him the book. "There is a section on the Mad Hatter and the March Hare. Do we dare read about them and see if it matches our interactions with being silver cuppers, or whatever it was they called me?"

I chuckled to myself as I flipped to its corresponding page. The chapter title page had some loose illustrations, showing these were no doubt the folks I had encountered at the tea party. I turned the page and the first thing read in big bold red letters, *Don't drink the tea*! I wilted.

"Oh, dear," I sighed, closing the book and placing it back on the shelf. "I certainly hope that doesn't mean I've poisoned myself. Though, even the most delayed poisons probably would have taken hold by now. In any case, I suppose I can't very well do anything about it now."

I turned around and whistled for Toto to follow. We plodded down the steps in tandem and looked around. In a little alcove, I saw a desk with books stacked up, one laying open in the middle. Some little voice in my head was telling me I was being too calm and accepting that I may have drank poison, but it was swimming in a sea of dizzy thoughts, ebbing and flowing like the tide.

"All the more reason to find this Alice, and find a way

home," I said, approaching the desk. "I do hope she shows up soon though. I don't really want to be here long enough to test that poison theory…"

I trailed off as I caught sight of what the previous desk-occupant had been reading. Clear as day, I was staring at a picture of the very same slippers I was standing in. I scanned the page, my eyes latching on to a familiar couple of words— my name.

"Oh, Toto… I don't think we are so safe here after all. Whoever was reading this book must have been the one who sent those monsters after me. What a fool I've been," I rambled, feeling panic well in my chest, as cold, fearful logic encased me once more.

Why would I go West when I knew those monkeys came from someone called the Wicked Witch of the *West*? Where had all my sensible thinking gone?

Those flowers had probably lied to me to set a trap! This Alice girl probably wasn't even in this castle and I had been a trusting fool, sitting here waiting like a sitting duck.

I scooped Toto into my arms, whirling around at the sound of a loud bang behind me. A girl, about my own age, in a deep indigo blouse tucked loosely into a pair of white cloth pants faced me in the doorway. She had ice blue eyes, and long blonde hair secured back into a ponytail with a ribbon.

I swallowed hard. Was this the queen?

Twenty
Alice

"**L**ook, Hatter," I said crossly as I pinned him by the neck with my forearm. He was giggling like an idiot. I tried to swallow down my irritation. "It would be extraordinarily easy for me to just kill you."

Peter chortled a little from where he leaned against the little picket fence. He'd accompanied me after the flying monkeys had reported that Dorothy had run West.

I shot him a glare, not wanting him to ruin my intimidation tactics. Sure, I didn't want to kill anyone. But, this was different. No one else had ever been standing so blatantly in my way of getting home before. It might be the compass talking, but deep down I knew now that I would do anything I needed to do to get home. I had a new understanding of Avrilia's intense methods of getting home the moment I saw Dorothy's name appear in the book. Why should this new arrival had a better chance at getting home than the rest of us who had been trapped here for so much longer?

Ignoring Peter's interruption, I brushed my fingers gently along the Hatter's cheek. "But, that's not good enough for me, I'm afraid." I released him and paced away slowly for emphasis.

He was still laughing. I gripped the table and it buckled,

cracking into a splintered heap, the assortment of tea-ware and crumpets also meeting their doom in a toppled pile.

I checked the Hatter. He had stopped laughing and was now staring at the ruins of his tea party with a look of stupid awe and horror smeared across his wrinkled face. I pulled him close to my face with an invisible hand as I sat in his chair.

"I can tell by all of those laugh lines you are still a pretty foolishly blissful individual," I observed.

The Hatter grinned and nodded. "It's the tea. Tea… T. U V W X Y and Z. Y X… Xylophone!" The Hatter shouted loudly.

"Xylophone," The March Hare meeped from his hostage position in another chair.

"Silence!" I bellowed. I was about to just give up and kill them both. That was what the compass wanted, and it was very exhausting to fight against the urge all the time.

The Hatter gasped and stuffed his knuckles in his mouth.

I rubbed my fingers in circles on my temples. Had he always been this frustrating? "As I was saying… No more nonsense, Hatter. Did you see the girl or not? Tell me or your happy little crow's feet are going to become actual crows and will peck your eyes until they are nothing more than a bloody pulp, and then some." I tugged in agitation at my compass.

"Well, this is certainly new," Peter laughed, coming to slouch in a random seat at the broken table. He grabbed a scone from the pile, and dipped it into the nearest toppled jar of jam. "Don't drink the tea, but there is no law against the scones," He mumbled happily to himself, stuffing the scone in his mouth.

"What girl?" The Hatter said around the fist in his mouth.

"Whoops," A small voice squeaked. Peter had accidentally shrunken himself and was wandering around the plate of crumpets.

He ate a crumb and returned back to his normal stature. "That's right. It is the cucumber sandwiches that don't change your size."

I'd had enough. The red was leaking into my vision. These fools were going to die and it would not entirely be my fault. I let out an exasperated scream and, trying to remain in control, managed to only set the Hatter's top hat ablaze. He began hopping around and was fanning the flames instead of putting them out. I smacked my head with my palm. There was no torturing these fools. I would just kill them. Someone was going to die.

"The girl who defiled the Grandmother's teapot?" A new voice spoke and I knew it well.

"Hello Cheshire," I sighed dismissively, until his previous statement registered, causing me to sit up straight. "Wait, did you a say a girl defiled someone's teapot?" I turned away from the hopping Hatter and faced the Cheshire Cat.

"Yes. She wasn't a very *committed* guest— If you know what I mean. I daresay she had never been to a tea party in her life. Let alone a *mad* one," He drawled in a dramatic, judging tone.

"What did she look like?" Peter interjected around a mouthful of cucumber sandwich.

I furrowed my brows at the sound of a crash behind me. Turning my head, I saw that the Hare had escaped his binds and was standing on a chair pouring tea on the Hatter's smoldering hat.

I rolled my eyes and turned back towards Cheshire. "What shoes was she wearing?"

"They were very pretty shoes," The Hatter gushed, dripping with Earl Gray.

"I do believe they were, Hatter. So vibrantly silver. They had a real *magical* quality to them even," The Cheshire Cat gave whimsical laugh. "You haven't seen a mouse around here have you?" He licked his lips.

I was close and I knew it. "Which way did she go?" I asked. No one answered me.

The cat shrugged and the Hatter was trying to piece together a silver teacup while mumbling nonsense about silver cuppers. The March Hare was hopping about in circles. Enough was enough! I tackled the hare and pinned him to the ground.

"I am going to rip your ears off and hang you by them! Pay attention. Which way did the girl go?" I shouted in his face.

"I haven't a clue. She took the only exit." The Hare pointed with his ears to a tiny gate. "Who is to say where she went from there?"

I was fighting the urge to smite the creature when I noticed some small paw prints on the ground. "Was there anyone with her?" I mused, still sitting on the Hare.

"She had a boisterous little critter with her. A Toto dog, I believe," The Hatter threw in from his teacup restoration project.

I smiled. "Brilliant." I got up and made to leave for the forest again.

The Cheshire Cat appeared on my shoulder and cleared his throat, pointing with his tail to the ruined tea party.

"What?" I demanded.

"You might as well put it back. It keeps them harmless. You know that," He answered and then disappeared. I sighed and flicked a wrist. The table and tea-ware all restored to new once more.

Leaving the madness and infinite tea party behind me, I followed the dog prints towards the Fungi Forest. Peter trailed along behind me, still chewing the remainder of his sandwich.

"Say what you will about those two, but they do make excellent sandwiches," He gushed as we crossed an arm of Nonsense

Falls. "That whole threatening side of you was interesting," he commented after a moment of silence.

"I was just trying to get information," I replied, waving away his insinuations.

"I didn't say I didn't like it," Peter laughed quietly, quoting something he had once said to me back before things got so messed up. "It was just interesting. I think you have been really finding your way here, despite everything. Not that you need to be killing folks willy nilly, but having a commanding presence will help you keep Wonderland in line. Makes for an easy reign, so long as you aren't *so* commanding that it comes off as hostile. You'll have a mutiny on your hands if you go too far in that direction."

I bit my lip and didn't respond. I didn't need to find my way in this world, I needed to find my way to my world. We followed the remaining prints in silence until they disappeared against the mirror-rocks. She must have gone through and ended up at the Red Castle. I looked around and cursed.

"Come on, if you want," I called to Peter before stepping through the glass portal.

Peter quietly followed suit and we both paused at the entrance to the ever-changing hedge maze. I didn't have the time nor the patience to wander through it.

"Can I have some dust?" I asked Peter.

He smiled and wagged a finger at me. "I don't think any of the thoughts you're having right now are happy enough to make it work."

I fixed him with a glare and folded my arms across my chest. He was right that the pixie dust magic thrived on happy thoughts but my mood was already bleak without his silly attitude and infernal obstinance to allow me to fly on my own.

"Fine," He sighed. "Come here, I'll just carry you to the entrance. You can check the maze while we go."

"Thank you." I grinned and threw my arm around his shoulder.

True to his word, Peter zipped me over to the entrance of the castle. He hovered in the courtyard, looking a bit fidgety.

"Aren't you coming?" I asked, pausing to look up at where he was hovering.

"What? Oh, uh, yeah. I mean no. I've been here all day. I need to get back to Neverland for a bit. Fairy demands and whatnot," Peter rambled distractedly. "Good luck."

With that, he flew away before I could say another word.

"Curious," I muttered with a frown, then turned back towards the castle and continued my search.

I wandered around a bit, looking for any sign of a trespasser. I hadn't seen her while flying over the maze, so she should be in the castle somewhere still— Hopefully. Eventually, I made my way to the foyer where I had battled the Jabberwock and stopped cold. All of the glass from the wall was scattered along the ground.

"Here we are," I said, smiling as I had caught the trail once more. She must have gone down the hall and was behind one of the doors. It only took a couple of tries before the flowers gave up the mystery-girl's location. The library. I was one door away from the shoes, and I knew exactly which door it was.

I stood in front of the door, hearing a noise from within. I inched the door open to see her, and she was wearing the shoes. My shoes. Her back was to me, but I could see her curly brown hair, pulled into neat braids. She wore a patterned blue dress and was clutching a little black dog in her arms.

I pointed a finger, ready to blast her with lightning when a thought flooded my mind. My magic could not kill another witch and this Dorothy girl, by way of shoes, was most certainly a witch. If I tried to zap her, I could very well end up deformed and pallid like Avrilia, or become something worse like a dreadfully cheerful yellow. Worse still, it could make my compass go even more askew, or turn me into a Jabberwock like the Red Queen. No, I would have to get close. It would be done by force, like the other three witches who had fallen by my hand.

I opened the door the rest of the way loudly, letting it slam into the walls. Dorothy spun around, her large brown eyes full of fear. I walked smoothly and gracefully up to her, not showing a hint of irritation that she was there.

"Hello, Lovely," I said sweetly, adopting Avrilia's pet name for me. It had been disarming enough for me when we met. I sat down gracefully on the edge of a nearby reading chair. Dorothy just stared back at me, probably sizing me up. "My name is Alice, and you are?"

"Dorothy." She looked stunned for a moment, before finally stating her name, still standing in her rigid stance. "Sorry for the intrusion. You see, this boy told me to find you. And then the butterfly was flustering and I walked through some weird rocks…" She trailed off, swallowing hard. "The boy said, though, that you might be able to get me back to Kansas. So, can you or can't you?"

I felt my smile falter for a moment. "Boy? What boy?"

I knew she must have met Peter. He probably never even went to the Tweedles, and went to find the girl. Probably at the crossroads, just like me. That made it less special if he greeted every lost girl there and sent them into Wonderland. After all, there had only been two new girls in a long time. This was looking like a pattern of behavior. Though that silly girlish thought was the least of my concerns, I still felt ruffled. Never mind the fact that Peter had neglected to tell me he had met her.

"Peter, I think."

Right, clearly my arrival was not so special to Peter. My stomach lurched at the thought. I quickly reminded myself that he did send Dorothy my way— which might have been more helpful if he had told me. I wasted a good deal of time dealing with those mad fools and he had known the whole time where she was! He sat there and ate sandwiches. Anger roared alive within me once more. Why was he sabotaging me when he knew how important this was to me? My temper was rising, and a dull sense of panic sliced through the preexisting butterflies associated with Peter. I would deal with him later.

"What exactly did he tell you, Lovely?" I asked. Then, as if on cue, he waltzed in through the door, whistling a stupid happy little tune.

"Well, now it is just a party isn't it?" I said, letting the smile melt from my face. I rose to my feet and Peter stopped, realizing we were not alone. He grinned at me, then at Dorothy, and then back at me.

"Alice, I hope you realized that you can't *kill* her," He said cheekily, leaning hard on the most alarming word in his statement.

Fan-bloody-tastic. All subtlety was gone now.

"I beg your pardon?" Dorothy gasped, taking a step back.

"I did realize that, but thank you for announcing it to all of Wonderland, Peter. Why didn't you tell me you had already found her?" I demanded, rising to my feet. "I had to deal with the Hatter. And you watched!"

"And ruin the fun?" He shrugged. "Why? Jealous, Alice?" His grin widened as he leaned forward on his tiptoes, and he wiggled his eyebrows up and down suggestively.

I was pretty fed up with everyone for the day and was quite through with being nice. Not when I was so close. My compass was spinning, and this time, I did not bother to fight it. I threw a fireball at Peter's face, which he narrowly dodged.

"I do not have time to deal with wild goose chases!" I shouted at him and shot another fireball at him, this time aiming considerably lower. A book about the King of Hearts had taught me that is where you aim at boys.

Peter floated in the air, missing the ball again. "You know, I can't quite decide if you're less or more attractive when you're trying to set me on fire," He mused, tapping his finger on his chin. "Plus, I believe in a world that isn't dictated by a sense of time, you have all the time in the world! Let's smell the talking wildflowers, shall we?"

He was infuriating. Why was he picking now to flirt like a schoolboy and spoil everything?

"Are *you* that mutiny you mentioned?"

"Not in the slightest," He keened. "I only wish for what's best."

I shook my head. I was about to pluck him from the air and squash him against the floor like the pest he was being when Dorothy interrupted.

"What the hell is going on? Who are you people?" Her eyes were wide as she witnessed Peter's and my quarrel. "Look, I just want to go home. There is no need to be jealous of anything to do with me, because, hopefully, I won't be here much longer. But, for goodness sake, can someone tell me what the hell is happening here?"

I glowered at her, my eyes narrowing into chips of blue ice.

"Let me introduce you to Alice, The Wickedest Wicked Witch of the West," Peter landed beside her, threw his arm around her shoulders, and gestured broadly with his free arm to me. "Welcome to Wonderland, Dorothy. We do hope you will stay a while. At least, I do anyway."

Twenty-One
Dorothy

Alice was the Wicked Witch of the West? This certainly did not spark my hope of getting her to help me. Vibrant fireball remnants twinkled on her fingertips and her pretty face puckered into a scowl. She gave me a long look, and I could do nothing but blink back at her helplessly. Another wave of dizziness crashed over me, and my poison theory reared its head.

Peter squeezed my shoulder lightly and stood between me and Alice, his hands in his pockets. There was an annoying smirk on his face that slowly spread back into a brazen grin as the silence stretched on, like this was something he had hoped would happen.

He cleared his throat. "Seems like you two dolls have a lot to talk about then. Should I call on the Hatter for some tea?" He gave me a meaningful look. This was the second odd reference towards drinking tea. I had drunk a lot of tea at the Hatter's.

"You can leave now, Peter," Alice said through a returning forced smile, though her eyes were blazing.

Peter wagged his finger at Alice, and squinted his eyes playfully as he backed towards the door. "Play nice, Love." He closed the doors behind him, leaving me and Alice completely alone.

I honestly couldn't tell if they were a couple or not. But,

clearly I had come in the middle of something between them. I didn't have the current mental capacity to rationalize why the glowing boy at the crossroads would send me to Alice, only to try to spoil the encounter.

"You are not from around here, are you?" Alice asked me, her tone cool and casual, breaking through my spinning thoughts.

I shook my head. "No, I'm from Kansas."

"Ah, American then. I was from England. Peter too, originally, I think. He's never said, but you can hear it in his voice. I hope you will forgive his behavior and commentary. He is from a part of the world that has prided itself on never growing up. I can only assume while he is there, he spends his time with those called the Lost Boys— very young boys— and absorbs some of their irritating immaturity. That is honestly why I have not ever ventured very far South. What about you?"

"What?" I asked, surprised by her apparent friendliness.

"Why West?"

"I couldn't go home," I answered simply.

Alice's face seemed to harden for a moment before softening again. "You want to go home then? So do I. I have been trying to figure out some way for a long time now. Others even longer than me."

"I was wondering if you knew how to get back," I responded honestly.

Alice returned to her reading chair and flopped down. "I am afraid that I have not been successful yet myself. Any current plan I might have in the works, unfortunately, only will work for one I think…" She trailed off and looked at me fixedly before continuing, "And, I intend for that to be me. I'm terribly sorry, of course."

She summoned another chair from the corner of the room

next to her and patted the seat.

I complied and sat down. Toto hopped off my lap and ducked under the writing desk.

"There was a problem with some mirrors out there," I said awkwardly, not knowing what else to say. She wasn't trying to kill me with anything besides kindness, currently.

Alice, like everyone else, had no way to help me. Her presence unnerved me, like there was something sinister under her skin, waiting to leap out. I wanted to leave but she didn't seem to be done talking to me, and fear was setting in my bones.

"Oh, dear. That should have been dealt with already. You'd think the Card-guards would be programmed to hop to more quickly. It is not as though the cards are not used to being decapitated," Alice sighed, tucking a stray strand of blonde hair behind her ear.

"Decapitated?" I gasped, instinctively clasping my throat.

"Well, the Queen of Hearts did have a distinct fascination with beheading her subjects. Sorry, the Red Queen did the beheadings. Intimidation seemed to work well for her, so I don't see why I should change things too much."

"The Queen of Hearts? Red Queen?" My head went from feeling light and dizzy, to suddenly submerging into a heaviness, like I was swimming in letters and words.

"Yes, she was Queen of Wonderland before her sister died. She went insane from grief, separated herself into two people, and the dark side killed the Good. I daresay, you look a little ill." Alice squinted at me suspiciously. "You aren't going to die from this ailment, are you?"

"What? No! I think something didn't agree with me earlier. It is giving me a bit of a headache." I held my head in my hands as I spoke.

It must be a delayed symptom from the twister. If Peter had brought up the tea casually to Alice, then the warnings probably just had to do with the evident addictive qualities it possessed. I truly needed to believe I had not poisoned myself so easily. *It is just a concussion from the tornado*, I told myself firmly.

Toto poked his head out from his hiding spot and raced up to me. He kept looking back at the door, as if trying to tell me to leave. Alice didn't make me feel safe either, but Peter had said she couldn't kill me, right? Then again, why should I trust anything he had said?

"But you're feeling weak then?" Alice pressed on. Was that *hope* in her voice?

"I suppose, but what does that have to do with—"

"Where did you get those shoes, Dorothy?" Alice said suddenly, her voice shifted from friendly to aggressive in an instant. "And, how is it that you have them and are still *Good*?"

"My house fell on some witch that was bullying some munchkins. Apparently that glued these things to my feet." I tasted the faint flavor of the tea I had drunk on my lips. "I didn't mean to—"

"I can get them off for you," Alice cut me off again. There was an unnatural edge to her voice. I rose groggily to my feet and stumbled away from her. "No magic in this entire world can get them off, but there is another way."

"What's that?"

Quick as lightning Alice had me pinned to a bookcase with her elbow pressed against my throat. "You die." And, with that, she produced a long, sharp dagger from behind her back.

She was about to plunge it into my defenseless body when something went off like a timer in my brain, restoring me with deranged amounts of energy. I managed to catch her wrist and stop the knife from sinking into my chest. Anger and fear were boiling in my stomach, and I started shoving back against her. Everything was pulsing in radiating colors.

As I had hoped, years of being on a farm had made me just a little bit stronger than Alice, and I was able to redirect her weapon-wielding hand. The blade caught on her arm and carved a long gash, blood rolling down the silver blade.

"Ah!" She cried out, releasing her grip on me for a moment, and dropped the blade on the ground.

Her face flushed and her eyes narrowed. She gave a puff of frustration. I noted the little compass that was dangling around her neck was going haywire. She looked the picture of terror.

"That does it," She hissed through her gritted teeth. "Time to really let the Wicked out to play."

Her hand reached up, but before she could do anything, I was suddenly engulfed in a cloud of shimmering dust, with the words, *think of Kansas,* echoing in my ear. Instinctively I visualized my family farm in Kansas. Images of Aunt Em, Uncle Henry, and my cousins with their families flashed in my mind.

"What in the…" I trailed off as I realized I was suddenly floating off the ground. I screamed and began flailing my arms and legs around, too late realizing I was propelling myself towards the grandiose window I had previously been admiring, which was suddenly open. My vision started spinning, toggling shapes and sizes of what I was seeing in flashes of bright colors.

For one clear moment, I caught sight of Peter behind Alice, grabbing her arms and holding her steady as she fought for freedom. He was helping me escape? I thought he had wanted me to find Alice, now he was helping me get away from her. Perhaps he was trying to be helpful in a very strange way.

Toto returned to his hiding place, and the knowledge that I'd have to find my poor dog sank in as I floated over mushroom forests and tumbleweeds of water, obscure little houses glinting below me.

Alice's eyes burned with fury as she rushed to the edge of the balcony. A strand of flaming lightning burst from her, the wave of heat scoring me with the vehemence of her anger. But, I was out of actual striking distance. I closed my eyes as I floated out of sight.

~*~

I was back in a cyclone of colors, shapes, and lagging motion. The hues swirled and vibrated, pulsing with an energy that felt very alive. I registered only for a moment that I was on my hands and knees, crawling through the mud. My mind whirled and nothing made any sense.

I floated a moment in front of a mirror, then tumbled through it. Red beat in front of my eyes, a thumping sensation that made me throw my hands up to protect my face. The motion of fingers curling and uncurling slowed, transparent echoes leaking from the original hand as it moved.

Follow the Yellow Brick Road… a foreign voice hammered against my skull. I closed my eyes for a moment, instantly feeling like I was falling through the dense earth, dirt and worms sliding past my body in rapid succession as I sunk deeper. Hearing a cackle above, I opened my eyes to see a flash of a captor pouring dirt into my perceived grave, burying me alive. I closed my eyes once more.

Behind my eyelids I saw two floating balls of yellow hovering towards me. They were quickly joined by two other pairs of yellow orbs.

I heard banging on a door, followed by nails scratching

underneath floorboards. A sudden sensation of spiders crawling over my arms made my body shudder.

I opened my eyes to see that the perceived balls of yellow were actually eyes belonging to those cursed flying monkeys from earlier.

In an instant, I was shrunk down to the size of a mouse. Coughing, I spat out a mouthful of teeth, only to reach up and feel that all my teeth remained in tact. Another wave of pulsing red crashed over me and I was once more normal sized.

I lurched to my feet to escape the hovering monkeys, noting I was standing on the glimmering Yellow Brick Road from my departure of the Munchkin village. My vision was suddenly bubbling with iridescent yellows. I took a step forward, squinting as a shape began to form in front of me. It appeared to be the size of a munchkin.

"Biscuits leapt from the woods and toppled into mushroom towers," I babbled. I tried again, "Butterflies and lemons don't make good letters."

"Are you alright? Come here, and let us help you," A voice cooed.

I sighed and rushed to throw my arms around the munchkin blob, only as I touched their skin, the body evaporated, and everything blacked out. I shook my head and saw I was standing in a giant field of scarecrows. They moaned and reached their arms towards me clumsily from where they were pinned to their stakes. I screamed and turned to run away, slamming smack into one, and knocking its straw-filled head off its shoulders.

It landed at my feet, staring up at me with dark voids for eyes, and began speaking to me, its voice hollow and undefined.

"Sorry, Miss. If I only had a brain. Lend me yours?" The

voice slowly turned into a dense cackle, escalating in shrillness. I quickly picked up the head and placed it back on the body.

"I think I've lost my head too," I murmured and dared to take another step forward.

This time the ground fell away from my feet and sent me plummeting into darkness once more. I had the sensation of falling upwards, but realized I was sinking downwards.

I opened my mouth to scream but no sound came out. Instead, grating voices bounced off the hollowness. My feet thumped hard on the ground and the world bounced around me. I was once more standing on the Yellow Brick Road.

I heard a thudding in my ear drum like a war drum. The shuttering movement of wings caught my eye above as the flying monkeys descended upon me. The hard sound of marching clattered in my ears, and I saw varying shapes twisting and contorting from hearts to spades, then monkeys to diamonds and clubs. Red pulsed behind my eyes again and a fearful, psychotic rage bubbled in my chest.

I blinked and was standing inside my house. Something shadowy was slithering down the hall towards me. I tried to run away, but felt like I was running through water, tripping and tumbling to the ground.

"Enough!" I screamed at the top of my lungs. Everything fuzzed into red with flurries of black, until the black took over and I fell to my knees. Something was running down my face, I assumed it was sweat. I wiped it away with the back of my hand, but started in horror as I saw my hand was stained red, tufts of fur and feathers stuck under my nails.

Shaking, I looked down to see more scarlet splatters and stains on my dress. I looked to the sky through watering eyes and saw a looming castle, shimmering and green, as if it were made entirely of emeralds. Then it was gone and I was in the clearing next to the Munchkin Village.

Taking a breath, I slowly looked around me, choking down bile as I saw the scattered remains of the assaulting monkeys, and what I could only assume were the torn up bodies of the Card-guards, littered across the Yellow Brick Road. There were miscellaneous munchkin bodies strewn about as well, still and lifeless.

I sobered, feeling my sensibility rattling to a standstill back in logic once more as I took in what had happened. "What have I done?" I whispered.

"She's killed in cold blood. She's a Wicked witch now." I turned at the sound of a tiny voice. Behind me, Boq, the munchkin man from my arrival, was poking his head out from behind a tree.

I shook my head desperately. "No, no. I didn't mean…" Tears poured down my cheeks, choking the words back down my throat.

He stepped out solemnly. "All hail Dorothy, the new Wicked Witch of the East."

Keep watch for the sequel:

When Wicked Runs: *East*

Turn the page for a sneak peek of Chapter One!

One

Alice

I rushed to the grand window of the Red Castle library, that overlooked the Eastern side of the world, and saw Dorothy floating over Wonderland.

"Peter!" I screeched in dismay, seeing my hopes of going home drifting away on the breeze. Who had been my most trusted friend, and favorite person, had just sent my only option to get home flying away. To add insult to injury, he had used the very dust he never shared with me in all the years we'd spent together to do so.

"You could't just use magic on her, Alice," Peter insisted firmly from behind me.

Dorothy Gale had arrived in this world and instantly taken ownership of the only potential lead to getting back to the real world. The magical slippers I needed to get back home were stuck on her feet. I needed those shoes to undo all the Wickedness I had committed in the several years since my own arrival here. It was my only shot at getting a clean slate again, and to return to my own family.

I had been searching for a way out of this world for years, and this new girl had been here all of five seconds. It might be the altered moral compass dangling from my neck—the very thing that had turned me into The Wicked Witch of the West in the first place—but something inside me told me it was either her or me, and I fully intended it to be me. The only way for me to get those shoes from her would have to be by force.

Normally, I was opposed to killing and violence, but something inside was changing with each tug of my compass' arrow. I'd already convinced myself that unleashing my Wicked side to get the shoes was a means to an end. Just one last time of letting the compass skew me.

I was seething and was certain my face was flushing several pigments of red. When I turned to face Peter he took a step back. "I was going to *stab* her!"

"What happened to not killing? She was fighting you off, anyway. Look, you cut yourself in the process of wrestling with a long and sharp blade, for bloody sake. You would have used magic and then who knows what could have happened to you. I thought you didn't want to be green," he huffed, his voice escalating in volume.

"It was yellow! I did not want to be yellow." I stamped my foot for emphasis.

He snorted, his usual detached air gone. "Hate to break it to you, Love, but your hair is already *yellow*."

That did it. I'd had enough of everything that day. I'd suffered through interrogating the insane Hatter, Peter's willful sabotage, and

Dorothy with her stupid slippers. I glared at Peter and, with a flick of my finger, he began to shrink and turn a grass green.

"Alice! Seriousl-rrrribit." His outcry of indignation was morphed into a monotonous croak.

"You want to behave like a toad then you can be one too. And it is blonde, not yellow!" I shouted at him and then sat down, flopping angrily on the beautiful marble flooring of the library, its surface cool against my boiling skin. I sighed heavily, trying to collect myself.

I had underestimated this girl. I had handled her all wrong. Trying to ambush her by force without a proper plan had been impulsive and foolish. What was even worse was that I knew Peter was right; I would have used magic. He had only been trying to save me from myself.

But, that did not excuse his behavior earlier. He sought Dorothy out, sent her my way, didn't tell me, let me wander around looking for her, then sent her flying away when I finally had her. What was he playing at? He was wrecking everything! He was trying to actively stop me from leaving now that it was real possibilty. That realization struck me with a slap.

I pressed my hand against my forehead and groaned. Then why had he put his arm around her? He was her rescuer now. That curly mop of brown hair and her freckles. I knew I was definitely jealous of there being another young girl around. For so long it had been just me. Well, me and Peter with our adventures. Could I really be replaced once I left? Not if she dead in order for me to leave, I supposed.

Still, I'd met him first, and as childish as the feeling of jealousy was, this Dorothy girl was not going to just take that from me. Peter had been the only truly good thing I believed to have come from this long tumble down a rabbit hole.

My own foolish behavior certainly had not helped, but neither had Peter. He should have manned up and just told me he did not want to help me! But, would I have heard him even if he had? I puffed another sigh and looked down at him.

He was doing his best frog-glare at me. It was hardly intimidating but I sighed and turned him back to his human form. We stared at each other.

"Don't ever turn me into a frog again," he said in a dark tone, his eyes void of their usual sparkle. Peter was normally very chipper, carefree, and accepting of my nonsense. But, not in that moment. He really detested magic being used on him.

I was not doing myself any favors.

"I am sorry, Peter," I managed to croak out.

Part of me felt I should not have to apologize. I was the way I was because that is what this place turned me into. Peter's stern face faltered. He groaned and flopped down on the ground beside me.

"You know, Alice, it's getting really hard to help you. I'm telling you now that I'm not going to be coming around anymore if you think you can just stamp your foot and turn me into an amphibian."

"Help me? You have done nothing but the opposite all day," I countered, keeping my voice level. The awkwardness of the serious quarrel felt palpable.

He laughed and I looked at him like he was mad. "I sent Dorothy your way, didn't I?"

"But, you didn't tell me when you found her, you let me interrogate half of Wonderland, and you told her I was thinking about killing her and—"

"*Thinking* of killing her?"

"Alright, I was going to kill her."

"Which honesty isn't like you, Alice. It is one thing to become more callous, or have no control from the compass… But you needn't lose yourself altogether," Peter cautioned. "I showed you the shoes because I thought there was no way you would set out to kill someone in cold blood. I was honoring my promise, but I guess I didn't really believe you had it in you. I didn't realize you would really go to any length to go back."

A small furry black body erupted from under my writing desk and yapped at me. "Ugh, and she left her dog here," I grumbled, feeling jealous that she had a piece of home with her. That's where all of this stemmed from. I just wanted to get back to my family.

The dog bounded over to us, pausing to give cautious sniffs in our general direction. Peter reached out and stroked its head, until it rolled over and melted into the floor with simple happiness.

I returned my attention to Peter. "Peter, you literally sent her flying away. That isn't really in line with promising to help. You lied about going to Neverland and then showed up moments later to sabotage. Why are you deliberately making it as difficult as possible for me to get those shoes and go home?" I boldly asserted my question and held my breath. My words were met with an unusual silence that stretched on for several moments.

Peter inhaled deeply, then sat up and looked me in the eyes. "Technically, I promised I would help fix this situation. Your idea of fixing it, and my idea of fixing it just so happen to be a bit at odds. I don't want you to go back to that place. This," he gestured around us, "Wonderland, is your home now. We made it your home, a place to return to when we made that fort your first night, remember? I like having you around, Alice," he said sincerely.

I was unsure of what to make of this directness and honesty. I had been wishing for it moments before, but now, I wasn't sure how to react to it actually happening.

"Seriously?" I asked, squinting at him. "I can't tell if you are telling the truth or if you are just making excuses."

He smirked and looked at the ground for a moment, then rose to his feet and shrugged. "I know it doesn't happen often, but I'm not always messing around, you know. I'm serious, Alice. You don't need to go back. Stay here. Stay with me."

$$\bullet \ \bullet \ \bullet$$

Keep watch for more!

Other works

Chasing Figments
Available on Amazon, Bn.com, and other online book retailers

The Grim and The Fantastic
Available on Amazon, Bn.com, and other online book retailers

About the author

Marissa Miller is an author/illustrator with two illustrated children's books under her belt. She currently resides in northern California with her husband, two little dogs (Diggory and Phineas), and three cats (Burt, Winry, and Jinx). Most days you can find her frolicking outside, drinking her weight in tea, immersing in Disney antics, or doing something to a creative end.

Miller's first published work is the wonderfully imaginative children's book, *Chasing Figments*. Following her picture book, Miller published an illustrated middle grade book, *The Grim and The Fantastic*. Both books embody Miller's motif, which is finding the splendor in one's life, no matter the circumstance, and using imagination to overcome obstacles.

Follow the author
on Social Media

Instagram:@marissamillerbooks

Twitter: @BooksMiller

Facebook: Marissa Miller Books

Goodreads: Marissa Miller

Youtube: Marissa Miller Books

For more content, check out my website!

www.marissamillerbooks.com